To Facebook:

*for the inspiration, motivation, tools and fabulous
support network that led to this book.*

I could've done without the distractions.

First published in Great Britain in 2018 by
Pollok Glen Publishing.

Copyright © Heleen Kist, 2018
moral right of Heleen Kist to be identified as the a
work has been asserted in accordance with the Co
Designs and Patens Act 1988.

CIP catalogue record for this book is available fro
British Library.

Paperback ISBN: 978-1-9164486-1-2
eBook ISBN: 978-1-9164486-0-5

s book is a work of fiction. Names, characters, plac
ents are either a product of the author's imaginatio
d fictitiously. Any resemblance to actual people liv
dead, events or locales is entirely coincidental.

r design by JT Lindroos (www.oivas.com). Flower:
or photo: Scott Cadenhead (www.headshotglasgow

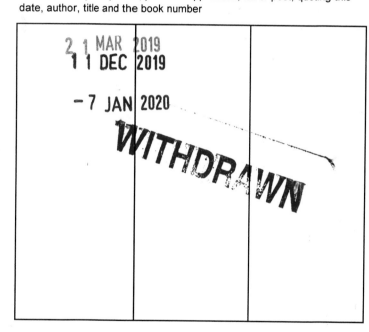

IN SERVIT

IN SERVITUDE

Heleen Kist

CHAPTER ONE

Glory was dead. It had to be her in the burnt-out carcass of that stupid, silly car of hers...but it couldn't be. Not my sister. *Not you.*

Dave caught me as I collapsed, the phone falling from my hand, and held me like only a strong boyfriend could. I screamed and raged, fists banging on his shoulders, first at the injustice; then for release.

I had to go.

He stayed on his knees, panting and bruised, knowing he wasn't welcome at her house. Knowing he couldn't help. 'I'll be wherever you need me to be,' he said, as I raced out the door, my tears and snot merging into the damp Glasgow air.

With the rain gone, the clouds dissipated in furtive wisps as if clearing the stage for the moon's headline act. I hurried across the railway tracks into leafy Pollokshields, still trying to make sense of the news. The roads and houses widened in affluent unison while I wove through them to Sutherglen Drive. A journey I'd made a hundred times. For her. What now?

Sobbing and shaken, I replayed Stephen's call in my mind. 'She's dead, Grace...Glory's dead. What am I supposed to do? The boys...they can't...the car…down banks…police…she's dead…fire.'

I'd never heard my brother-in-law so distressed. Stephen, the stable one. The always-steady counterweight to his—our—glorious butterfly. Never much of a sharer: why speak when a raised eyebrow would do? But on the phone he'd sounded bereft, words and cries shooting out of him in almost random order as though held inside for years, under pressure, waiting for that one emotion so strong that he would succumb and let them free. Then crumble.

I'd pieced together this much: they had found Glory's VW Beetle mangled against a tree in the sloped bank of the road up to Drymen. She had died instantly; her ancient car's safety features no match for the impact. An accident.

'Stephen…Stephen. Stop! Are they sure it's her?'

'Yes. It's her. There was nobody else. No other car. She crashed alone. Oh my God, she was alone when she died…my love…never forgive myself...' His sobs drowned out his words, but I needed to know why she died. I needed to know everything.

'What did the police say? They must have said something?'

'Nothing. They have no idea…What will I do? They can't tell me what happened. All they're saying is this stretch of road is a death trap.' The line went quiet for a while. 'And they're running tests. Tonight. I don't know…I don't know anything else…Grace, she's dead.'

What happened, Gi? What the hell happened to you?

As I ran, flushes of adrenaline funnelled up my spine, coursed sideways and up through my shoulders, and gathered, pounding, at the base of my skull. I tried to regain control, forcing myself to breathe and exhale rhythmically to avert an attack—like when I was little. But the sadness kept hitting me in the guts at a boxer's tempo, making me feel sick and allowing in only intermittent gulps of air.

Breathe.

But what if she—?

Breathe.

I focused on the force of my feet hitting the ground. I had to get a grip. I had to take charge. Glory would need me to. Stephen was a mess. So I made a list, and unconsciously synchronised my steps with the tasks at hand.

One. Help Stephen with the boys. Do the school run. Buy food, cook, clean. *You loved taking care of them so much.* Would he even know where to start? Christ, did I?

Two. Learn how to take care of the café. *Your other baby.*

Three. Move some of my personal training clients to evenings to fit this all in. Thank God I was self-employed.

I kept my attention on the practical issues because I couldn't let other thoughts snake their way to my brain, to my heart, to the pain. To the boys. My parents. Oh God, our parents. Would they already know? A rush of saliva flooded my mouth, pressing against my clenched teeth as I battled nausea again.

Keep it together.

My knees wobbled as her Victorian sandstone house came into view, its tall windows reflecting the light of the distant sun. I paused to steady myself and leaned against the tall hedge as I was tormented by visions of my beautiful sister. I breathed through it. Tried to blow it all away. I had to clear my mind, to create a free space for the upheaval to come. The aftermath of a death that still did not ring true. Couldn't be true.

Not you. Anyone but you.

It took two attempts to punch in the gate code with my trembling hand. I darted up the long drive, golden gravel crunching under my feet. Immobile silhouettes appeared in the window and while I tried to make them out, Blue barked.

Shit. The dog. I would have to walk that damned dog.

'Be strong,' I repeated mantra-like, as I reached the side door to the kitchen. Was it right to still use my key?

CHAPTER TWO

Blue met me at the door. I struggled to remain upright as the velvet grey Weimaraner circled my legs, battering my calves with his enthusiastic tail-wagging. He still hadn't figured out he liked me more than I liked him. Jumping towards his bowl, he gave me an expectant look, turning plaintive when I didn't follow.

'Not now, buddy. I'm sorry.'

Unfamiliar voices sounded from the front of the house. Four, maybe five people murmured in hushed tones. News travels fast. Police cars were uncommon in this sleepy part of town and blue lights flashing outside must have attracted the neighbours like moths to a candle.

Whoever it was hadn't bothered to make themselves useful. Three plates of half-eaten chicken nuggets covered the kitchen counter, ketchup still smeared on the stools, casting off an acrid smell. God knows how they would cope without her. A pile of tea bags languished in the sink. The tell-tale sign of adults assembled.

I peered across the open-plan dining area, through the glazed doors into the living room, curious but not quite ready for people. I saw the neighbour, Jean, and a handful of people I may or may not have met before, congregated in a small circle. Sipping their cups of tea and feasting on the misery of others under the banner of 'community'.

Their chattering stopped as I entered.

'Where's Stephen?'

'Upstairs, with the boys.' Jean launched her short frame off the sofa to meet me. 'I'm so sorry for your loss,' she said, with what must have been her best expression of pity. She stretched out her arms and leaned in for a hug, hands hovering above my shoulders. When I recoiled, she used them instead to smooth out her dress, and stifle a little cough.

'How are they holding up?' I asked.

'He hasn't told them yet. Stephen had parked them in front of the TV in the attic after dinner, right before the police came. They didn't hear a thing. As far as they're concerned, their mum's at the spa for the weekend. And Stephen wanted to keep it that way, so we're being quiet. I can see why. Poor boys need to sleep before they can take it all in.'

I frowned, disapproving of the deceit, the giant omission. Then again, this would buy Stephen and me time to gather ourselves before having to crush their little souls. I closed my eyes to stop the tears from escaping. I couldn't lose it. Not now. There was too much to do.

'Can you get everybody out please, Jean? I'll update you later.'

'Wouldn't you like me to stay and—'

'No.'

'Are you sure?'

'I'm not sure of much right now, but I know none

of you are needed here.' It had come out more unkind than intended, but I didn't have the energy for pleasantries. Thankfully, she seemed to understand, and with a gentle squeeze of my arm, she returned to the lounge, herding the others towards the door.

I braced for the next encounter and turned towards the stairs, the visitors' indignant whispers fading behind me.

Stephen reversed onto the landing and closed the door to Adam's room as I reached the top. In jeans and a light blue jumper, he looked like he would any other Saturday night.

'Hey.'

He jumped. 'Grace! That was quick.'

'Yes, I came straight away. I got rid of everybody else.'

'Oh God. Yes. I didn't know how to. Not without causing offence. Thank you.'

Our embrace lasted longer than it ever had. We weren't close—not helped by what he'd done to Dave—but in this moment we were shipwrecked, clinging to each other's debris.

He let go and nodded towards the door. 'I haven't told them yet.'

'I know. I understand. Was she going to a spa?'

'Yes, for an overnight pampering. They'll be expecting her again tomorrow night.' He rubbed his temples with the palms of his hands, dropped his eyes and swayed slightly as he rambled on in a daze. 'Will you stay? Take the guest room. Noah's in with Adam. I had parked them in front of Nickelodeon in the attic after dinner and then the officers came. I panicked. Didn't know what to do. The police want to come again at ten tomorrow morning. They said they could help me with telling the boys. Can you stay?'

'Yes, of course.' I reached for his arm. 'Don't worry. We'll take care of everything in the morning. You need to rest.'

'I'll try. Yes. I'm just in shock, I guess. I can't believe she's gone.'

'I know. Me too.'

As his hiccups carried him towards his bedroom, he turned. 'You're the only one I called.'

The meaning of this didn't escape me. He was leaving it to me to tell my parents their daughter was dead. It filled me with terror. I wasn't ready for this.

I slid downstairs and found some relief in tidying up, bringing order where I still could. Postponing the inevitable.

The kitchen was silent. The rubber-neckers had gone, no doubt planning their casserole-shaped excuse to return to where the action was. Blue dozed on the mat by the door, unperturbed.

When I scraped the leftover nuggets into the bin, I noticed a box of medicine buried among the rubbish and fished it out. Zolpidem. Sleeping pills. I flipped the package both ways but there was no prescription sticker. There were still tablets in the blister pack.

Were they yours?

The phone buzzed in my pocket as I threw the box away again. It was a text from Dave. '*RU OK? Here 4U.*'

I typed back, '*Coping. I'll be fine x.*' But I wasn't fine. I wondered if I'd ever be fine again.

The text had sucked me back into the dark reality of the situation and, with the phone already out, I shuddered. I couldn't hold off any longer. 'God help me,' I said to myself as I pressed the speed-dial for home.

As the line rang and rang, part of me hoped I'd never need to tell them. That somehow I could hide it forever. But Dad's voice came through just as I was about to give up.

'Sorry darling. I was in the shed clearing out some—'

'Dad. Something terrible has happened.'

'What is it? Are you okay?'

'It's not me. It's Glory. She's been in a car crash...She died. At the scene. Instantly.'

I heard him gasp. Then nothing. I strained to listen for a response, a suppressed moan perhaps; but the insistent tone of a dead line took over and said enough. Why would today be any different?

I put the phone down and covered my face with my hands. Seconds later, my heart jumped at the sound of buzzing.

'Dad? Did we get cut off? I thought you'd—'

'Are the boys alive?'

'Yes. She was driving alone to a spa.'

'Thank God,' he said. I held on for more, but he merely sighed.

'Dad? ...Dad! Speak to me. Please please speak to me...Dad?...I need you to talk to me.'

'I can't.'

'I know it's hard but could you pl—'

'You need to grab her papers.'

My ears tingled. This made no sense. 'What?'

'Don't let Stephen find her papers.'

'What papers?'

'Her bank statements. Legal documents. That sort of thing.'

'Dad, what's going on?'

'I don't want to tell you over the phone. She opened

some accounts and Stephen mustn't find out. It's money she wanted to keep for the kids.'

'What? Why?'

'Come round tomorrow and I will explain everything. But right now, your mother needs me. Goodbye, Grace.'

I stared at the handset, wondering if he would call back again. Or did he really have to go? I pictured him, crushed but calm, kneeling by my mother, brushing a hair from her face while her slanted mouth requested the thousandth small bit of assistance since the stroke last year. How would she take Glory's death?

A little later, I made my way upstairs for an early night, knowing full well my racing mind wouldn't allow much sleep. I struggled to decide what had shocked me more: that Glory had been scheming behind her husband's back or that she'd confided in our father, and not me.

CHAPTER THREE

The silver-framed photograph weighed in my hands with a newfound heaviness. I gazed at the two preteen girls sharing a casual embrace we could never again recreate. Close in age and with the same wavy red hair and high cheekbones, it was no surprise people had often mistaken us for twins. The difference lay in the eyes: similar in shape but not in colour. Or in spirit, I thought. Her blue pair stared straight at the camera, with a playful twinkle inviting adventure, whereas mine—a muddy brown—struggled to project my heart in the same way, always creating an impression of aloofness.

With a deep sigh, I placed the frame back onto the sewing table by the window of the guest room, where it beamed among other childhood snaps. Glory smiling with a gap-toothed mouth surrounded by melted ice cream. Mum and Dad sitting barefoot by a tent. A Polaroid of her first dance recital, protected against fading inside an acrylic cube. Simple pleasures captured for future smiles.

Resting my hand on the white plastic sewing machine, I twisted a spool of thread between my fingers.

This was your spot. Are you still here?

I sat down at the untidy crafting corner. It had been nibbled away from a room otherwise designed to convey polished, suburban success. What Stephen wanted people to see.

Around me, deftly placed accessories broke the furniture's clean lines, and the walls showcased the fruits of the family's annual pilgrimage to the photography studio. Played out against a permanently white background, guests witnessed the journey from chubby cherubs to boisterous boys, posing alongside their parents who grew only in loving devotion.

A tailor's dummy stood beside me, draped with colourful scarves that reflected the sunset in shimmering patterns, as if calling for my attention. I ran both hands through the soft fibres, creating dancing shadows on the wall and releasing a smell that punched me in the lungs, calling up a memory so vivid that I became light-headed.

Glory's young voice.

'Look at me! I'm Scheherazade!'

Loose strands of long red hair enveloped her face as she twirled around, her hands waving multi-coloured strips of fabric in fluid, hypnotising motions along her eleven-year-old body. She bounced towards me, covering her nose and mouth, batting her eyelashes in cartoon-style seduction. 'Oh Aladdin, my hero! Shall I dance the dance of the seven veils for you?'

'Stop it, Glory.' I grabbed the so-called veils she'd been dangling in front of my face, too close. 'Plus, that wasn't Scheherazade. I'm fairly sure the dance of the seven veils was Salome.'

Glory shrugged and kept the choreography going. 'I

don't care. It's exotic! And foreign! And marvellous!' Each phrase was punctuated by a defiant jiggle of the hips.

'And a little blasphemous,' I said, failing to suppress a large grin.

'Okay, miss party-pooper. Your turn to do something with this.'

She heaped the mix of polyester, silk and cotton we'd rescued from our parents' store onto my head and sat on the ground. Bright blues beaming in anticipation.

'Fine, Salome. You think you're so sexy. Well, you've got another think coming.' I wrapped layer upon layer over my shoulders and across my waist, waiting for the inspiration that came so easily to her.

Once I could move no more for the bulk, I plonked my elbows on my side and stood legs apart like a superhero, bellowing, 'For I am…Heidi!' My heart leapt as her unrestrained laughter filled the room. 'And I am on my way to meet my own man…' I paused, basking in my sister's approval, while I searched for that goatherd boy's name—or any goatherd name. She roared as I broke into song instead. 'High on the hill lived a lonely goatherd, yodelay-hee yodelay-hee yodelay-hee hoo!'

'Oh Grace, you're so funny,' she said, then launched into yodels that merged into mine. And I wished it would last forever.

But the memory faded.

At the dummy's side, I kept my eyes shut and stroked my cheeks with the fabric, hoping to hold onto the image a while longer. I yearned for the closeness of years gone by, when every afternoon, we downloaded the day's events in our shared bedroom and analysed each conversation, each frown, each wink. When we exploded into whoops and laughter at our wild and cruel strategies for coping with the mean girls.

Admiring desirable qualities in each other, we joked that if they put us in a mixer, we would make one fabulous person. We even gave her a name—GiGi—a rich and sophisticated-sounding combination of our initials and so, in private, we called each other 'Gi'. I smiled as I remembered how this splendid creature had been destined for great things—far removed from dreary old Perth—and how we took turns making up her adventures, indirectly exposing our dreams for the future.

Well, we made it to Glasgow, didn't we, Gi? That's something.

I folded my jeans and socks and wriggled my bra from underneath my T-shirt, which I kept on to sleep. The sheets were cold, accentuating my loneliness, and I hugged my legs to stay warm. The floorboards on the landing creaked as Stephen wandered about, probably unable to sleep, possibly checking in on his kids, certainly feeling lost. I remained still as I heard him scuffle by my door, not sure what to say if he knocked.

What was it about him, Gi? Did he make you feel safe?

Lord knows we both needed security after moving to the city for college. She'd found it in straight-laced Stephen. Stephen with the steady job at the council. Stephen with the side parting able to withstand a hurricane. We'd thought Glasgow would give us a 'GiGi-esque' cosmopolitan lifestyle, but we hadn't been prepared for the grime and crime of the metropolis. Two naïve girls from the provinces.

Remember our tiny flat in the West End? We had so much fun.

She'd left after four months to be with her man. I'd had to fill the second bedroom with messy strangers, who touched my stuff. Made noise. Invaded my space. But forgiving her had been easy: she was happy.

When you're happy, I'm happy.

That was our thing.

Yet while an unending stream of tears cascaded onto my pillow, I reflected on what my father had just told me, and realised that maybe, somehow, she no longer believed I was the other half of us.

CHAPTER FOUR

I didn't expect to wake to the sound of giggling, but here were two smiling pyjama-clad boys standing at the foot of the bed, daring each other to shoot me with water pistols, their silhouettes back-lit by the open door. Adam, the elder at eight years old, looking very much a leader, legs spread wide, ordering his brother to hit me from the side.

'No. No. Don't shoot.' I held up my hands.

In contradiction with all military conventions, they shot me anyway. Once they'd discharged their ammunition onto my sodden face, the boys jumped on the bed and pounced on me for a double bear hug. It was torture. My now damp hair was caught under an elbow and tugged at my scalp; I struggled to find a gap in between the body parts through which to breathe, and I experienced the full force of a knee pushed into my bursting bladder. But despite my discomfort, I recognised this moment for what it was: an offering of pure, youthful love. So I let it unfold.

They were the sweetest boys, and I enjoyed being an aunt, but I struggled with the concept of unconditional love—the giving or receiving of it. It felt like such a huge responsibility. And once you'd given yourself over, there was no turning back. Sometimes I wondered what was wrong with me: my ticking clock should be deafening by now. Why couldn't I let go more? Trust it would all work out, like Glory had?

'Your door was open, Auntie Grace. Why are you here? Is it because Mummy's at the spa? Did you know they're going to cover her whole body in mud?' asked Adam. I felt a kick in the gut when that image confirmed how close to the truth he'd come. Mud. Earth. Ashes to ashes. It took all my might to stay composed.

'I don't believe for one second that door stood open, you cheeky monkey.' I gave him a quick tickle and changed the subject. 'Look at this clock over here. What kind of time do you call this?'

Six-year-old Noah beat his brother to it. 'Six thirty! We've been up for twenty-two minutes already.'

'Oh, you have, have you?'

'Blue was whining. I gave him some food, but I think he needs a walk. I'll be his carer until when Mummy's home.' Adam sounded surprisingly cavalier about his mother's absence.

'Poor Blue. We forgot all about him last night, didn't we? And aren't you a good boy for remembering?' I jumped up to put on my jeans and sniffed at yesterday's socks, deeming them acceptable. Opening the curtains a little to gauge the weather, I made a mental note to bring some clothes and toiletries over from my place. 'Well, I think we're going to have to take him for a walk, then, don't you? Go put some wellies on. Let's go to the park. And as a special treat you can stay in your PJs. Now make sure you—'

The boys were racing downstairs before I could

finish, gleeful sounds filling the house with the characteristic liveliness of happy families. I stood for a moment clutching the door handle, gathering strength to maintain this good-naturedness. Stephen would wake up soon and reality would inevitably come crashing in. There was only so long we could pretend.

A morning chill licked my face. Wellies had been a good call. Rain had fallen overnight and the paths in Maxwell Park had flooded in the areas where the surrounding grass couldn't withstand the frequent downpours. Blue ran freely, sturdy paws creating little water fountains as he raced across the soaked ground. The boys rushed to scale the climbing frame in the play park, then bounced like bees in a meadow from one multi-coloured metal structure to the next. Their boundless energy contrasting, unknown to them, with the dead weight I carried inside.

My wet feet squelched inside the light, woven trainers that formed such an inadequate barrier to rain, they should never have been marketed in Scotland. 'Come on boys. Let's go.'

Nothing.

'Come on boys, don't leave Auntie Grace hanging.'

They stayed spinning on the roundabout, heads tilted back to accelerate getting to peak dizziness, the obvious object of the game. I marvelled at why anyone would choose to become nauseous.

'We need to get Blue before he catches one of the ducks in the pond,' I attempted again. Glory had taught me that with boys, distraction was the best tool to get your way or to prevent a tantrum. It was harder with girls, she'd asserted, who were more stubborn and wanted to cling onto their drama for longer. A flush hit my cheeks as I remembered Glory's own fondness for drama, how she relished its emotionality. She'd always known how to draw the attention towards her—part of that magnetic spell she'd cast on others. On me.

After using my sleeve to mop up nascent tears, I noticed that the boys had gone from the play park. I eventually spotted their two small bodies running towards the pond, oblivious to the fact that Blue had been standing by me all along.

Damn. I didn't have the patience for this.

As we finally returned home, the boys were in high spirits, comparing the length and smoothness of the sticks they'd picked up. We found Stephen sitting in the kitchen, staring into the middle distance, nursing a cup of tea.

'Hey.' His bleary eyes rose to meet me but faltered halfway.

'Hey,' I replied.

'Auntie Grace let us wear our PJs to the park. Blue was whining so we took him for a walk.'

'It's okay, Adam, did you have fun?' he asked, running his hand absentmindedly through his son's hair.

I left the boys to update their father on the morning's activities, gesturing that I was going to clean myself up.

Once in the privacy of the shower enclosure, I stood and wept, letting the warm water caress my head and cover my shoulders like a comforting throw.

How were we going to tell them?

I turned the side jets to the most punishing setting and suffered through my body being pelted by hail. It was time to get real.

CHAPTER FIVE

It wasn't yet eight o'clock and the clouds were refusing to let the morning sun through, leaving the kitchen in the kind of shade that has married couples arguing whether the lights should be on or not. But Stephen and I were mute as we danced around each other like awkward teens, preparing breakfast while the boys played in the living room.

The rich smell of coffee penetrated my lungs and kick-started my senses, as it always did. The one unhealthy habit I allowed myself and I needed it now more than ever after such a fretful night. Though sleep had come in the end, it was only once the last tear had been drained from me.

Pop. The triumphant sound of the toaster presenting its achievements brought relief from the silence.

We'd so far avoided commenting on the day ahead. Although he'd pleaded for my help when he first called, it was up to him to decide when and how to tell his kids that Glory had died. As we were both new to this, I didn't even have any advice to give. I would have thought it was akin to ripping off a plaster, best done in one quick painful move. But maybe he was right, and it made sense to hold off until the police came, with the grief counsellor from social services. Still, this charade didn't sit comfortably with me.

I grabbed the bag of wholemeal bread and fished out a few spongy slices, grateful for the excuse to speak. 'How many pieces of toast do you want?'

'I don't know. Three?'

Anger flashed across my temples. Three? Who has three pieces of toast? There are two slots in the toaster. Two. What kind of messed-up person leaves a slot empty? I closed my eyes and sighed. Wow. This was all becoming too much. Pulling myself together, I said, 'I'm going to Perth later.'

'Yes, of course. Of course. I'm sorry.' He looked away, folding and re-folding a tea towel. I was puzzled to see the unmistakable look of guilt on his face. A look I'd seen a hundred times, when my clients admitted they hadn't followed their exercise schedule the previous week. Why guilt? Had he sensed my rage? Was he conflicted about making me do the dirty work with my parents? I had to admit thoughts of blame had fleeted through my mind, but they had been suppressed as quickly as they had come. None of this was his fault. He was the victim, I reminded myself. We all were.

But it was him you were hiding bank accounts from, Gi. Why?

I watched him for a while, shuffling in his pyjamas from one cabinet to another, unshaven and expressionless. It's how the movies always portrayed a widower: crumpled, empty shells of men unable to take care of themselves. Perhaps there was truth to that, but the image before me clashed with the cinematic version because this man was about thirty years too young.

He perked up a bit when the boys came into the room, though a heaviness continued to hang in the air. Spirited chat about Transformers turned into arguments about who got the yellow spoon today and knees colliding under the breakfast bar.

'Go get dressed,' the impatient command came when the last of the juice had been drunk. And off they went.

Hesitating for a moment, I gestured to catch his attention. 'Stephen?'

'Hm?'

'When I was tidying up last night, I found sleeping pills in the bin. Whose are they?'

His eyes opened wide at first, then a frown creased his forehead as he seemed to take too long to choose his words. 'They're Glory's. She hasn't…hadn't been sleeping well. The café was really stressing her out lately.'

'How come?' I asked, relieved I hadn't been meddling into marital problems.

'I don't know. She wouldn't talk about it much, but I could tell it was taking its toll. That's why I booked the spa for her.' He seemed to gulp back a sob. 'I thought it would help…and it got her killed.'

He hunched forward and clasped his hands around his head. The guilt I'd sensed earlier now made sense. I reached over and stroked his shoulder. 'It wasn't your fault, Stephen. You could never have known. It was a horrible, horrible accident. What you did was lovely. I bet she was very excited.'

A grateful face looked up. 'Yes, she was. We joked that she wouldn't need the pills anymore after this and she binned them theatrically. She did that for me. She knew I didn't approve of them. I don't even know where she got them. We had cup of tea together before she left, and I kissed her goodbye.'

We sat in silence for a while longer. I wondered if he was thinking of that last kiss. Looking at the sky for inspiration, I searched my brain for my last moment with Glory.

Had I even said goodbye to you?

The sun started to tear through the clouds, more confident in its claim of daytime.

'Are you keeping an eye on the clock, Stephen? The police will be here soon.'

'You're right. I'd better go shower.'

I climbed up the stairs shortly after him and listened at the bathroom to confirm the jets were on. The door to their bedroom stood open on the other side of the landing. I had been in here before, but never uninvited.

There was no time to waste.

A vast teak-framed super king-sized bed filled most of the space, with matching bedside cabinets on either side. I checked the drawers. Nothing. It seemed unlikely that she would hold her secrets in this shared room, but then again, she wouldn't be the first to hide things in plain sight. Glory's presence was everywhere: in the romance book on the table, in the collection of earrings in the wonky child-made ceramic pot, in the content of the overflowing wardrobe. And the smell.

Glory's scent enveloped me as I rummaged through her clothes, as if giving me permission and drawing me in further. I caressed the folds of her dresses and buried my head in her jumpers, suddenly overwhelmed by the knowledge I would never see her again. I imagined her elegant and beautiful and full of joy, showing off a new purchase, twirling.

And then it hit me. The shoes. I reached up to the top shelf looking for one particular shoe box: treasured Jimmy Choos that she'd concealed from Stephen at first. Even though they'd been on sale, she'd feared they were too extravagant. She'd told me she'd waited for her birthday to disclose their existence, so he couldn't give her too much of a row.

'What are you doing?' He'd finished sooner than expected and stood in the doorway in his bathrobe; his tone, to my relief, indicating surprise more than annoyance.

I was overtaken by an urgent need to take the shoes.

'I'm sorry, Stephen. I was just…just remembering, you know? Is that okay? I'm sorry…Could I keep these shoes for a while? She loved them so much.' I held the box up inviting, but dreading, scrutiny.

'Yes, sure. All right.' He looked everywhere but at me, not registering what I had in my hands, fidgeting with the belt of his robe.

'Sorry. I'll go now.' I scuttled away.

In the guest room, I cursed my impatience. Why didn't I wait until he was out? Whatever would he think? I opened the lid and took out the velvety pouch Mr Choo enclosed to keep the shoes safe and the prices high. From its odd shape, I could see at once this did not hold only shoes. Prising apart the drawstrings confirmed the power of female intuition: there were rolls of twenty-pound notes stuffed inside and around the shoes.

Jesus, Gi, what is this?

CHAPTER SIX

When the police came, I needed all my resolve to keep from falling apart while witnessing the boys' anguish and Stephen clutching for help as he tried saving them from the abyss while himself plummeting. It would only make matters worse to expose my own immeasurable sadness, so I shut off.

Focus on the practicalities.

'Do we need to identify the body?' Clueless, I'd reached for what I had seen on TV and branded myself an idiot the moment it came out.

'No,' said the thirty-something police officer in a neat blue uniform. If she was annoyed by the clichéd televisual reference, she was kind enough to hide it. 'An identification was possible based on the items on her person.'

The woman from social services interjected in a quiet voice. A portly maternal figure, she'd broken the news to the semi-orphans in masterful child-friendly terms and seemed to know what she was talking about. 'We normally encourage the children to be brought to the deceased to say goodbye. It makes it more real. Sometimes kids struggle to understand the finality of death.' I balked at the idea of bringing the boys to the morgue, but she pre-empted my response. 'However, as Glory has been in a car accident and sustained severe injuries, I don't think it's a good idea.'

The horror of hearing of my sister's disfigurement clashed internally with the intense relief of knowing we'd be spared another emotional roller-coaster.

'And you're really sure she just lost control of the vehicle? That it wasn't anything else?' I asked.

'We can't be entirely sure. But there is no evidence to suggest the contrary,' said the officer.

Towards the end, they handed over the items that had been in the car with Glory: her little orange handbag and a large overnight tote.

'We checked with the network to see if she was using the mobile phone while driving, which is standard practice. The device appeared not to have been used all day. There is no reason for us to keep it for further investigation. Or any of this.'

And so the verdict fell, with perplexing efficiency. Glory died in a fluke accident and that was that. No alcohol, no common recreational drugs, no texting or phoning, no witnesses, no culprit. But I still had another mystery to solve and I eyed the phone lying on the coffee table with its promise of emails and banking apps. 'Did you unlock the mobile, officer?'

'No. That would require special approval and there wasn't cause.'

Slipping into my most casual tone, I turned to Stephen. 'Do you know the code?'

'No. She hardly used it.'

I picked up the handbag and audited its content. 'I'll take the keys to the café and put up a notice saying it won't open for a while. Okay?' Talking shop presented an opening for an innocent sounding request. 'Do you know her computer password?'

'No, and I really don't give a shit about the café, Grace.' His raised voice shook the boys who had been curled up against him on the sofa. Red-ringed eyes looked up in confusion and I immediately regretted my actions. I'd taken it too far. It was all very well having a mission to distract me from my grief, but Stephen needed to deal with all of theirs.

Half an hour later, having seen the visitors off and ensured the others were stable, I stepped out of the house. I lingered on the porch to reload on fresh air, replacing the single stagnant breath I'd held during this worst endurance test of my life.

I headed to my flat for a quick change before facing the next challenge up North. At least I would soon understand what the hell was going on.

CHAPTER SEVEN

Traffic was light on the M9 up to Stirling and disappeared on the stretch of the A9 that ushered me home to Perth. Or 'the Fair City of Perth', as the locals called it. It hadn't carried the official status of city long, but its residents had always held an unshakable confidence in the superiority of their town because it had once been declared a 'royal burgh' by King William the Lion. So just 'Perth' would never do.

Being alone for the hour-long journey did me good. I knew the route so well that it required no mental effort, but I still had to concentrate to remain safe, meaning that thoughts couldn't wander too far. I was ripped from this meditative cocoon, however, as soon as I turned into Viewlands Road and my old high school came into view. Memories fluttered as I drove past the imposing concrete structure, now surrounded by professional-looking playing grounds I would have killed for in my day.

Back then, when the kids gathered for Games on what was not much more than a flattened surface with faint white lines, I had outrun them all. The PE teacher identified my potential early on. I could be a great athlete. She had tried to convince my mother to let me join a range of clubs in the area. But the religious Mary McBride wouldn't hear of it. Her daughter running around in skimpy clothes? No, sweat belonged on horses, not on women.

The Catholic ethos was a constant guide to my parents, yet they had chosen this non-denominational school for us. Perth being primarily a Church of Scotland area, they wanted us to fit in better than they had. But being called Grace and Glory had put a target on our backs.

Do you remember how they teased us at first? 'Look, the Hallelujah girls!' and 'Why aren't you wearing your halo?' But we showed them, didn't we? You were so popular in the end, and they learnt not to mess with us.

I cruised into Buchan Grove, a small cul-de-sac a few streets away. My father's blue Vauxhall estate rested under the carport that gave access to the garage, the garden and the rear door. Dad took exceptional care of his cars and liked to change them every two years—a luxury he curtailed after selling the shop to fund their retirement. Only every three years, now.

They kept the little bell that hung above the door to announce the arrival of a new customer and its spirited chime welcomed me as I entered the kitchen. Dad appeared at once, conditioned over many years to drop everything on being summoned by that sound.

'Hello darling.'

Exhaustion had ravaged his face, his complexion dull grey and wrinkles etched into his features like notches on a belt, each representing a heroic but mundane effort in caring for his ailing wife. And now this.

'Hi Dad.' I rushed to him and sunk into his giant

frame, bathing in the comforting familiarity of his hug and the faint cigarette smell that always pervaded him. I smiled. Dad had pretended for years he didn't smoke. And we'd pretended to believe him.

I was home.

'It's awful Dad. I can't believe she's gone. How are you?'

'No parent should lose a child.' He turned away. Not going there. Again.

'How's Mum?'

'She's in the living room. I'm not sure she has processed it altogether yet. Let's talk in here for now.'

Just as we settled at the kitchen table, a shout came through: 'Who is it?'

'It's Grace, dear.' He let out a sigh of regret for his foiled plan. 'Come,' he said, getting up again.

The inner door led to the narrow, carpeted hallway lined with a mixture of family portraits and kitsch floral prints. Left was the open-plan lounge and dining area in varying shades of burgundy. Mum was sitting in her armchair facing out, scrutinising the immaculate garden beyond the glazed double door. She craned her neck and moved side to side as if searching for something.

'Hello Mum.' I reached over the padded armrest to hug her.

She stroked my shoulder for a while and patted my arm twice to signal the greeting was over, while she zeroed in on the pigeon she had discovered trespassing among her plants. 'It's good of you to come.'

Dad hovered in the doorway. Eventually, he cleared his throat. 'Would you like a cup of tea?'

'Sure, thanks Dad. But I'm also happy to make it.'

'No, no, you stay here.'

Perhaps he wanted out of this room as much as I did.

Mum kept her eyes on the garden while I noticed more dust than usual on the fire surround. Dad came back, carrying a tray with tea cups and the biscuit tin reserved for real guests. I took it as code that there would be no open sharing of emotion, only dignified lamentation.

Don't judge them for it, Gi. They're just being who they are.

He sat down. 'So,' he said.

'So…' I waited, praying he'd say something that would give me permission to break through the platitudes and bemused murmurs, and let my grief pour out.

'God took her too soon, darling. And we'll never know why.' He sniffed and sat upright. 'Now we need to make sure Adam and Noah survive this. How are they? Are you helping? We would, of course, but we're tied to the house.'

'That's okay, Dad. Mum, it's fine. I went to the house straight away. I was there when the police came to help us tell the boys. They were very good at explaining what might have happened, and what would happen next.'

My mother stirred. 'Typical of Glory to get herself killed. She was always an irresponsible child. And now she's abandoned her children, too.' A cold chill raced through my veins as I took in the most heartless thing I'd ever heard come out of my mother's mouth.

'Mum! That's a horrible thing to say. It was an accident. You know that.'

She gave a barely perceptible shrug and kept her gaze on the pest outside. I turned to my father in horror, looking for support or an explanation—

anything. His desolate expression and gentle shaking of the head suggested such an outburst was nothing new. My confusion grew as he changed the subject, casually whitewashing the last few minutes. 'Now, did you find those bank statements?'

'No, no yet. God, Dad. Will you please tell me what that's about?'

'Do you remember Alastair Evans?'

'Your old accountant? Sure.'

'Well, he came with a clever tax structure for Glory, one that worked for people who owned their own business. Your mother and I had to buy shares in the café for a token pound. And then we had to gift those shares to trusts set in the boys' names. It was all very complicated. Glory would then be able to transfer the profits of the café into these trusts tax free. Now, the money could only be used for the benefit of the boys. School fees, that sort of thing. But the sense we got is that nobody ever checked.'

'But why can't Stephen know? This just sounds like a tax thing.'

'I think she was leaving him.'

My eyes jerked open and I squeezed them shut a few times, as if the correct retinal focus would help it all make sense. Thrown by my apparent shock, Dad tempered his statement.

'Well, she never said so. Not in those words. And we didn't want to pry. We reckoned that if she had something to tell us, she would do so when she was ready. But there was something about her behaviour. Jumpy. Terrified Stephen might find out. She even swore us to secrecy.'

Those secrets, again. Secrets kept from Stephen but also from me.

Why didn't you tell me?

The yearning for my sister—the sister I thought I had—rendered me adrift and I rested my head in my hands until the undulations abated and I could think clearly again.

Glory had wanted to leave her husband.

Of course.

A new wave of energy filled me as a logical plot appeared to unfold.

'I found over three thousand pounds in cash stuffed in a shoe box. That must have been her escape money,' I said.

The juvenile thrill at holding this piece of the puzzle was doused by Mum's icy cold words. 'She'll be off with another man. The slut.'

'Jesus Mum, what's gotten into you?'

'Always with the boys, that girl. Sex, sex, sex.'

Too stunned to respond, I soon noticed she wasn't even speaking to us. Her words were being cast into the void, her volume rising like a priest spewing threats of damnation to an invisible congregation of fornicators. 'Harlot. Jezebel.'

Dad got up, lifted me by the arm and swooped me into the kitchen.

'What was that all about? What's wrong with Mum?' I pointed towards this unrecognisable, possessed being. 'Is it grief? This can't just be grief can it? I mean we're all sad, but this…Do you think it's true? Was Glory cheating?'

Two large hands pressed down against my shoulders, acting like a pause button. He bent through his knees to be at eye level with me and waited until I seemed ready to listen.

'I'm sorry. I've never found a good moment to tell

you girls…Darling, Mum has dementia. She's had it for a while. Since the stroke. It comes and goes, but since I told her about Glory's accident it's gotten worse. Right now, I don't think she even knows you're here. You need to forgive her.'

He stepped forward to comfort me, but I slapped his hands away, head shaking in disbelief. My legs were jelly and my arms scrambled for support as I sped towards the exit. I had to get out.

CHAPTER EIGHT

Alice's door had only just come off the latch when I burst through, my childhood friend pushed aside by this sudden invasion. I stood in her hallway, tears drowning my face, not remembering why I had come, why I'd run the three streets from my parents' to land on her doorstep. But then her hands touched my forearm and her familiar hazel-green eyes rested on me, projecting a myriad of questions but not a hint of impatience. Sanctuary. I'd fled here for peace and a listening ear, as I'd done so often in the past.

'Grace? What's wrong?'

'It's all too much. I'm sorry, Alice, I didn't know where else to turn.'

'It's okay, come with me. It's nice to see you. It's been a while.'

She took my hand and guided me to the kitchen. The sprawled-out cat was shooed from the rattan seat near the radiator as she settled me down. Almost instantly, the cat returned and leapt onto my lap.

Although the decor was very different to when her parents owned it, the house maintained its comforting intimacy, its walls harbouring the secrets, laughter and mischief shared between teenage girls many years ago.

'What's all too much?' she asked.

It did not take long to describe Glory's death and my mother's increasing infirmity. And Alice wept freely, both with and for me. It took a second pot of tea for me to spill the rest: the money, Stephen being kept in the dark, Mum's shocking insults.

'Your mother was always a hard woman, but she loved you girls very much. You shouldn't take it too personally. She'll be in shock, and these kinds of patients can exhibit strong behavioural changes.' She had shifted into professional mode, speaking in the warm but authoritative tone to which her therapy clients no doubt responded well.

'Do you know the saying *in vino veritas*?' I fidgeted with a damp tissue, shredding it beyond recognition.

'Yes. In wine truth. Why?'

'Well, could it be a case of *in dementia veritas*?'

'Do you mean is it conceivable that Glory took a lover? That your mum sensed it? I couldn't say. What do you think?'

I smirked. That was the oldest trick in the psychologist's playbook. To bounce the question back. 'I wouldn't put it past her. I mean, you know what Glory was like.'

And Alice did know. She'd seen that my sister, as the youngest, had enjoyed less anxious parents and had learnt to charm everyone into giving her what she wanted. And by age fourteen she wanted boys. While other girls donned flannel and jeans in true 1990s grunge style, Glory wore flowing dresses in colours that flattered her skin and hair. Boys fell over themselves to walk her home after school and she let them, even though she only lived two streets away and it meant abandoning two of our supposedly inseparable trio.

'Still, she's been married for years. She's got adorable kids, a beautiful house and a café she loves. She seemed happy when I saw her only a few months ago.' Alice sounded unsure but seemed determined not to sully her dead friend's reputation by speculating.

'But come on…can't you imagine her growing bored with Stephen? You know how much she liked bad boys. Surely Stephen is too dull? Remember how she forever asked us to cover for her while she hung out at the Inch with the guitar players and the bottle smashers?'

'Yes, but I bet she learnt her lesson, don't you?'

Straight away, I understood the incident she was referring to. I'd gone to fetch Glory from the park and brought a clean pair of trousers because some bastard had torn off her skirt and forced her into the mud—all for smiling at another man. I had taken her to Alice's to recover, and with Glory shaken and humiliated, we vowed never to speak of it again. I'd even washed her clothes and stacked them into her wardrobe again, so she wouldn't have to face that. She'd recovered well, and my mistrust of men outlasted hers.

'Okay. If she wasn't leaving her husband for another man, what's with the cash? The secrecy? What if Stephen beat her? I mean, I always thought he could be quite controlling.'

'Jesus Christ, Grace. Next you'll tell me he found out about the other man and killed her. Look, I get it. You're angry. You need it to make sense. To fall into place. But sometimes life doesn't all make sense. You know that. Your mind has gone racing, and you need to stop, or you'll blow things out of proportion. Even start resenting her.'

'I guess.'

'Trust that she'll have had her reasons. Maybe she was ashamed.'

'Ashamed of what? She should have told me. I could've helped her.'

'Well maybe that's it. Perhaps this time she didn't want you to save her.' That comment stung. She must have seen it in my expression because she came over for a hug. 'I'm sorry. The truth is I can't second guess why Glory was keeping secrets. All I am certain of is this: she's gone now and we must let it lie. And remember her with love.'

We remained huddled, letting the finality of her death sink in, our long hairs intermingled, moist cheek against moist cheek. Bored with the cramped darkness, the cat wriggled free and jumped away with an accusatory look that made us both laugh.

'More tea and biscuits,' Alice said and bounced up.

'And I need a wee.'

When I came back from the toilet, she poured another cup of tea and I opened the biscuits. 'How are things with Dave?' she asked.

'Ugh. I was hoping to avoid that particular subject.'

'How come?'

'Well, it's been really awkward lately. I think I love him. I really do. I certainly love being with him. But we can't live together right now, and he won't accept that.'

'Why can't you live together?'

'My landlord doesn't allow me to have anybody else living in the flat and even though Dave is there all the time, that's not a permanent solution. So he wants me to live with him. But his apartment is a bit of a shit hole. And in the Gorbals, of all places.'

Alice scrunched up her nose in sympathetic repulsion. 'Ugh.'

'Right? I mean, I understand he's from there and all. And to be honest, his is one of the nicer homes in the neighbourhood. But I just don't want to live there. I don't feel I belong. Until we can scrape the cash together to do it up and sell, we're stuck in limbo.'

'What's *your* plan?'

'I prefer to wait for us to be in a position that we can afford to move to a nice place together. But Dave says I'm stalling.'

Without missing a beat, my ever-intuitive girlfriend pounced on what I didn't want her to ask. 'Are you?'

I squirmed. 'Surely it's not stalling when what you're suggesting makes the most sense? And who thinks it's a good idea to start a life together in a place that's too small? We'd just get on each other's nerves.'

'Of course you're going to get on each other's nerves, but that's going to happen wherever you live. I mean, we've always known you're a control freak. Look what you've done to the biscuits.' She chuckled and pointed at the plate.

I stared at the Custard Creams forming a neat pyramid and shook my head. Nothing ever slipped her attention.

Alice leaned forward and rested her chin on her hands. 'What are you really afraid of?' she continued. Why are you not letting this man in?'

Why indeed? That is where I drew a blank. Dave was fun. We loved working out together. Had great sex. What's more: he didn't need me. And maybe that's what unsettled me most.

'I don't know…I don't know how it will play out. I guess I'm worried that once I let go and re-plan my life to include him—you know, permanently—something will go wrong. What if I open myself to him and then for whatever reason he leaves? You know I couldn't cope with that.'

She leaned forward, frowning. 'Sweetie, we all worry about that. That's completely normal.'

'Besides, what kind of freak puts up with someone who does this?' I pointed to the carefully stacked biscuits and we both chuckled.

'Who cares? Grab him while he does!'

'Maybe I will,' I said. 'But now I have to go. Stephen will need me.'

Alice nodded and led me to the door. We hugged each other goodbye. 'I'll come visit soon,' she said. 'Let me know about the funeral. And if there's anything I can do to help. But in the meantime, honey, take care of yourself. And remember: love isn't only about giving, it's also about being willing to receive. You deserve love, my friend. He's a good man. Take the plunge.'

CHAPTER NINE

Was I stalling? Alice's question haunted me the whole way home, the intermittent drizzle on the windshield mirroring my feeble indecisiveness.

Thoughts of Dave, Glory, her secrets, mum, the dementia merged into a distressing, unfixable tangle, like wind-struck streamers on a kite that had flown far and fast out of reach.

Once in Shawlands, the struggle to park the Fiat anywhere within two hundred yards of home compounded the exhaustion from my arduous morning, so that by the time I'd turned my key in the lock of apartment number 2/1, I was too weak to push. I stood with my head resting against the cool wooden door for a minute or so; then it opened from inside.

'Oh. It's you. Good,' said Dave. 'I wondered if maybe it was someone at the wrong door.'

He was wearing a black T-shirt and tight jeans. Both accentuated his muscles. His short brown hair was wet and smelled of shampoo. It was the freshly showered look that won over the housewives when he came to quote for a job. A nice change from the grotty workmen you didn't know whether to trust or not, it gave the added subliminal message that this plumber would also clean up after himself.

It didn't hurt that he was handsome: large twinkly eyes and a wide, genuine smile displaying rows of perfect, straight teeth which clashed implausibly with his thick Glasgow accent. He was short though, which fit the stereotype a little better.

I was still using the door for support while Dave approached with care, like a zookeeper primed to catch a fragile species.

'You look like you've been through the wars,' he said.

'I have.' I let go into his arms.

He brought me to the sofa, my head finding comfort on his lap. His arm was wrapped around my shoulder and he stroked my hair, waiting for me to speak.

I didn't.

The room was in the semi-darkness of early evening when I woke with a start, a sharp pain radiating in my neck and my cheek flushed with the warmth of another body.

'How long have I been asleep?'

'About two hours.'

'And you sat here all this time? In the dark?'

'It's okay. You needed it. I sang some songs in my head—the Stone Roses have a surprisingly big repertoire.' He smiled.

'I have to go.' I unbent my aching limbs one by one. 'I have to get back to Glory's.' The sound of her name made my stomach jump.

'How are they doing?'

'As you would expect.'

He offered to make a pot of tea while I showered.

The casualness of his movements around my flat irked me; as did the noisy banging of cupboard doors. But I was grateful for the offer and his presence.

Once clean and with a bag packed, I sat with him at the breakfast bar where the tea stood steeping. Having mulled it over while soaping myself, I'd determined there was no easy way to ask what I wanted to know.

'Dave?'

'Uhuh.'

'I know you don't want to talk about why you and Stephen fell out, but can you tell me this: was it to do with violence?'

'What do you mean?'

'When you guys grew up in the Gorbals, did Stephen ever get into trouble? Fights?'

'Wow, Grace. That's some prejudice right there. What? You think anyone from the Gorbals must have a violent streak?'

'No, of course not. I'm sorry. I didn't mean to imply...I know you're not. And your friends are all great. But, you know, it's just got a reputation. I'm sorry. I really just wanted to know about Stephen. When you were young.'

My apology seemed to have done the trick. He looked less insulted.

'No, not Stephen. No fights. Christ, his foster parents would've killed him if he'd laid a finger on anyone. Why do you ask?'

'So he never assaulted anyone? Or had a temper?'

'No. I told you no. He was fine. What's this about, Grace?' He searched my face for an answer, his eyebrows sinking into a deep frown.

'Never mind.' I got up.

'I thought you said it was an accident. Did he hurt

her? Tell me.'

He turned the barstool to free his legs. I placed my hand on his shoulders, intended to signal reassurance, but with the added benefit of keeping him there.

'Ignore me. I'm talking shite.'

CHAPTER TEN

The funeral was awful: watching the boys cling to their father while surrounded by strangers twice as tall, smothered by a relentless flood of sympathies. Stephen a perfect picture of sorrow. I had hardly been able to look at my parents—let alone speak—for fear of breaking down and was grateful for their trusted friends from Perth caring for them.

Alice had stood by me while the mourners gravitated towards immediate family: parents who lost a child, children who lost a mother, a husband who lost his love. Me merely a sister; once in adulthood, relegated to second-degree kin. A slap in the face I hadn't seen coming.

But we knew better, didn't we, Gi?

I moved back to my flat once the boys survived their first few days back at school. The little troopers navigated the innocent but misguided celebrity status thrust upon them with an amazing resilience.

You would have been so proud.

Stephen re-joined his colleagues within days of the accident, quoting important deadlines. Who could blame him wanting to escape the house?

The last commiseration casserole made way for veggie burgers and pasta selected from Glory's list of 'favourites' at Tesco, its delivery man oblivious to the reduction in portion size from four to three.

With mornings a struggle, I still came round to help pack the kids off to school and exercise the dog. I didn't mind. It took only fifteen minutes to walk to Lochiel Academy junior school. There, I observed the boys race inside with their friends, a scene repeated across the street by a stream of mothers entering McDonald's for coffee. The fast food place bore testament to Glasgow city council's greedy hypocrisy towards its child obesity targets, sandwiched as it was between two primary schools.

The mums had been kind to me at the gates, offering commiserations and help with an awkwardness that seemed to grow as the days increased. I wasn't one of them. I knew that. I brought the stench of death to their jasmine- and patchouli-scented lives. I'd offered them respite by stating I didn't drink coffee, and they never invited me again.

This morning, the boys had barely given me a glance before darting off, their little heads and Spiderman backpacks disappearing into the crowd.

'Come on Blue, time to run.'

On hearing this, the dog skipped in place, keeping his shiny eyes on me as he awaited my first step. Then off we went. His enthusiasm for me had ballooned these last two weeks as he worked out that I always kept up, no matter how hard he pulled on the lead to go faster. We ran down Pollokshaws Road and turned into Queen's Park, skirting the pond to prevent a possible incident with the swans. Still at pace, we headed for the flagpole atop the hill to admire the ten-mile views in three directions.

'Look, buddy, you can see Ben Lomond today. I still want to climb that one.' Dark clouds were forming up ahead indicating imminent rain but, for now, we stood side by side catching evasive rays of sunshine and breathing in the cool spring air.

I gazed down and smiled. I had grown fonder of him too, admiring his ability to stay in the present and to rebound, unshaken, from even the foulest smelling tree trunk only to try his luck again. Channelling my inner canine, I had stopped getting sucked into the rabbit hole of crazy theories. I now chose to accept that Glory had probably merely been bored and, in sneaking around, had likely only wanted to engineer a bit of financial independence.

'Right. We can't stay here forever. It's time to go back down and face the world. You and me, buddy. Looking out for each other.'

We took the shortcut described to me by Adam, slicing through the senior school's playing fields and past the hockey club, where he played with his pals on Friday nights. I headed for a last lap of Maxwell Park to round off the walk, in keeping with Glory's usual schedule.

Blue pulled at the lead. I let him off once I'd scanned the area and noted no loose dogs. Only a lone figure loitering. His eye line crossed mine as he also took stock of the park and paused on me long enough to raise a creepy sensation.

To break the connection, I moved to a bench by the play park and pretended to tie my laces. When I straightened up, the man was striding straight towards me. I searched for Blue, hoping for a semblance of protection, but he was nowhere to be seen. Nor was anyone else.

Before I could stop him, the man sat down next to me. He whistled and shouted, 'Here boy!' then faced me with a disturbing grin. As if he knew the dog wouldn't come. I jumped to my feet and looked around. What had he done?

On my second attempt blowing silent air through my dry mouth, Blue appeared from behind a tree thirty yards away. Safe. He showed no interest in me or the man, instead sniffing out the ground's many treasures.

I turned back to the intruder. Sensing an edge in standing over him, I raised my chin and my voice when I asked: 'Do I know you?'

He chuckled. 'Nah, hen. I'm only the messenger.'

'What?'

His smile faded. 'We're not very happy about you closing the café for so long. You need to open up again. There's a delivery coming on Thursday.'

'What do you mean? How do you—'

His eyes turned to ice as he grabbed my wrist in a flash. 'We'll be very disappointed if you're not there to receive the goods. Ken what I'm saying?'

He rushed off, his dark coat billowing behind him like a cape, almost engulfing Blue who circled his legs, tail wagging, until he turned towards the road.

I collapsed onto the bench, my leaden limbs welded to the frame. Who was this man? How did he know about the café? How did he know who I was? Then it dawned on me: did he think I was Glory? Even then, none of it made sense. Why would a supplier come find you like that?

Blue sniffed around my shoes and placed his head on my knee, his expectant stare coaxing me to come run again.

'So much for looking out for me. Fat load of good you are.' I pushed him aside, wincing at the slabber left on my trousers.

My nerves remained on edge as I dropped him off and made for my first client appointment of the day. Since moving to Glasgow, I'd experienced my fair share of encounters with vagrants invading my personal space, asking for change, a meal, a kiss. The alcoholics were most likely to hurl lecherous compliments at you and try to cop a feel, whereas the junkies slung cocky threats of physical aggression their broken bodies couldn't possibly deliver. I learnt that it upset men the most when you didn't smile on demand. I also learnt that, naturally, this made me a cunt.

But this was different. This man had been looking for me.

I walked with an overly straight posture to signal, should anyone be looking, I was not afraid. 'I will not be intimidated, I will not be intimidated,' my mind recited, but I flinched whenever something dark flashed past in the corner of my eye. Mental affirmations not working, I started a light-footed jog, swaying to Taylor Swift singing in my head. '*Something something something, shake it off.*'

Although the fear subsided, the knot in my stomach persisted. The incident had woken a repressed sense of duty. The café. I could no longer pretend the café wasn't there, wasn't being neglected, wasn't another part of Glory we would need to pack away.

I'm sorry, Gi, I know how much you love it.

I vowed to resurrect it, if only until Stephen was ready to decide on its future. Though him wanting rid of it would be no surprise.

CHAPTER ELEVEN

'Is my bum okay?'

'Hm?' The question jerked my thoughts back to the exercise room and the red-faced blonde struggling to sustain a one-minute plank, fishing for a gold star for posture.

'Grace is everything all right? You're a million miles away today.'

'I'm sorry. Yes, your line is great,' I looked at my watch. 'Time's up. Well done. Let's do the burpees again, shall we? And this time, speed it up. Starting with sixteen.'

'Were you…thinking…about…your sister?' Her words came out in breathless chunks as she squatted and jumped.

I'd made all my clients aware that I would need a break because of the accident. In true British style, most enquired about it once out of politeness, for it never to be mentioned again. Others saw it as carte blanche to pry into my state of mind at every opportunity.

'That's it. Only nine more to go.' Ignoring her enquiries, I projected the professionalism she was entitled to for her thirty-five pounds an hour.

'I can't…imagine…what you're…going through.'

'Yes. It's been hard. And eight more, please.'

Once she was sucking on her ionised-water bottle for recovery, I took my chance. 'With everything going on, would it be possible to move your session to later in the afternoon? I've got Glory's café to deal with. I don't know what's required yet or how long that will take. So I'm just testing the waters.'

'Oh.' She took a few more sips and eyed the door, her caring persona disintegrating and revealing the me-first, elbows-out attitude that explained why she had the big house with the gym and I didn't. 'Thing is, Grace, I really like working out with you, but it's hard for me to fit in me-time already, what with the kids and the house and the Heart Foundation. I need to keep it at nine, if it's all right with you?'

Shit.

'I understand. I'm sorry to have to ask. If I can't make it work, I'll introduce you to another trainer I know. You'll like him. He's very good with bums.' I gave her a conspiratorial wink and she giggled at the innuendo. 'And you'll need it with a bum as big as yours,' is what I didn't say.

She grabbed her towel, dabbed her flawless face and showed me to the door.

'Okay. Well, I hope it works out. Let me know on Monday. If not, maybe I'll see you at the café when it's up and running again? I really like that place.'

Of course she does.

CHAPTER TWELVE

As I left my client, thinking about the café, I was reminded of the time I'd dared to challenge Glory's concept for her new venture. It must have been three years, yet I could still picture her sitting opposite me, affronted.

'I know you find this hard to believe, Grace, but I'm not an idiot.'

'I never said you were. But I don't see why it has to be vegan. There are not that many vegans around. And the vegans I know don't even drink coffee.'

'It's only pseudo-vegan. It's psychology. I've been around the yummy mummies for years now and I know exactly how to make them part with their not-so-hard-earned cash.'

'Well, I don't get it, so maybe that makes me the idiot.'

'Are you expecting me to comment on that?' She laughed. 'Here's the thing. Shawlands is going through a phase of massive gentrification. Crappy pubs are being replaced by hipster gin bars, right? The dead giveaway is that half the greengrocer's display is dedicated to avocados.'

'God forbid we run out of avocados!'

'This is serious, Grace.'

'Sorry. Tell me more.'

Her eyes lit up and threw herself into a rehearsed-sounding explanation of her terribly clever plan.

'I've been reading up on marketing. The proposition needs to be right. It needs to be bored-mummy heaven. We'll serve single-source artisan coffee and throw cushions over some mismatched chairs and hand-carved wooden benches. That will also attract the actual artists that are still around, and the students. And then I'm tapping into the clean eating fad. Oh my God, Grace, you can't believe how much energy is spent talking about what foods are forbidden and why. And not just for the mums. The kids too! It's all posturing. Loads of nonsense allergies.'

'Some of them are—' My point was lost.

'We put unprocessed-sounding dishes with lots of veg and chick peas in the name. And we offer every possible substitution for dairy and eggs. They're not actually going to order it, but it allows me to charge higher prices. And ta-dah! You've got a winner.'

'Let me get this straight. It's a place where they can look like they have special dietary needs, even though they don't have them? And you're going to make them pay extra for it?' It sounded ridiculous. Why did these well-to-do married women always feel the need to adopt every latest trend? They seemed constantly looking for purpose? I didn't get it. Luxury problems.

'Yes, exactly,' Glory said.

I rinsed a nascent bad taste from my mouth with a sip of water. 'That all sounds pretty scheming, if you ask me. Aren't you supposed to be nice about your customers? Aren't these your friends?'

'Okay, you got me. Here I am trying to be all calculating, hard-nosed business-like, when in reality, I'll probably go broke handing out free coffees to my posse. Who am I kidding, right? But I really think there's something there.'

'I, for one, am pleased you're not the monster I thought you were a minute ago. Have you decided on a name?'

'Not yet. I'm torn between *Glory's Greens* and *Veg&Might*.'

'Veg&Might is funny. And it sounds more hipster, you know, something-and-something. I'd go with that.'

'It might attract the men with beards. I do like a stubbly chin...' I caught a naughty twinkle in her eye.

'Yuck. How does Stephen feel about this?'

'About facial hair? He hates it.'

'No.' I laughed. 'About you running a café.'

'He's not so keen on that, either. But he's given me a little "play money", as he calls it.' She shrugged. 'And he's resigned to me wanting more out of life right now, so we'll both have to make do with that.'

'Well I'm right behind you,' I said, not fully believing she'd be successful.

'I'm glad someone is.'

CHAPTER THIRTEEN

Later that day, I retrieved the staff's phone numbers from the emergency contact list at Veg&Might. Glory employed two people. I called Sascha first. The more reliable one—in contrast with her career-anarchist look. Thank heavens she was keen to start work again straight away.

The other one was a part-time yoga instructor who'd decreed that showing up to work was not always 'compatible with his chi energy'. Glory had performed a hilarious impersonation one day, which made us laugh so much that a 'lack of compatibility with chi energy' became our go-to excuse for anything. Seemingly oblivious to anyone but himself, he declined to return, having been offended at the lack of contact.

Good riddance. But how much more pressure would that put on me?

Dependably punctual, Sascha was waiting for me on the doorstep as I strode over three minutes late the next morning.

'Nice change from the green,' I said, pointing at her head.

She ran her hands through her hair. 'Glory liked

purple. I dyed it last night in her honour. I'm so sorry for your loss. I'll miss her a lot.'

'That's very kind. Thank you.' I'd learnt through trial and error how to accept condolences with the appropriate poise. 'As I said last night, today is about understanding how and when I would need to assist to keep the place ticking over.'

A residual smell of ground coffee greeted us as I opened the door, and the fresh air launched specks of dust into the sunlight, where they staged a welcome dance, as if to celebrate the end of their static neglect.

Having only been a visitor until now, it was new territory to find myself behind the counter as Sascha showed me around, explaining how to prepare the food and drinks. I wandered from appliance to appliance, stroking the cold metal, getting a feel for this new workplace.

'Between nine o'clock and eleven, it gets busy,' she said, 'so it would be great to get some help.'

'What's it like at other times?' I tensed up, bracing for the answer that would determine how many more clients I stood to lose.

'Well, that depends. There are a few regulars who come for lunch, and Wednesdays are popular with groups of mums before the school pickup. That's about it. Sunday brunch is getting busier, but we had an offer on, so it's hard to tell. It's pretty quiet, overall. I can handle that alone.'

Relieved, I inhaled fresh hope. I wouldn't be needed much. But while my body relaxed, my brain perked up on spotting an inconsistency. How can it be so quiet? Grace was always talking about her 'booming' business. She'd been so sure it would be a success. It wasn't unusual for Glory to exaggerate, but it made me wonder why she'd put in place the complicated structure for distributing profits to the kids if there weren't any.

'So is this not profitable, then?'

'I don't know. Glory took care of the business side. I only had to make sure I rung up every order in the register.'

I thought of all the things that would have to be taken care off: paperwork, utilities, rent…How much of that was my job now?

'Who does the accounts?' I asked.

'An older gentleman called Alastair. Do you want me to check for his details?'

'No, thanks. I can find him,' I said, recognising the name, 'He's a family friend.'

'He often comes in on a Friday, if that helps. Our only customer in a suit.'

I searched through the folders of papers under the counter. There was not much of interest and I started to lose faith in ever finding the hidden bank details.

Sascha retreated to the small kitchen area. 'The fridges need a complete clear out. All the food has gone off,' she yelled from the rear.

'Yuck. That does not sound fun.' I came closer, breathing only through my mouth to keep out any foul smells. 'Where do we get this stuff from?'

'Some of it we buy from small craft traders, like the jams and honey. They show up and we choose on the day. The organic veg is sourced from Locavore, the social enterprise a couple of streets away. But to be honest, most of it is pretty standard stuff and comes from a wholesaler called Excelsior. Deliveries are once a fortnight. We'll have to call them to replenish.'

'No need. I happen to know they're coming

tomorrow.'

'Oh?'

'Yes, some asshole accosted me yesterday. A real creep. I'm minded to give this supplier a lesson in customer service.'

'Wow. That's weird. I wonder who that was, because Marius the delivery guy is a sweetheart. He's Romanian and doesn't speak much English, but Glory liked him. He's been our man from the start and I think she was so excited to be opening that she invested in becoming friends with anyone that mattered.'

A rush of warmth filled my chest and a grin spread across my face as I pictured Glory's ebullience in greeting every person crossing her threshold. 'Always the charmer.'

'Ha! You should have seen the charm bomb she threw at the council's planning inspector.' I marvelled at her perfect choice of words, as if the expression had been made up for my sister. A charm bomb. 'The kitchen had the wrong extraction vent for this category of venue, or something like that, and the man had threatened to stop the launch. Glory worked at him for weeks. All sweetness and light, with a little flirtation here and there. It was so fun to watch. And then, all of a sudden, he sent a letter saying it was all okay, and we never saw him again. We could not have been happier if we'd won the lottery.'

We. That one word kicked me in the gut and turned the mood stone cold, her celebration poisoned by my envy of their shared joy. Sascha went quiet, looking perplexed by the sudden shift in my demeanour, her eyes searching for an explanation.

I faked a smile and reached for her shoulder. 'Well, you and I, my friend, are going to make this work and do her proud. And I'm putting you in charge.'

She beamed, the earlier chill interpreted as a pause for suspense—like when they make you wait as they announce the winner on talent shows.

'Oh, Grace, I won't let you down. I promise. It will be so great to have the run of the place. I have so many ideas, but Glory didn't let me—' Both hands rushed to cover her mouth as she realised how her enthusiasm had led her into inappropriate territory.

She is young, I told myself. She has no experience of loss. I chose to forgive her and concentrated on the blessing of having someone willing to take on this burden.

CHAPTER FOURTEEN

Alastair cleared a slot in his diary for me straight away. His firm's office stood on the corner of West George Street and Wellington Street, a short but steep walk from Central Station. The property formed part of an uncharacteristically jumbled Georgian terrace with buildings of different heights and styles fronted by equally mismatched 'To Let' signs, insulting my senses and spoiling the elegance of Blythswood Square ahead.

Order was restored in the corporate blue and grey entrance hall of Evans & Carmichael Chartered Accountants, where the receptionist greeted me with a professional smile that warmed upon hearing my name.

'There is coffee and tea set up for you in here, Miss McBride.' She guided me through a white panelled door on the right. 'Mr Evans will be with you shortly. Please make yourself comfortable.'

That wouldn't be difficult. The room oozed comfort, from the first step onto the deep woven carpet to the inviting plush armchairs bathing in the sunlight from the large square window, framed by silver-tinted curtains that caressed the floor. Opulent and intimate. I spotted a silver box of tissues on the side table as I sat down. This must be the room reserved for family matters.

After a short wait, Alastair ducked through the doorway—all six-foot-four-inches of him—dressed in a grey suit and holding a black leather-bound notebook. I looked up. The height difference transported me back to when he towered over me visiting my parents' store.

'Now, which one are you again?' he would tease, and the routine finished with me holding my fist as high as I could—usually halfway up his chest—and saying, 'Watch out, Uncle Alastair, because one day I will reach, and you will learn who's who.'

That day had come, sort of. I stood and reached his chin. But instead of a punch I offered a hug. 'Hello Alastair.'

'My dear Grace. It's been too long.' His monkey-arms encircled me almost twice. 'What a terrible tragedy.' He placed me into my seat as if I were a delicate package, and sank into the chair opposite. 'You must be devastated. I'm sorry I didn't get a chance to pay my respects to you at the funeral.'

'That's okay.'

'I spoke to your parents last week. They appear to have a lot on their plate already. With…umm…your mother.'

'Yes. It's awful. And all coming at once. I'm only holding it together because Stephen and the boys need me. And there are a lot of affairs to sort out, which is why I am here.'

'Of course. Is there something specific you are looking for?' He opened the notebook and fetched a Mont Blanc pen from his silk-lined inside pocket. I doubt my family would be given a second look if we met him now, but he owed his early success to the loyalty of his Perthshire clients, most of whom were childhood friends, and he was the type of man to value relationships.

'Can you explain the trusts you set up for Glory's kids, please? Dad asked me to find the paperwork, but I don't know what I am looking for. Nor what to do if I find it.'

'Happy to explain again.'

The use of the word 'again' jarred, but I figured he meant earlier conversations with my family.

'Our firm designed this structure for clients who are owner-managers with younger children, to help release funds from the business while minimising tax. I won't bore you with the process to set it up, which required the directors' and your parents' participation, but the upshot is that the two children own a certain class of share in the café through what's called an Interest in Possession trust. They are entitled to a fixed dividend from the business every year. Those funds can then be used to pay for school fees and associated costs to the benefit of the children, such as uniforms and summer camps.'

'I think I follow. But who manages the trust? Isn't that expensive?'

'That's the nice thing about this type of trust: the money can go into bank accounts in the names of the children. And as long as the dividends are less than fifteen thousand pounds each, there is no tax due or self-assessment required for HMRC. Glory would be the one making all the payments from the accounts, of course, as the boys are too young and probably wouldn't even be aware the accounts existed. She had wanted to be the sole trustee, but I warned against that and now she has passed, I'm glad I did. Your father is the other trustee.'

'Why Dad and not Stephen?'

'I don't know.'

'Do you think she was hiding things from him?'

He frowned. 'Well, that's not my concern as her accountant. Glory could choose anyone as trustee and she chose your father. She never said why. And it wasn't my place to ask. But if the funds were being used for school fees, I would be astounded if Stephen didn't know. After all, it would replace payments he would have been making beforehand.'

I sipped my coffee, my mind racing. Was Glory hoarding money in these accounts for future use? And if so, where the hell was it?

'Do you have the details of the bank accounts, so we can see how much is there?'

'No, I don't. I wasn't involved in that part. You could call Clydesdale since that's where the café has its account, and maybe she kept everything at one bank. But they're prohibited from releasing such information to anyone but the client, or in this case the next of kin. It would be best if you found the statements. Even then, unless your father is also a trustee on the account itself, it will be a rigmarole to get access.' I sank back into the armchair and rubbed my eyes. Alastair patted my arm. 'Oh, my dear. I'm sorry. This is all very complicated. I spent a lot of time explaining accounting and taxation to your sister and here you are having to absorb it all in one go. It doesn't seem fair for you to have to worry about this. Why don't I pick this up with your father?'

'No.' I was anxious to fulfil my task but also too

intrigued to let go. 'Dad asked me to take care of it. As you said, they've got a lot on their plate.'

'I see. One way to trace the bank details, of course, is to check the recipient details for the dividend payments out of the café's bank account. They will have been made around the time of your dividends, same as last year.'

'What dividends? What do you mean? I've had no money from the café. Why would I?'

Alastair cocked his head and looked at me with a puzzled expression.

'But Grace, my dear, you're the majority shareholder in the café. Which is why you get the vast majority of the profits. Do you not remember receiving two payments in the last two years? They were big sums: five figures.'

'What? I don't know anything about this. What are you saying?'

The blood drained from his face. 'You really have no idea? Glory told me you'd invested in the café and helped out a lot. That's why you were a shareholder. She brought me your signatures. She told me you were always too busy to come.'

'No, I never invested. I don't have any money.'

He shuffled in his seat. 'I've known you so long. I didn't bother to do the necessary checks. It all seemed so plausible. I've got your signature on the trust papers. Was that not you?'

'No.'

He brought his fingers to his temples and rubbed, his eyes closed. I was desperate to question him, but I didn't want to interrupt his thought. After a while, his eyes flashed open and his hands dropped to his knees like dead weights.

'G. The payments were made to G McBride. The account never actually specified "Grace", only "G". I'm sorry. Glory pulled the wool right over my eyes. I don't know where the money went. Why would she do this? This could have serious repercussions for me.'

'Uncle Alastair, relax. I'm sure it's fine. You've done nothing wrong.'

'Technically I have. I should have stuck to the Know Your Client process.' Alastair wrung his hands together and my stomach swirled. Trust bloody Glory. How dare she put this kind man in this position? And what for?

'It's okay. I won't let anyone find out.'

He forced a smile. 'Thank you.'

'But let me get this straight…the café is mine?'

'Except for the few shares held by Glory, which will pass to Stephen, yes. Because you have all the voting rights you need for control, you already have the ultimate say.'

'What am I supposed to do with it?'

My quest for advice seemed to revive him and he grew into himself again.

'You could sell it. It has a surprisingly healthy bottom line for a place that size. And I suspect that with the vegan angle fashionable right now, someone will want it. That is, if you can bear to part with it?' He paused, testing for my emotions. 'It feels like a decision you shouldn't rush.'

I grimaced, baffled this was my decision at all.

CHAPTER FIFTEEN

The next day was my first on the new job. Sascha was pushing folded napkins under wobbly tables when I heard a knock on the rear door.

'That must be the wholesaler,' I said.

'I'll check.' She left for the back while I stayed at one of the tables, examining a pack of receipts to educate myself on what sold well.

What was your miracle formula, Gi? How did you keep this place going?

Whilst I was still frozen in indecision whether to keep or sell the café, I'd worked out that either option required me to do my best to keep it financially sound.

'Marius is here.' Sascha stood by my side, holding paperwork. 'He is offloading the boxes and needs a signature. Glory would normally—'

'Give it here.' I took the clipboard from her and scribbled on the designated line. 'Once the goods are inside, I'll help you put it all away.'

I yawned. The weight of all the new demands hindered my sleep, leaving me perpetually on edge. One constant thread strangled every option I thought of: sooner or later I had to tell Stephen that his wife had gone out of her way to complicate things and—for reasons I could not fathom—had minimised her ownership of the business; leaving him with little say and me with one giant headache.

Dammit, Gi. This would all be easier if you'd just bloody talked to me.

'Grace?' Sascha walked in. Her eyes darted between me and the papers in her hand as she plopped another problem at my feet like a cat's gift bird. 'I've counted the boxes and there are fewer than there should be according to this list. I'm so sorry I should have checked before you signed, but I only came to ask how you wanted to handle things and then you signed it and then Marius left and he was so upset because I told him about Glory and it's only then that I saw—'

'Don't worry,' I said. I managed to fake a smile while mentally cursing the heavens. 'I didn't even look at the damn paper. And besides, I put you in charge, and here I am snatching things out of your hands before you even get a chance to speak. I'm the one who should be sorry.'

'Okay. Sorry…Thanks.' She came closer. 'I've marked everything that's here, but about thousand pounds' worth of goods is not accounted for. That's like half. Which is weird because it actually looks like the usual set of boxes. Shall I call Excelsior?'

'No, it's fine, I'll take care of it. I want to talk to them anyway.' Aware I was stepping on her managerial toes again, I added, 'But you're the boss…so why don't you show me what you want me to put away?'

'Just those, thanks.' She pointed at a mound of twenty-odd boxes that wouldn't present much of a challenge.

'Why don't you go online and see if you can make

people aware we're open again from tomorrow. I've seen we have a Facebook page but what else?'

'Great idea. We've not got much else. I've been thinking for a while we should set up a Twitter account and put out photos on Instagram. Those pastel-coloured macaroons we have would make a great shot next to a perfect latte.'

As she made a beeline for her iPad, I got stuck in, reminding myself to ask later for her advice on getting new personal training clients through social media. They hadn't been as loyal as I'd hoped.

Because I'd cleared a stinky mess from the fridge before, I remembered the system for where the different fresh foods were kept.

There seemed to be no such schema for the small storage room, its shelves housing inbred families of condiments, tins and cleaning products. My hands itched at the prospect of restoring harmony.

Exactly what I needed.

'Have we got any labels?' No answer. 'Never mind. I've got some labels at home. I'll bring them in.'

Once the shelves had been redistributed, I started unpacking and placed the new items face forward in the correct spot, behind any older ones so that they would be used in the right sequence. My shoulders became lighter and my movements flowed as I bent and stacked, lifted and folded, and hummed an airy tune as blessed order prevailed.

When the pile was down to four, I noticed a series of black stars drawn with permanent marker, pulling my attention to a box of paper napkins. I swooped it up and fixed it against my chest as I picked at the tape to prise it loose.

The paper inside seemed an odd colour at first, but

when I lifted the flap further, all five litres of blood dropped to my toes and the room swirled.

No.

No more.

Please.

CHAPTER SIXTEEN

All the hot water bottles on Earth wouldn't make my stomach ache go away. Bloated with stress, I had spent two hours contorting myself, seeking relief by concocting stories that would somehow make collecting boxes of cash look okay. But it was hopeless. This situation stank, whichever way I looked at it.

What were you up to Gi? And who are these guys?

When Dave came round, I was sprawled on my sofa, partially undressed, pressing a heat pad to my belly. He fixed a gentle kiss on my forehead. 'Can I make you a hot chocolate?' he said, in the hushed and understanding tone men put on for 'women's issues'. I saw no point in setting him straight.

'That would be great.'

I was slowly getting used to letting someone do things for me, even if it had made me uncomfortable at the start, when I'd needed him to understand I wasn't some delicate flower that needed caring for. But he knew I wasn't weak. He was just nice. And mine—something that also required getting used to.

He stroked my hair and disappeared. I listened to his footsteps padding into the kitchen, the hum of the kettle, a cupboard door banging, the clinking of a spoon…followed by silence. Despite the smell of cocoa, he returned not carrying my drink, but the napkin box.

'Grace? Why is there a box full of money by the sink?'

He stood. Silent. Blinking. Like an owl. For some time. When I could stand it no longer, I confessed. 'There's another one in the bedroom.'

'Did you…win the lottery?'

I squirmed with each step Dave made towards me. I hadn't planned to discuss with him what I'd found. Had my subconscious left the box in plain sight to force the issue? After all, if I ever intended to live with this man, I had to discover if I could trust him.

'Sit down. I need to tell you something,' I said.

He kept his gaze on the box glued between his hands, as though the answer would pop out like a jack-in-the-box. I zipped my trousers up and sat facing him.

'I believe Glory was doing something fishy. Today, there was a delivery at the café and the invoice had a lot more items than they brought. And then when I was packing stuff away, I found…that.'

'Okay, who—'

'There's more. Stay here.' I got up and retrieved the Jimmy Choos from the other room. 'This one I found in her closet at home. Three thousand pounds stuffed in between her shoes in neat little rolls. Dad thinks she was leaving Stephen, but that's news to me. Also…apparently, she's been squirrelling money away for the kids in special bank accounts with trusts and everything, but I can't find them. And then the accountant told me the café's making lots of profit but there are hardly any customers.'

'One thing at a time, babe. Take it slow.' He caught my hands. 'This delivery, who was it from?'

'A wholesaler called Excelsior. This guy snared me in the park on Tuesday, saying how I needed to open the café or they wouldn't be happy. I didn't understand then. I thought maybe he was looking for Glory, you know? But now I can see why he needed someone there.'

'Wait. Some strange guy accosted you in the park and you didn't tell me? Why wouldn't you tell me that?'

'It's fine. He didn't hurt me. He was just creepy. He made no real physical threat. But then again he didn't need to.'

'Did he say anything at all? Or whoever it was that made the delivery?'

'No. It's like I'm supposed to know what to do, but I don't.' I sagged forward and landed face down on his lap, wishing I could block out the last few weeks. 'I have no idea what's going on.'

'Well I do.'

I jerked my head up. 'What?'

'I hate to say it, Grace, but your sister was into dodgy shit. I think she was laundering money through the café. Easily done. That's what this box is.' He rattled it for identification. 'And when you launder money, you get to keep a share of the profit. And that, I expect, will be in that one.' He pointed at the Choos.

'How do you know this?' I was careful not to angle too much for tales from his past, to not insult his underprivileged background again.

'I watched *Breaking Bad*.'

'What?'

'On Netflix. It's about a chemistry teacher who sells drugs but ends up with too much cash. So he buys a car wash to launder it with his wife.'

Astonished at this ridiculous admission, I launched onto my feet. 'TV? You're expecting me to believe something from TV is happening in my life? For Christ's sake Dave, it's my sister we're talking about, not some cartoon criminal mastermind.'

'Calm down. Listen, we'll work through this. We don't know why she did it, but the priority is for you to make it stop and not get involved.'

'But how? If what you're saying is true, these guys are criminals. What if they want their money? What if they come after me?'

'Then we inform the police. Plain and simple. I know that lands Glory in it but she is dead and you did nothing wrong. We have to focus on you.'

I pressed my fist against my eyes to prevent the tears from coming, but they came. Boy, did they come: gushing like an exploded tap, spraying circular fountains around my hands. 'I can't go to the police.'

'Why not?'

'Because I own the café. For some reason, Glory put most of the shares in my name. The cops will never believe I didn't take part. I've even been paid dividends somewhere, according to the accountant.'

He rose slowly, his voice nothing more than a hiss. 'That bitch. That holier-than-thou, self-absorbed, scheming bitch.'

'Dave…no.'

'No what? She gets to be sweetness and light and everything nice, and somehow buckets of money accidentally appear wherever she goes? Come on!' He paced like a lion, venting his frustration into the air. 'And to think all this time I was the one who wasn't good enough. Oh yes. God forbid this lowlife would come anywhere near their precious children, carrying the putrid stench of the lower classes.' He shook his head. 'Bloody hypocrites. And all this time I was the one you wouldn't trust. Ha! Face it Grace, your sister was a cow and she has landed you in it...on purpose.'

'I knew it was a mistake to tell you,' I shouted, slamming the door behind me extra hard.

CHAPTER SEVENTEEN

In hindsight, storming out of my own apartment was probably not the best idea. It was dark, and without a coat the wind burrowed through my jumper's twisted fibres and nipped at my bare arms. As I walked, the occasional gust shoved me from behind, propelling me like a parent coaxing a dawdling toddler. Move.

Where to?

My loose hair wrapped itself around my face and I was lucky to avoid a red van as I careened, blind, across the road. The current of air thrust me along Dixon Avenue towards Holy Cross Church, a red Romanesque sandstone with tall stained-glass windows bursting with symbolism. Lost and wounded, I wondered whether I would find solace in my long-abandoned Bible. Then I remembered, with Mary and Martha, Cain and Abel, and Joseph and his conniving brothers, the gospel was hardly an authority on sibling harmony.

Dave's outburst had been unacceptable. I should have kicked him out. But I'd been so shocked by his vitriol, this angry side of him I had never seen, that my instincts jumped to 'flight' rather than my usual 'fight'.

How can I fight for you, Gi, when so much of what he said is true? What am I supposed to think? The evidence is all there.

I'm stuck in the middle of your criminal activity, with no concept of why you have done this, what you were planning with all that money, or why you've made me an accessory.

And Dave wasn't welcome in your home and that was horribly unfair.

As I looped back along Queen's Park, face-on to the wind now blowing my eyes dry, I reflected on how forgiving Dave had been, much more so than me. My jaw tightened as I replayed in my mind the awful conversation Glory and I had at Veg&Might some eighteen months ago.

'I told Stephen about your man Dave and it turns out they know each other,' Glory said. She stirred the foam on her cappuccino into a brown-and-white swirl, licked the edge of the spoon, stalling for time. 'Were you aware?'

'No, it hasn't come up. Not sure I've shared Stephen's last name.' I wondered why she didn't sound more pleased about this coincidence. 'How do they know each other?'

'Stephen's from the same part of town as Dave. He doesn't like to talk about it.'

'Oh. I knew he was from Glasgow, but you wouldn't guess the Gorbals from his mild accent. Where are you going with this?'

'They went to the same school. Were in the same year.' She stirred the foam again, pulling little peaks from the surface. 'But they weren't friends.' She let that phrase linger.

'Just spit it out. What's wrong?'

'Thing is, Stephen doesn't want to see Dave. Doesn't want me to see Dave. Or the kids.' She took a sip of her drink, burying her eyes in the cup.

'What? Why? That's ridiculous.'

'He's worked hard at erasing that part of his past. You know he was in foster care, right? His parents died when he was little.'

'Yes, you've told me that before, but I don't understand what that's got to do with anything. Are you trying to tell me something about Dave here? Is there something I should know?'

'No, Gi, I like him. He's nice, and he's got a great smile. Those teeth! But Stephen and Dave have some sort of history that Stephen doesn't want to be reminded of. And he doesn't want him in his life. I accept it's not fair. And I'm happy to come see you guys at your place once in a while. Hang out. It'll be fun.' She smiled sweetly, and my hackles rose.

'Well, I think Stephen's being a dick. Unless there's something specific that Dave did to offend him, I think he's being an utter cockwomble and I can't believe you're taking his side.'

'If your man's done something, then Stephen's too much of a gentleman to say. And—no offence—it's not like you're the best judge of men, are you?'

I walked out, and we didn't speak for two weeks after that. I'd later confessed to myself that even though I was furious she'd given into her husband, part of my resentment stemmed from not knowing enough about my new boyfriend and worrying this was yet another guy I shouldn't trust.

Because you were right, then. I did suck at men. I did, and I do.

As if on cue, the image of Dougie Campbell sprung into my head. A repressed vision of the square-jawed, fifteen-year-old hunk who broke my heart. Smitten, I'd been in thrall to his football skills, cocky charm and the attention he showered on me—even in front of his friends! My sister had warned against him. She told me he was trouble, but I wouldn't listen. 'You're jealous,' I'd said, chuffed to be the desired one for a change. But it was her instinct that saved me from humiliation. Turns out, Dougie had taken bets he could get under my shirt at Alice's party and had been planning to dump me straight after. Having heard rumours, Glory flirted with him that night and, guiding him upstairs with a promise of getting into her pants, she took his off instead and threw all his clothes out the window.

While the party-goers laughed and pointed as he fetched his underwear from the garden, I celebrated his very public punishment—but my heart still bled. Glory left her applause to console me. 'I'm sorry, Grace. I didn't mean to hurt you. It was the only way I could think of to prove to you he's a shit.'

It hurt, though, Gi. I ached for a long time. But you'd only been looking out for me and for that I was grateful. It was always you and me against the world and now…now I don't know what to do.

I searched the sky and strained my ears for an answer that didn't come. I yearned to hear her explain how everything she'd done had been in my best interest. An 'honest, just wait and see.' The alternative was too unbelievable, too unbearable. Feeling abandoned in the evening silence, I headed home. I would make up with Dave when I saw him again—he was unlikely to have stayed at my flat—but for now, I had bigger problems to deal with.

CHAPTER EIGHTEEN

The wholesaler sat on the edge of Govanhill, within a concentration of semi-industrial outlets. I knew the area from visits to the Polmadie recycling centre and languishing in traffic on game days when football fans flooded the streets to Hampden Park.

I parked twenty yards away, near the car wash for McGraft's private hire cabs. Everyone said the firm was run by the mob, but with Glaswegians caring more about saving cash than their safety, it still enjoyed a near monopoly. Supposedly, they kept fares low because the cabs were merely a front for money laundering. Like I was now, it seemed.

The box lay on the passenger seat. I had struggled half the night with what to say and half the morning with what to wear. Pathetic. As if your outfit matters when quizzing gangsters about your dead sister. A visitor exited the shop and drove off, leaving the parking lot empty. The building's yard was also quiet. It was time. I picked up the box and walked towards the entrance, my resolve to end this nightmare growing with every step.

'Can I help you?' said a voice the second I entered.

The woman behind the payment desk examined me. She wore a garish golden blouse that matched her over-sized hoop earrings. Her hair was that shade of black you only get from home dyes, her roots disclosing that she was in her fifties while her cosmetic-laden face tried to pretend she was a young thing.

'I need to see the manager.'

'Is that so?'

So much for service with a smile.

I craned my neck and looked for a door or staircase leading to the office but saw nothing. Every inch of the place heaved with pallets of goods, aisles so narrow that any customer would volunteer to pay the additional Pick & Deliver charge not to manoeuvre a trolley through them. A clever ploy to increase takings, no doubt.

'There's a matter I can only discuss with the manager, so would you please say where he or she is?'

'Oh, an important matter is it? Aren't we special. You're still gonna to have to deal with me, hen. So what can I do you for?'

Should I run? I could reach the rear of the store before the woman had squeezed her pudgy shape around the desk, let alone taken a step in what I guessed would be improbably high-heeled shoes. I stared up at the cameras mounted on the walls, their red lights blinking at me. Chances were security would be on me in seconds. Plus, I didn't even know where to go.

'Yes, I am very special, and I've got a problem with a very special delivery I want to talk to him about. So if you don't mind…' I nodded to the phone.

'What's yer problem?' She narrowed her eyes, her tone a curious cross between question and threat.

I decided I would not get far without coming clean. 'I don't like the napkins you delivered.'

'What wrong with them?'

She'd taken the bait.

I plonked the box onto the desk, removed the tape in one swift pull and spread the flaps out, exposing the pile of cash. 'They're a little on the luxurious side.'

'Jesus wept, woman, close that up!' Shaking her head, she grabbed the phone and pressed a red button. 'A ginger lassie calling for Mike.' A pause. 'Okay.' Turning to me, she said, 'They're coming for you.' That tone again.

My insides screamed for me to leave. I hoped the flush of nerves wasn't visible on my face as the woman held her false-lashed eyes on me. Christ, didn't she have work to do? I swallowed hard as I felt a burning drop of stomach acid raise to my throat.

After a minute or two, a young man wearing a shiny track suit approached from the rear of the store. A classic Scottish 'ned', pasty white, with a skeletal body belying a diet of bacon rolls and Irn Bru. He strolled through the middle aisle, playing with his keys and kicking aside loose pieces of cardboard along the way.

'Alright?' he asked the cashier.

'Aye, love.'

The boy-man moved in and stood too close. He jutted out his chin, like a pit bull ready to pounce. 'Alright, hen?' The scars on his cheek underscored a capacity for violence. I took a breath and feigned nonchalance.

'Aye.'

He grabbed my elbow. 'Let's go.'

The young chap nudged me to the rear, up the metal stairs and along a narrow corridor with open doors on either side. As we neared the end, I could hear raised voices. Judging by the lack of reaction from the workers we passed, this seemed to be nothing new.

He stopped a few yards short of a room whose entrance was being blocked in its entirety by a leather-clad body. 'Boss?'

The biker type stepped aside, which revealed his pock-marked face, sweat pouring from his temples, presumably as a result of their heated exchange. He sneered and peeked back inside the room. 'Now what?'

Behind him, the boss lifted himself up from behind the large antique-style mahogany desk facing the door. As I strained to see past the perspirer, I could make out the green tartan carpet and burgundy-striped wallpaper that completed the heritage look. I thought it a curious choice of decor for an otherwise modern structure and noted one of his gold-framed oil paintings hung askew.

'So now you go and tell that shyster I won't put up with his underhanded dealings and he'd better come clean about the lorries. Tell him to come in an hour. In the meantime, I'll need to deal with this bloody distraction,' the boss said, pointing at me.

Not sure whether to be grateful or offended, I chose to wait for their exchange to finish; my chaperone having resumed his box-kicking and key-jiggling. The boss spat out some more instructions as the biker pounded along the hall. I snapped flat to the wall and raised the box so that he could squeeze past. His body odour stirred my low-lying nausea.

I was summoned inside. 'Who are you and what do you want?' The owner readjusted his green velvet waistcoat, retreated to his desk, and indicated for me to sit down. I slid into an empty seat, holding the box, while he clasped his hands in expectation.

'My name is Grace McBride. I believe you know my sister Glory.'

'Yes, I'm very sorry to hear about her passing. What a waste.'

'Yes, well, thank you.'

'Marius tells me you've taken over the café. I guess you're here on business?'

'I guess I am. For starters, I'd like to understand what this is about?' I opened the box.

He stared at the contents. 'Well that is the price of a lot of cups of coffee you are going to ring through your register. I'm told it's very nice coffee, too.' A grin spread across his smug face.

'And so by paying you a big fat invoice for goods I did not receive, I've effectively laundered money for you?'

'Bingo. Glad to see we're dealing with a pro.'

'I don't think you understand, Mr whatever your name is.'

'You can call me Mike.'

'Fine. Mike. I want no involvement in this. I came to return the cash. I would appreciate receiving a correct invoice which I shall pay forth-with.'

'Pay it forth-with, will you? Want a receipt, too? A nice handwritten one, perhaps?' The sarcasm wasn't lost on me, but I persevered, despite feeling out of my depth.

'Look. I don't know what kind of arrangement you had with my sister or why she was consorting with you. But I am telling you, it stops now.' I raised my voice at 'now' to regain some credibility.

'Oo, consorting. Nice word. Listen, my dear, I don't think you know what or who you are dealing with. Or should that be 'whom'? I bet you know. I don't care if you want to play ball or not. I'm running a business here, and you'll do as I say.'

At this point, I'd had enough of being patronised by this gentleman-wannabe lording it over me in his faux-Victorian parlour inside a shitty industrial park. I stood from my seat, ready to leave, and gave him one last chance to end this well. 'I'm here to give you back your dirty money. If you don't want it, I'll take it to the police.'

'What is it with you law-abiding people and the police?' He threw up his arms. 'Do you really think they care? That they're on your side? My dear, half of them are on the take.'

Was he bluffing? He had to be. It was my only way out.

'Tell me, then…' I paused, trying to re-order my thoughts. 'Why did Glory get involved with this?'

'That I cannot tell you. Brian Scott sent her to clear a debt he owed. Need to know more? Go see him. He runs his business from the Prince William. All I know is your sister and I made a deal to get her out of a pickle and I expect you to honour it.'

'And what if I don't?'

'Well then I wouldn't be very happy, would I? I might need to come see you…maybe when you're watching those sweet little boys.' He squeezed his eyes into menacing slits. I stood nailed to the ground. I'd never been on the receiving end of a real-life-actual-credible threat before, and I couldn't breathe.

'Got you scared, have I?' His snarl relaxed into a look of pity when I didn't respond. Couldn't respond. 'Listen. Be a good girl and don't do anything stupid. Do this for another…let's see…six months and I'll let you go, okay? I'll even keep your commission as it is.'

CHAPTER NINETEEN

'Come on,' I pleaded as the vomit remained ingrained in the fabric of the passenger seat. The bowl of soapy water dribbled with each energetic rub and I was getting hot, which made the experience even more unpleasant.

I'd made it out of the wholesalers', through the car park and into my parked car in one piece, but fell apart as soggy chunks exploded from my lips and I purged myself of the last encounter—and breakfast. Desperate to get out of there, I'd rushed back to Pollokshields, the puke-infused air a sour reminder of my contemptible weakness.

My hair snagged on the rear-view mirror and the tug, together with the smell, brought up a vivid memory of Glory holding my hair as I retched.

I must have been thirteen. She'd walked into the bathroom on hearing noises.

'Oh. Again?' she'd said. 'Here, let me hold your hair. You'll get sick on it.'

I mumbled thanks and tipped my head over the toilet bowl. After, I wiped my face and rinsed the awful taste away with a glass of water.

'Why are you anxious? Is it the exams?' she asked.

'I lost my notebook for history. I can't find it anywhere and the exam is tomorrow. And I'm going to fail and then—'

'Relax. You'll be fine. You're good at history. Come, I'll lend you my notes.'

'It's not the same. I have colour coding. Your writing is a mess. I've mapped it all out. I know where everything is and—'

'Hey. Hey. There's no need to get worked up.' She stroked my hair. 'Relax. Breathe…'

My mother's voice sounded from across the hall. 'What's going on?' I threw her a warning look.

'Why don't you want to tell her?'

'Because last time I threw up she said it was all in my mind. That I had to just snap out of it.'

'So?'

'I don't want her thinking I'm weak.'

'You're not weak, silly. You're one of the strongest people I know, Gi. But you care too much, sometimes. Life is fun. Stop expecting the worst to happen. Let go a little.'

I felt a cold tickle as the cleaning liquid seeped over the rim of my yellow rubber gloves, the stained car seat coming back into focus.

Well look at me now. After all those years learning to control my anxiety, it's got the better of me again. But I'll push through it.

You need me.

Blue escaped the house and sniffed around, trying to squeeze through the door frame to nuzzle the oh-so-enticing wet patch and my mystery box. 'Shoo.' I pushed him aside and cursed Glory's unreliable rear door. Although I was late for his walk, he would have to wait until I'd wiped away every memory of that awful man.

I wondered if he'd threatened Glory too. I couldn't stomach the idea of him laying a hand on her. And I hated that I would have to meet him again. But I'd first arm myself with more information. If I could only find out how much she'd owed, maybe I would be able to buy my way out. He ran a business after all. Not that I had any kind of money. And I still didn't know where she'd been keeping the profits.

My shoulders were sore from the tension and the scrubbing. I reversed out of the vehicle to stretch on the pavement.

There was little traffic along this street and I didn't care what the learner drivers and small red van might think as I bent over, head between my legs, hands clamped behind me, bum sticking out.

Inside the house, I rinsed the sponge under the kitchen tap, picking at two stubborn oat flakes. The morning's plates had been left to steep in the sink again. Stephen had arranged for a housekeeper twice a week and it seemed the three males had relinquished any responsibility.

I placed the dishes in the machine and uncluttered the counter, helping myself to leftovers.

Wanting to leave a note, I searched for pen and paper. A pile of partially opened post lay on a side table and I snatched an envelope to write on. I found a ballpoint and scribbled my message: *'Dear Adam and Noah, there is no such thing as a dish fairy. Pull your finger out. Kisses, Auntie Grace.'*

My movements had disturbed the jumble of letters and they cascaded to the floor. As I collected the strewn sheets from the ground, my eyes were drawn to the golden logo of the Highland Arms, the spa hotel Glory had been due to attend. They'd sent a credit card receipt showing a refund. How typical of him to care about the money.

Poor Gi, you never got to go. And it had been such a special treat.

The ratio of processed to closed envelopes suggested Stephen was making slow progress in the painful administrative tasks that followed death. My lungs constricted as I realised he would soon show interest in the café. After all, as her husband, he would expect to inherit everything.

What the hell would I tell him?

I knew I had to deal with the crime issue before he reached that point. If I succeeded in getting out of the money laundering, I could probably reverse the ownership issue and present the children's accounts as a clever tax ruse by Glory.

'We can explain all of it away, then, can't we buddy? And nobody will be any the wiser,' I said to Blue who, eyeing the peg housing his leash, didn't seem to appreciate the complexity of the situation.

Our outing took us along St Andrews Drive and into Pollok Park. Rhododendron Walk was in full bloom and a colourful array of flowers danced in procession. I breathed in the freshness, exhaling through my mouth to blow out any remnant fumes from my earlier sickness.

'After this, Blue, I get to meet another gangster,' I said with a false enthusiasm that was lost on him.

I crouched down and cupped his face, holding it close to mine and shook his head to make his ears flop.

'No? You think it's a bad idea?'

Pouting, I scratched his cheeks and grabbed his jaw

to make him nod.

'Yes, I think it's a terrible idea, too, but I've not got much choice. Have I?' I pushed on one knee to get back up and lengthened my spine. 'In fact, Auntie Grace is going to have to put on her big girl pants for this one.'

CHAPTER TWENTY

I didn't need to look up the location of the Prince William. As its red, white and blue frontage proclaimed, it was the most famous pub in Scotland. Well, maybe in Glasgow. A sacred institution for many: the one true home of loyalist Ranger fans. These were 'The People'. And judging by the fully obscured, barred windows, the people disliked other people knowing their business.

These were the people whose Union Jack and Red Lion-decorated facade left no ambiguity as to their politics—the Orange Lodge nearby being no coincidence. These were the people who, I suspected, had graffiti-ed 'Go Home' on the red brick office building across the street, in front of which a dozen migrants queued for assistance on housing and benefits. These were the people whose antics had no doubt signalled to the founders of the freshly opened prosthetic clinic around the corner that Govan was the place to be. These were the people who would choke on their pints if a Catholic woman stepped inside their hallowed hall.

'Right. Here we go,' I said to myself, but my limbs

were paralysed in position, my hands gripping the steering wheel. I flexed my biceps several times as if this pumping would somehow propel me out of the car like an untied balloon. With my propensity for sports and physical endurance, I'd always thought of myself as the tough one; but it seemed my delicate sister had fewer qualms dealing with Glasgow's underworld than I did.

Had she flirted her way out of danger? I bet it helped.

Twenty minutes of procrastination later, I stepped through the door to face a nearly deserted room. Two patrons were perched at the bar facing a wall packed with gold-framed photographs of their footballing heroes. The TV showed the day's news on mute.

Sashaying as best I could in the hoodie and leggings I now regretted choosing for the occasion, I asked the burly bartender for Brian Scott. Without saying a word, he withdrew the tea towel from his shoulders and leaned sideways to peer into a semi-dark room at the rear.

'Willie,' he yelled with enough volume to lure out a bald-headed brute, but not so loud as to disturb the room's inner proceedings. 'Lassie wants to see Brian.'

'Thank you.' I gave him a big, bright-eyed smile. He shrugged and returned to his wiping.

Middle-aged Willie shuffled towards me, carrying the weight of the world. What would his story be? As he reached me, he slapped the wooden bar and took a deep breath, inspecting me as if I were a shipment of meat of unknown origin. I grinned again and struck a pose with my hand on my hip.

'Please could you take me to Brian? I have some business to discuss involving Veg&Might on

Pollokshaws Road.' A flicker of recognition shot through his eyes and he spun the blue velvet-topped stool in front of him to the right height before dropping his weight onto it.

'He's busy. We can sit here.'

'Well…um…Willie, is it? That's great. I know I'll enjoy your company while I wait for Brian.' I cringed at what was coming out of my mouth. 'Any chance of a drink?'

He sighed and gestured for his colleague. I ordered a lime soda and found that I was to drink alone. I brought the glass to my lips, but the damp cloth smell on the rim warned me not to sip.

'Do you think he will be long?' I asked.

'Depends.' It was clear he had a limited appetite for conversation.

'That's okay. I'm not in any hurry.'

I twirled my curls while we sat alongside the other silent drinkers watching the soundless screen.

'Aye, he'll not soon tire of those tits,' boomed an amused voice, exiting the rear room. Three men flowed out, each wearing what appeared to be the current fashion for thugs: jeans, T-shirt and a bomber jacket. They joked on as they left, pausing only to check if my breasts were the kind one might tire of. I couldn't hear what they said once they'd passed, but it sounded complimentary.

Creeps. But it was all I had, so I pulled my hoodie tighter and tossed my hair.

'I think we're good to go, don't you?' I said to Willie.

He led me to a bolt hole that exhibited more gold-framed portraits and an illuminated stained-glass shrine to a player he would be horrified to know I did not recognise. An L-shaped bench skirted the walls facing the entrance and the man I guessed was Brian occupied the middle, his muscular arms and legs extended along its blue velvet frame. That way, any visitor had to place themselves on the wooden chairs opposite, their backs vulnerable to the men minding the door.

'Hello there. To what do I owe the pleasure?' He grinned, his teeth showing just that little too much. His brown hair, tamed by lashings of gel, remained immobile as he ran several visual scans over my body.

'I'm Grace. My sister Glory Paterson died in a car crash on the nineteenth.'

'I heard. Very sorry for your loss. What a waste.' He lowered his eyes with the slow shake of the head convention required.

A thrill shot through me. He recognised her name. Maybe I would get my answers now.

I eased forward, expecting an invitation to take a seat, but he appeared to be enjoying the view. His lower half shifted to expose his crotch, this vulgar display of appreciation thankfully blocked by the table between us.

'She was a beautiful woman. Must run in the family.' He grinned and sought a new angle from which to leer. This, combined with the beer fumes in the small space, made my stomach turn again. I crossed my arms and kept my eyes on his hairline so as not to encourage his letching, all ideas of using flirtation now abandoned.

'I'm trying to pick up the pieces, to help her husband, and I understand you had dealings with her?'

'Yes, you can say that. I'm the landlord. For that café—what's it called again? Something with vegetables. I don't know. I own a lot of property in Govanhill and around there.' He waved his hand in a large circle, an illustrative perimeter to his sizable portfolio. If this was meant to impress, it had the opposite effect. Landlords in that area were notorious exploiters of Eastern European immigrants, piling multiple families into squalid flats. So much so that the newspaper had reported the city council was building a fifty-million-pound war chest to serve compulsory purchase orders on the biggest offenders.

There was no doubt I was dealing with scum. I clenched my fists, focused on the floor and breathed in, filling my lungs and feeling the oxygen course through my muscles: a method of mental and physical strengthening I used for lifting weights. I stepped forward and seized a chair. 'Mike over at Excelsior tells me you had an arrangement.'

Brian's eyes widened in surprise. Unsettled, he seemed to ponder how much I'd already learnt. He rolled his drink between his fingers. 'That man's nothing to do with me anymore, hen. But I do have business with you.' That last statement came served with a cold stare. I didn't bite.

'Why did you bring her to Mike? What did she owe you?' My voice sounded confident despite my quavering insides.

'Turns out the lovely Glory didn't have much of a head for business and got into arrears on the rent. At first, I'd let it go because she'd convinced that husband of hers to give me the right planning permission, against the rules. Very convenient. The place wouldn't shift before, so that was worth a few months.'

Upon hearing Stephen mentioned, the room closed in on me. Visions of him knowing, scheming, conspiring screeched inside my skull, clashing with the Stephen I knew. Had he known all this time?

Brian continued, 'Three months later my patience

ran out. Your precious sister pleaded for more time. So, being the gentleman I am, I told her if she fucked me we could call it even. For a while. Now, if somebody had told me she had a twin, that would have bought her another month, maybe two.' He sniggered then brought his arms forward, his long fingers making a squeezing motion reaching for my ass. 'Are there any more of you?' he said, salivating at the prospect of triplets.

The earlier mild nausea built into a torrent of revulsion. 'That's disgusting. She would never do that.'

'Disgusting.' He lingered on the word, rolling each syllable over his tongue, dripping in scorn. 'I'll tell you what's disgusting: the way you posh birds believe your shit smells better than mine. Well it doesn't. Put you in a sticky situation and you're as crooked as the rest of us.'

'So what did you do?' I responded to his increasing irritation with exaggerated calm, so as not to agitate him further.

'As she wouldn't plant her sainted lips on my cock, either, I told her she could do me a different favour. At this point she was out of options and desperate. She confessed her husband didn't know she owed money, and she was too embarrassed to admit she'd failed. What the fuck was she thinking, anyway? I mean, vegan? In Glasgow?'

Tears pricked my eyes as I imagined my poor sister in servitude to this man while her dream of a successful café was falling to pieces. Even though I had warned her, I experienced no pleasure from being proven right this time. All I could picture was her trapped in a cage, with these men clawing at her through the bars. Too ashamed to cry for help—or too afraid?

'And in comes Mike,' I prompted.

'Yes, yes, Mike. I had a deal with Mike that went South. I won't bore you with the details, but let's just say we've never been on the best of terms. He operates several money laundering establishments, so I decided, why not one more? I had introduced her to Excelsior when she was looking for suppliers, so connecting them was easy.'

'And in exchange for the rent she owed you, she cleared your debt with Mike by cleaning his cash.'

'That's right.'

Everything explained, I felt oddly at peace. It all made sense now. Why she'd ended up mired in crime. He too acted at ease, as if this was a run-of-the-mill account of people interacting. I still considered him vermin, but at least he'd given me what I'd asked. I realised, however, I hadn't yet established a way out.

'What is the amount she owed? I want to take care of it.'

'Oh, you can't expect me to remember that. It was a lot. And knowing Mike, it won't have shrunk.'

'What do you mean?'

'Ever heard of Casheze?' he said, referring to the payday lender famed for outrageous interest rates. 'Well they are Santa Claus compared to Mike. Why do you think I wanted rid of my debt?' He chuckled, seemingly proud of his ruse, and oblivious to my fury.

'You bastard.'

He shrugged. 'Serves her right for rejecting me. She came crawling back though, once she figured out she'd been shafted. But by then it was too late. The deal suited me. She was livid and threatened to shop Mike to the police, but I warned she was playing with fire.'

His callous entrapment of my sister made me jump

96

up and lunge towards him, ready to tear off that greasy head. I hurled myself across the table for a punch, but his heavies pounced in an instant. They dragged me away by the elbows, kicking, while I spat an encyclopaedia of filth at the sack of shit who sat, hooping with laughter, savouring the scene.

'I'll call you about the rent,' he yelled after me.

Only once the entrance to the pub was opened for my expulsion did I hear the unmistakable sound of my Fiat howling for attention. I prised the men off me and slammed the metal door in Willie's weary face; a final act of defiance in response to this humiliating exit.

CHAPTER TWENTY-ONE

I sprinted to the corner where I'd parked, to investigate the noise. The alarm grew louder with every step. Soon I discovered what ailed my car: a dark gaping hole stretched across the rear window, cuboid particles of glass scattered inside, over the trunk and onto the street. A thunderous roar escaped my lungs and startled the nearby pigeons, who flew off abandoning their bounty of salted crisp packets.

Locals assembled from various alleys and venues to watch me repeatedly kick the rear bumper, spewing obscenities; the blasting distress signal unmoved despite this new assault.

It all came out. All the pent-up bile poisoning my organs since the accident, since I'd been forced to deal with shit I wanted no part of and did not even understand. Tears of rage and frustration clouded my vision as I stomped against the black carcass.

'Bloody Govan. Bloody bastards. What the hell did I ever do to you? Bastard criminal bloody scum. Why the fuck am I even here? Damn you, Glory.'

As if being stared at by a bunch of amused low-lives wasn't bad enough, one guy had the gall to stroll past and instruct me to 'cheer up, sunshine.' Tempted to transfer my anger onto him, I settled on striking my inanimate Panda instead, until it wailed no more.

There.

My heart pounded against my chest, my breath coming out in short, sharp bursts. I bent over, hands resting on my knees. I watched my poor defenceless vehicle standing naked and abused, fragments dropping from its frame like crystalline tears.

Who did this?

I had been too busy venting my resentment about my day, my week, my month, to find out why my car had been targeted. None of the onlookers would admit to seeing the perpetrator, of course, and a quick mental inventory confirmed that I had left nothing inside. The boxes of cash were secure at home; my phone wedged in my pocket.

I wondered if it might have been Brian's men teaching me a lesson. I was still reeling from my encounter with that scumbag. As I scanned the pub to check for self-satisfied observers, its obscured windows taunted me like a winking hemline.

The crowd dispersed, leaving me to clear the debris so I could drive away. I wiped the glass off the rear, protecting my hands with my sleeves, then tried to rake it all into the curb with my feet. A large blue fragment stuck to my shoe, and I stooped to peel it off. The limp block of shattered screen held together the shredded remains of my 'Yes' sticker, showing support for Scottish independence. Its significance instantly apparent, I cursed my stupidity: I'd waved this red rag outside the watering hole for unionist bulls, asking for trouble. Part of me was relieved the damage was probably nothing more than a simple act of vandalism in the heart of 'No' country, but the other part couldn't shake the feeling I was in more danger than I cared to admit.

And that Glory had been, too.

'Not staying here', I muttered to my phone after Google declared that Strathclyde Windscreens would come to you for an instant replacement on site. Instead, I would go see Andy. He wasn't far away and could fix anything.

CHAPTER TWENTY-TWO

I turned the steering wheel to turn right onto Paisley Road West and tried to remember who had introduced me to Andy. It must have been four years earlier when I'd needed that first repair to a less-than-reliable Fiesta. Despite the recommendation, I'd been a little apprehensive when turning into the drive. His garage was nothing more than a large metal shack tucked away behind the shared yard of two medium-sized retail units.

Andy had explained that since setting up shop in the sixties he'd fought off more offers for his land than he had fingers on his hands; his biggest fight having been when Asda placed a superstore next door. 'Call me a creature of habit,' he'd said, in his defence, 'I like where I am.' And I liked him, remaining a loyal customer ever since.

Cold wind was blowing in through the missing screen, hitting my neck. Hair flapped around my face like laundry on a line. I spat the curls from my mouth and smelt the exhaust fumes penetrating the car. I should have covered the hole up before driving. Had I cleared the glass enough not to get hit?

I had rushed to escape the hooligans, but with Ibrox Stadium looming on my right—the home of Rangers football club—I sensed a menacing reminder that Glasgow was in fact a very small town.

A siren wailed. A patrol car tailed me in my rear-view mirror.

Shit.

Was it illegal to drive without a rear window? It hadn't even crossed my mind and here I was, parading my illicit vehicle less than one hundred yards from Police Scotland's headquarters. I slowed into the bus lane and came to a halt.

A female officer stepped forward, inspecting the rear. My finger darted onto the button opening the driver side window, to expose my friendliest smile.

'What happened here?' She sounded matter-of-fact. Her lips moved more, but I struggled to make out the words through the deafening thumps of my heart. 'Ma'm?' This time more concerned.

'Yes, sorry. The window got bashed in and I'm taking it in for repair.' I said it as though having one's car smashed in was a minor nuisance.

'It's illegal to drive a car in this condition. And dangerous. We can't have you shedding glass everywhere.'

'No. I'm sorry. I did my best to tidy it up. There shouldn't be any loose bits. I've been really careful. And I'm going straight to the garage. I've not come far.'

The officer eyes me up and down, stepped away from the car and talked into her radio. I couldn't hear. When she came back, her face gave nothing away.

'All right. We're going to let you off because you're on your way to get it fixed. But next time you really should have a windscreen service come to you.' She nodded towards the yellow brick building with blue-framed windows ahead, featuring the force's checked logo. 'You'll also need a police report for the insurance. Do you want to come in?'

'No, that's all right, thank you.' I paused, my brain performing a frantic search for an acceptable excuse. 'I doubt my third-party insurance would take care of it.'

As I maintained this conversation in the most neutral tone possible given the pounding my arteries carried across my body, another voice rose inside me screaming, 'Go! Tell her! Tell her everything. Let the police take care of it. Then it will all go away.'

But that voice had to be suppressed, muffled and shoved deep back down like a body being disposed of in the river. I wanted nothing more than for this nasty business to be over, but I couldn't let others find out what Glory had done. For her heedless crime to shape her legacy. What she'd be remembered for.

And how ludicrous would it be if I tried to convince the cops to go after the bad guys? Honest, Guv, my sister was an innocent bystander. Never mind all that cash. And yes, everything is in my name—but I knew nothing about it.

Yeah, right.

And what if it got back to the landlord? His men? What if it was true the cops were in the gangsters' pockets?

I couldn't risk it. I had to find another way out.

The officer rested her hand on my roof and leaned in for a girl-to-girl talk. 'Ma'm, this looks like intentional damage. You've got dents in the bumper, too. Are you sure you're okay? If someone is harassing you, you should talk to us. I can't help you if you don't tell me what happened.'

I dismissed her with a casual wave of the hand. 'Honestly, I don't know who did this. It's just one of those things. I had a 'Yes' sticker on the rear and I think that pissed someone off. I was in Govan.'

The officer grimaced and shook her head. I couldn't tell if it was to convey remorse over the current division among Scots, her dismay with the frequency of random acts of vandalism in the city, or that she thought I'd been a complete idiot to display my political colours in such hostile territory. Either way, she seemed to accept she wouldn't get much more out of me. 'How far have you got to go?'

'Not far at all. I promise. The garage is right around the corner on Helen Street.'

'Going to Andy's?'

'Yes, that's right. Andy's a good man.' Why had I felt the need to add that endorsement? As if associating with an honourable mechanic would somehow make me less suspicious.

'That he is. Tell him Samantha Murray said hi.' And with that, she smiled, closed the notebook and returned to her partner who'd stayed seated while observing the exchange.

Shoulders straight, I brought the window up, grinned my best grin and waved as the police car drove past. I crossed into the right lane, merged onto the roundabout and entered Helen Street, turning into the second alley, where I stopped, collapsed over the steering wheel and dared to exhale.

CHAPTER TWENTY-THREE

Oh my God Gi, I've just lied to the police!

I hadn't defied authority like this since that one time in school when I was thirteen. Mr Kendall, the headmaster, had summoned us both to his office for what we later termed 'frog-gate'. I could still hear his voice in my head.

'Girls, it won't come as a surprise why you're here. Miss Stuart is very upset one of you has let her frogs escape the terrarium. We're still missing one.' He pinched the bridge of his nose and sat on the side of his desk. 'Please can the guilty party confess so you can get back to class?'

We both stayed silent; me completely in the dark.

'Come on...speak,' he pressed.

'Why do you think it was us? It could have been anyone.'

'As Miss Stuart has already told you, Glory, she saw someone with a mop of red hair leaving the lab immediately before discovering the amphibians leaping loose. So as luck would have it, there are only two people in this school that fit that description: you two.'

'It wasn't me,' she said.

'It wasn't me either.' And that was true.

'Did Glory do this, Grace?'

'No.' That may or may not have been true.

'Right. It's going to be like that is it? Well, here's what I'll do. I'm going to split you up and give you a chance to confess or point at the other, in which case you will be free to go. If you don't identify the culprit, you'll each be punished more than if you'd put your hand up to begin with.'

The prisoners'-dilemma-style situation he'd tried to create failed. He'd not counted on the discreet, twinkly-eyed shushing gesture Glory made before we parted, which instructed me to trust her and stay quiet. After two hours of checking in on us in separate rooms and finding us mute, Mr Kendall called it quits. He threatened to call our mother, but Glory pointed out that the herself red-headed Mrs McBride might not be best pleased her daughters were singled out because of their appearance. What with equal treatment and all that. He'd groaned at the reference to the recent assembly on racism and let us go, probably determining a single frog wasn't worth the trouble.

She and I left the teachers' wing arm in arm, chuckling.

'How did you know he'd give up?' I kept my tone light-hearted, not willing to admit to having felt quite distressed during our isolation.

'I'd overheard Miss Bose and him discussing his need to leave early today, for his wife's birthday. So it was a waiting game. Plus, he had no real evidence: Miss Stuart is half blind! He'd just hoped one of us would give in. He couldn't possibly punish us both. Mum wouldn't have stood for it.'

'I genuinely didn't know if it was you. Why did you

do it?' And why did you put me through this?

'I saw she gave you a C, and I thought that wasn't fair.'

'Aw, that's so sweet.' I bumped her shoulder with mine. 'And a bit weird. Why the frogs?'

'To be honest, Zach dared me after hearing me complain about her. You should've seen his face when I walked straight to the lab. Never expected I would do it.'

'Thank goodness they didn't catch you in the act.'

'Yes. On that note, Gi…thanks for saving my bacon once again.'

'What are sisters for?'

CHAPTER TWENTY-FOUR

Andy was sitting outside on a pile of tyres reading the paper, catching some rare afternoon sunshine when I rolled up. Despite the lack of signage to direct customers to the garage, there seemed to be plenty of work for him judging by the vehicles in various stages of automotive undress parked around the entrance.

'Hello, my dear,' he said when he saw me step out. 'You've caught me red-handed. I was having a little break.'

He looked older than last time, tired and unshaven; his white hair now so fine it lacked the weight to force the curve on his comb-over and instead stood upright on one side like an array of micro-thin antennae. He didn't need special sensors, however to see what was wrong with my car.

'A scorned lover?' he joked, as he always did to take the sting out of the eventual price tag.

'Not this time, Andy. I've been good. How have you been?'

'No scorned lovers for me either, dear, unfortunately.' He winked. I'd learnt little about his personal life, having only needed his services a handful of times, but he had the air of a widower and I'd never dared to ask.

A quick inspection followed and after darting inside to consult his papers, he returned.

'The good news is I can fix this in an hour. The bad news is that hour will be Monday because I don't have the window in stock.'

He stuck a scribbled note into my hand, like a grandparent giving a secret fiver. I waited politely until he had walked away to look. He didn't like the money side, and this was reflected in his pricing, which had been stuck somewhere at mid-1990s level.

'That's fine, thanks Andy,' I reassured him, stuffing the quote into my pocket.

'Good thing it wasn't your sister's vintage Bug. I would struggle to find a spare for that again.'

A great sob escaped me and caught us both by surprise. He stood frozen, eyes darting from side to side as if looking for instruction on what to do. The sight of this kindly old man wondering what he'd done wrong amplified my sadness, and tears rolled out onto my cheeks.

'Sorry. Don't mind me,' I said. 'You weren't to know. Glory died three weeks ago. In the Beetle.' He approached, fishing out a crisp white handkerchief from his pocket, holding it out for when I was ready. 'Well at least you won't need to worry about parts for that car anymore,' I said trying to bring us back to more typical banter.

'What happened?'

'Her car fell into the bank off Stockiemuir Road and hit a tree.'

He grimaced and shook his head, recognising the dangerous part of the A809 North of Bearsden.

'Come with me.' He guided me towards the garage, his hand on my shoulder. I was made to sit in the tiny office at the side of the workshop, as narrow as a telephone box and only long enough to fit a chair and a desk built from a stack of crates. He grabbed the kettle and rushed to fill it from an outside tap, leaving me to gaze at the old calendars, invoices and crumpled notes on the wall through my waterlogged eyes.

Like a man who had been around his fair share of death, he seemed to guess what I needed. He handed me a cup of tea and stood far enough away to give me my dignity but placed his hand on my shoulder for comfort.

'There,' was all he said while he stood watch over me, neglecting all his duties.

After a while, when the tea was drunk, and the hankie had absorbed all it could, I took a deep breath and thanked him. He smiled and squeezed my shoulder, his hand strong from a lifetime of manual labour. He crouched to meet my eyes and his gaze changed from gentle old-timer to native Glaswegian hard man.

'Grace? Are you in trouble?'

'What gave it away?' I quipped, waving towards my car's glassless frame. But his frown made it clear he was in no mood for humour.

'Who bashed your screen in?'

'I was parked by Festival Gardens. I never saw them.'

'What were you doing there?' The emphasis on 'there' confirming that general area was already no place for a woman like me. 'Who were you seeing?'

'Nobody.' I avoided his gaze.

'Look, you don't need to tell me anything, dear, but

please hear me. Stop whatever you're doing. I've been around enough wreckage from so-called accidents to know what the wrong'uns are capable of. And it usually starts with a warning like this.' He nodded towards my Panda.

Promising to be good, I asked him to call me a cab. I needed space to think. His talk of deliberate wreckage awakened an underlying discomfort I'd felt for the last two days: a suspicion that maybe Glory's accident hadn't been an accident. I had pushed it aside because the thought that my sister might have been murdered also gave rise to the improbable, yet unbearable, possibility that, facing an inescapable plight, she might have veered off the road on purpose.

CHAPTER TWENTY-FIVE

The taxi drove through Dumbreck as murmurs from the Top Ten spilt from the driver's cabin, together with a stale smell of cigarettes revealing a 'do as I say, not as I do' attitude to his the ban on smoking the sticker on the door imposed. Resting my head against the window frame, I was treated to a parade of pink blossoms and wondered who, many moons ago, convinced every homeowner on this stretch of road to invest in the same cherry tree, choreographing this annual pageantry for generations to come.

The flowers usually lifted my spirits. I'd envision walking through rows of brimming branches, my cheeks caressed by the blooms' soft silky leaves, lustrous flashes of sunlight shooting through the gaps. But not this time. My imagination corrupted by recent events, I could only visualise my face being lacerated by twig after twig as the canopy grew so dark I lost my way.

A distant buzzing caught my attention and it took a while to recognise it as my phone. Once retrieved from my pocket and unlocked, it displayed a message from Dave. 'How are you? Call me. XOX.'

It was funny how people never phoned anymore. Only snippets of ever-reducing texts sent between handsets of ever-increasing complexity. But it suited me: putting the thing on mute every time I was with a client was too much of a faff. A missed call notification flashed in the corner of the screen. It was from two hours before. I dialled voice mail to listen to the message.

'Hello Grace, it's Alastair here. I hope you are well. I'll be heading home soon and I thought it easiest for me to drop the accounts at the café for you to collect. Saves you a trip into the city centre and I can then pick up any new post.'

How kind.

Since discovering that Glory pulled the wool over his eyes about my involvement with the shop and the itinerant dividends, he was insistent I became properly acquainted with the business and matters of money. He'd offered to compile the latest accounts and monthly statements, with a personal summary of critical information. I had also instructed Sascha to set aside any incoming mail that looked even remotely financial for Alastair to handle—at least until I gained a firmer grasp.

It would not be long before Stephen would want to wrap up this giant loose end, but he'd been too preoccupied with work and the challenges of his new life to bother with the administrivia of running the café. He'd asked me to deal with it and alert him if his input was needed. As far as I was concerned his input had never been needed, even when Glory was alive.

'Sorry. I'm going elsewhere now. Could you take me to Pollokshaws Road, please?'

This was met by a grunt from the front and a sharp

left turn that threw me off balance. Along Nithsdale Road, the grand Victorian villas were interspersed with unattractive rectangular apartment blocks that made you wonder what the planners had been smoking in the sixties. Once past the Muslim primary school that catered to the large Pakistani community in this area, the housing turned to tenements hosting a range of independent shops and restaurants at street level, none of which seemed to have the volume of trade as Pollokshaws, ahead.

Knowing it wasn't far now, I searched for my purse and made a mental note to get more cash out of the machine. My reserves were dwindling and my Gumtree ad hadn't yielded any new clients yet.

The driver cranked the handbrake. 'Thirteen fifty, please.'

He had stopped too close to the parked cars, meaning I needed to exit on the street side, where passing cars weaved in and out of idling double-parkers to avoid oncoming traffic. I hunched down and felt a strain in my lower back as I opened the door. The suspension on Hackney cabs was always set too tight.

I looked left, right and left again, my body flat against the black carriage. I thought I had a chance to go until a small van stopped abruptly three spaces down, causing the number 38 bus to jerk to a halt in front of me, with an admonishing toot for the offender. After four cars had passed in the other direction, the bus moved on and I was able to swivel around, the cab's exhaust scorching my calf.

On reaching the curb, I was perplexed to see a small crowd gathered inside Veg&Might—after closing time. Sascha was the first to look up when the door creaked open, and gave me an enthusiastic wave.

There were seven others, their chairs displaced to face the wall in an attempted semi-circle, thwarted by the tables fixed to the floor. A long brown-haired woman in a red floral wrap dress stood in front of three flip charts that had been tucked over the framed artworks so as not to damage the wall.

'Let's take a little break, shall we?' Sascha said to the group, no doubt inspired by my puzzled expression. 'There's cucumber water on the table over there.'

'Hi Grace. How are you?'

'What's going on?'

'It's our monthly charity night. I guess I've not talked to you about this. I hope it's okay. Glory didn't mind.'

'We have a charity night?'

'Well, I guess I should call it *my* charity night. You see, I've made a load of friends in the charitable sector and they all seem to face the same challenges in their work. So Oliver, over there...' She pointed at the taut behind of a swimmer's body standing with one foot on a chair. 'He and I decided to set up a little club, so we could all share ideas. I'm involved with SAFR, Scottish Action for Refugees. You've heard of it, no?' The name drew a blank but didn't want to discourage her from continuing the explanation, so I nodded. 'We meet here every second Friday of the month and one of us talks to the others about something that has gone particularly well for them or particularly badly.'

The group mingled, not minding the unscheduled break, while Sascha brought me up to speed on today's speaker. 'That's Julie. She's our star, really. She's from the Citizen's Advice Bureau in Parkloan and won the Fundraising Excellence Award last year—can you believe she's raised thirteen million pounds in her career?'

'Very impressive.' Out of politeness, I made sure to display the requisite admiration for this forty-something woman who, judging by the scribbles on the wall, had been discussing something called 'Practical Donor-Centricity'. I had no interest in getting sucked into the event. 'I'm only here for Alastair's papers. He was going to drop them round. You guys continue.'

'You don't mind? We only help ourselves to one cup of tea each.'

'No, that's fine.' I walked towards the counter. As I passed Oliver, I nudged his knee to force his foot off the chair. 'Please don't do that,' I said.

I looked into the startled face of a semi-bearded man with arresting blue eyes. Sascha became flustered, apologised on his behalf and, in her affable eagerness to please, decided the best way to overcome the awkwardness was to introduce us.

'Oliver, this is Grace, Glory's sister.'

His already embarrassed expression contorted further as he offered his condolences. 'I'm so sorry about your sister. I only found out today. I don't know what to say. Glory was a wonderful woman.'

'Oliver works at Invisible,' Sascha said, 'they deal with human trafficking and modern-day slavery. Let me also introduce you to Rachel. She's at Save the Children.' She grabbed my elbow and ushered me through Jill with the stained pink shirt, Damien with the giant gap between his teeth, and Felicity who wore a kaftan and had something to do with the mentally disabled. They were all uniformly sorry for my loss and complimentary of my sister.

'How come they all know Glory?' I asked Sascha as I picked up the thick envelope addressed to me.

'She was a real supporter. Sometimes she would invite her friends to sit in on our meetings, so they would get exposed to new charities and hear first-hand how hard our work can be. And then, bless her, she'd say her charity night wasn't about free coffee, to get them to make donations. All these guys have spent time with her one way or another.'

Through my clients I'd witnessed the charity one-upmanship that exists between the well-heeled ladies of the Southside, but I nevertheless felt a warm glow of pride spread across my chest.

You did good, Gi.

Speaker Julie was summoned to pick up where she'd left off and I bade my goodbyes to the merry band of Samaritans.

CHAPTER TWENTY-SIX

As I stepped outside, an unexpected gust of wind blew the package from my hands. It skeltered down the pavement for a good three yards before I intercepted it with my right foot. When I crouched down to retrieve the paperwork, my hair flew up and, squinting against the cold air, I noticed the double-parked red van that had caused the earlier jam start its engine. A stirring in my subconscious suggested this timing was not a coincidence. I had an eerie sensation I'd seen this vehicle around more than once.

Was I being watched? I looked in all directions, searching for a plan. The one-way road facing me would lead to Moray Place, a narrow lane with a picturesque A-listed terrace on one side and a wall flanking the railway on the other. I figured if somebody was following me, this would be the place to find out. You wouldn't get there without being seen.

I darted through traffic to cross and began my test. I increased my pace, looking behind me from time to time even though the van would not have been able to enter—they'd have to come from the other side. Many of the houses here had basement level gardens, and I toyed with the idea of hiding out for a while, but preferred to soldier on, to know for sure.

A flurry of questions set alight my synapses, which flashed frightening scenarios in response. Maybe Mike the wholesaler wanted to make sure I didn't go to the police with the tainted cash. Maybe they were looking to recover it—maybe even by force! Maybe they wanted me gone—though I couldn't come up with a reason for that. Perhaps I was seeing it all wrong. Perhaps it was Brian's men. I pictured hefty Willie and the other brute crammed inside the van's small cabin, on my tail since Govan.

My heartbeat quickened and sticky lines of sweat slid from under my arms. I grabbed my keys and threaded them between my fingers for a makeshift weapon. My phone was clenched in the other hand for an emergency call. What if they had guns? Hell, I knew they owned guns: I'd caught glimpses of them tucked under their bomber jackets at the Prince William.

The temperature plunged as the sun hid behind the trees and I was bathed in shade. I now regretted choosing this route, realising its peacefulness also meant no witnesses. I was easy prey. Up ahead, a front bumper turned into the street and the bottom fell out of my stomach. As the car came into view, I saw that it was just a blue Mondeo. No doubt a resident. The crunching of the tyres on some loose asphalt at the corner reassured me that at least I would hear them coming.

Mondeo-man parked halfway on the curb, like his neighbours, then bounded out with a friendly greeting and apologised for obstructing my path. I frowned at this clown distracting me with unnecessary conversation. Did he not see I was on a mission?

When I reached the junction, I peered round and all seemed quiet. I progressed into the middle of the lane and inspected both lengths for signs of life. Only a dribble of traffic passed in the distance where it met the main road again. No sign of a red van.

I hugged a street lamp and pressed my forehead against the cool black metal to steady myself. Had I imagined it? There were probably red vans everywhere. Christ, every postie drove a red van. The more I thought about it, the more I accepted that my mind had run away with itself after today's chilling encounters. Surely, I could be forgiven for suffering a bout of paranoia under the circumstances.

Suddenly aware of how ridiculous I looked embracing street furniture like a drunk, I shook my head and resumed my journey home. I speed-dialled Dave.

'Hi Grace. Hold on. I'm driving.' There was muffled rummaging, followed by a loud thud. 'Wait Grace,' came a voice barely audible over the ambient rumbling. 'I dropped the phone in the foot well. I can't pick it up right now. Let me call you when I get to my flat.'

'Okay,' I shouted to make sure he heard, and gazed at the handset with a mournful sigh. Of all the times to have to sleep alone.

CHAPTER TWENTY-SEVEN

Exhausted, I'd fallen asleep straight after getting home and slept like a baby. My alarm went off at six and I groaned. Saturday morning. Lots of clients to see; my last weekend lie-in a distant memory since becoming a personal trainer. At least the school run was off and I wouldn't need to walk Blue. Stephen was home.

Later, stirring my porridge, I reflected on how my work consisted, for the most part, of assisting people in a Sisyphean task. Every workday they sat on their bums ten hours at the office and three hours in front of another screen at home, then suffered through intensive workouts at weekends only to slide back into their bad habits.

Still, it keeps me in shoes, I thought as I tied my laces and started a quick on-the-spot jog to get me going. It was a dreich day and there was little light coming through the windows.

Once my door closed behind me, I had to cling onto the balustrade to make my way down the dark communal staircase. The light bulb must have blown after I got home. My senses kicked up a gear, still on edge after last night's alarming but ultimately imaginary pursuit. I scanned the road before stepping out.

No red van.

I decided to take the bike to help me relax, and pedalled off to my first visit. This one I liked: the gratifying case of an obese woman transforming into a butterfly with my help.

When I came home a few hours later, I spotted the door to my building standing ajar. Why was it open? My neighbours were usually very good about closing it. I locked the bike onto a streetlight before quietly nudging the door further to enter.

It was still shrouded in darkness and I flipped the switch. A quick flash of light came from the next level up and a man's voice gave me a fright.

'Hey! Don't do that.'

'Hello?' I inched forward, my throat constricted.

'Up here. Turn the light off.'

I did as instructed, and felt along the cold wall as I ascended the stairs. Around the bend, I could just make out the legs of a ladder first, then the man's legs, his body, and his raised arms.

'Mr Gibson? Is that you?' I'd recognised the helmet-like shape of his hair.

'Hi Grace. Just changing the light bulb.'

'Yes, sorry. I noticed that this morning, but I was in a rush to go to work. It must have blown.'

'Actually, it was odd. It was completely shattered. As if someone had smashed it. With a stick or something. The downstairs one too. The woman in 2/2 said she heard some commotion in the night and the front door slamming. Who knows what that was about.'

'Oh. That *is* odd. Thanks for taking care of it.'

I hurried up the next flight—insofar as the lighting

allowed it. I couldn't shake the feeling that maybe this was another warning—intended for me.

Safe within the confines of my apartment, I scoured the fridge for protein and wolfed down some leftover grilled chicken. I was running low on groceries and settled on the sofa to make a list. With the car still at Andy's, I would need to have it delivered or ask Dave to pick it up.

Right at that moment, the key turned in the door and Dave appeared as though summoned. He wore his work clothes—which was rare for a weekend—and took off his boots before leaning over me with a kiss.

'Hi.' I pulled on his hand for him to join me. 'Emergency?'

'No, merely a job I couldn't refuse.' He appeared distant, his usual cocky smile replaced by a droop, topped off by a furrowed brow.

'Have you had lunch? There's not much here, I'm afraid.'

'It's fine. I had a bacon roll.'

Attempting to lighten the mood, I put both hands on my hips and spoke in a tone of mock outrage, 'Mr David Baker, shame on you.' It did not have the desired effect. He managed only a weary smile then turned to me with a serious expression.

'Where is your car?'

The question confused me. How did he know I didn't have it? It's not like I always parked in the same place. Why was he looking for it?

'It's being fixed. The windshield got hit by a rock.'

He placed both hands on my cheeks and stroked them. Then he pulled my face towards his and stared into my eyes. A flush of nerves prickled at the nape of my neck. Something was up.

'Don't lie to me Grace, I know you were at the Prince William.'

'How?'

He let go and stood like a barrister presenting his evidence, a dark cloud hovering over where the wig would be. 'I was working there this morning. They've got a problem with their drains that keeps acting up. And there were these guys chatting and laughing about the woman who came in yesterday and how she'd tried to jump the boss and needed to be dragged away. How she'd have to be taught a lesson.' He paused, eyed me up and down and pointed. 'You. It was obvious they were talking about you: the hair, the clothes, the Panda. A fine piece of ass, they called you. And then they mentioned how you found your car vandalised and went nuts—which they thought was hilarious, by the way.'

I nodded and pulled him down to sit. 'Okay, it was me.'

'What the hell were you doing there? Are you insane?'

'Babe, you don't understand. It's the café. That Brian Scott man is the café's landlord. He's the reason Glory was laundering money. I needed to find out the truth and now I know.'

'And of course you thought this was a better idea than going to the police,' he said, his stinging sarcasm branding me an idiot. 'Why did you attack him?'

'I didn't attack him. He made me mad and I reached over to…I don't know…shout at him. Maybe a slap. But they grabbed me before I could do anything. I was angry…he said all this stuff about me, about Glory. He is a vile man.'

'Well what the fuck do you expect from one of the

city's leading gangsters? Grace, you need to stop this. It's dangerous. Go to the police.'

'You know damn well I can't go to the police. Even if you don't give a shit about what that would do to Stephen—and God forbid you'd ever tell me the story of what went on between you—everything points to me being an accomplice. Me. I'm the one that could go to prison. It's fourteen bloody years for money laundering! I looked it up. Don't you see? I have to find a way out. And that is what I am doing. Now, are you going to sit here and judge me or are you going to be my boyfriend and help?'

'I'm not here to judge you, babe, but you're playing with fire.'

'Playing with fire.' I repeated it, as it stirred a memory. 'That's what Brian Scott said to Glory when she threatened to tell the cops about Mike.'

'What? Who is Mike? What are you talking about?'

'I think Mike is the man who got Glory killed.'

Silence.

Dave shook his head slowly.

'I know it sounds crazy, babe, please bear with me.'

I led him to the breakfast bar, where I found a pen and the back of a letter to write on, hoping a full explanation would pull him in to help me. 'This is the café.' I drew a box. 'Mike runs the wholesaler that supplies the café. Here.' Another box, with an arrow to the first. 'Mike's guy delivers goods to Glory. This includes a box of cash and an invoice that is for more than the goods they have received.' A second arrow, with a pound sign. 'Glory pays the padded invoice through the bank. This means that Mike gets clean money in exchange for his box of dirty cash.'

Dave interrupted as I started to draw a circular

arrow within the café. 'Yes, okay, I get it. And Glory puts the box of money through the register as though they were clients paying for their coffee with cash, so that all looks legit, too. And she got to keep a share of the cash for the service. I understand the concept of money laundering. If you remember, I'm the one who told you about it. What I don't understand is where Brian Scott comes in. Or why in God's name you think Glory's accident was murder.'

I tapped my pen on the paper to direct his attention and scribbled some more: a stick figure, a pound sign, two more arrows, a police hat. A VW Beetle car with a cross through it. 'Glory owed Brian rent because the café wasn't going well.'

'Oh.'

'Yes. That was news to me too. So sad. If only she hadn't been too proud to admit she was failing.' The pen returned to the stick figure. 'So Brian says to Glory she can sleep with him instead of paying rent. That pig.' I glanced at my boyfriend who looked as if he was chewing on a worm. 'She refuses and he says he's got a solution for her.' I retrace one of the arrows. 'Brian owes Mike something—we don't know what. And they're not on good terms. But he agrees with Mike that if Glory launders money for him, then Brian's debt has been repaid. And this is where Glory really screws up: she agrees to it. I guess she thought it was a temporary problem and nobody would know. It would buy her time to improve the café's fortunes, if nothing else with her dirty cut.'

The pound signs multiplied on the page and I continued. 'It turns out Mike is a shark who charges giant interest so when Glory understands she'll never be able to stop, she confronts Brian, furious that he landed her in this trouble. He doesn't give a shit. It's no longer his problem. But when she says she'll got to the police…' I circled the police cap. 'He warns her she's in over her head. Playing with fire.'

I moved my pen to the crossed-out car. Dave stopped my hand and nodded.

He saw.

'And you think Mike killed Glory in a fake accident because he thought she was going to the police.'

'Yes,' I said triumphantly, as though we'd been playing Pictionary and we beat the other team to the prize. With this story building in my mind over the last few days, taking different shapes, adopting different outcomes, investigating different motives, it had taken an almost fictional dimension. As though I'd been outlining a novel. As though this wasn't about me or my sister. But looking at Dave's crestfallen face, I fell back to Earth with a savage blow.

It *was* about me.

And my sister was dead.

He reached over to hug me when reality struck and I started to cry. We sat for what seemed like an hour, neither of us speaking, until his phone rang. His exchange was short, but it was clear he had to go.

'Babe, I'm sorry. This conversation isn't over. Please don't do anything. I still think you need to report it. But I'll listen to your plan.'

My plan, he'd said, so confident I had one.

If only.

CHAPTER TWENTY-EIGHT

I hoped Alastair's envelope would produce missing clues to understand the scope of Glory's deception. With the paperwork spread out on the floor like a fan, I sat cross-legged and reviewed each document in order.

The most useful part of the pack was a summary note, which held an upbeat description of the café's finances and explained the share structure and dividends paid out over the last two years. In keeping with the profession's customary caution—and no doubt because his fingers had been burnt already—the note included his firm's formal disclaimers pointing out the assessment relied on information provided by the business owner and that no detailed audit had been undertaken.

Just as well, Uncle Alastair. Just as well.

The size of the turnover interested me less than the outgoings. Glory paid herself only a small salary, which I judged would be the only thing Stephen would be aware of. As one would expect, a big chunk of expenditure was dedicated to goods, staff and the property. It appeared there were no arrears on the rent during this last period.

The profits, which turned out to be considerable, had been allocated each year as dividends to the shareholders. The kids' class of shares had claim to the first ten thousand pounds. Eighty-five percent of the rest went to me, at least officially, which left very little for Glory as the remaining ordinary shareholder.

So where did 'my' money go? Copies of two bank statements from the café showed that dividends of twelve and fourteen thousand pounds, respectively, were transferred electronically to an account in the name of G McBride.

You made it look like me. How shrewd. Was it an old account from before you were married?

The bank account details were shown, so it would now be easy to find. But that led to a tricky question: with a mismatch between the official shareholder and actual recipient, who owned this money?

For a fleeting moment, I imagined it belonged to me. I pictured my hand signing a cheque for the deposit on a new house. I saw a blooming wisteria crowning the entrance of a two-story red sandstone, Dave smiling in the doorway, gesturing for me to come inside. There, we would cross an immaculate lounge to reach a sumptuous bedroom where we'd flop onto a giant bed with crisp white linen, into each other's arms.

With a deep sigh, I put the papers down and stretched my arms over my head. I'd been sitting too long, and my knees ached as I unfurled my legs. The basic-but-perfectly-functional kitchen I'd have to make do with beckoned for a cup of tea.

We can dream, can't we Gi?

What were you dreaming of through all this?

Was it Paris? That was the plan we'd concocted for

Gigi as little girls. Gigi would meet a dark Frenchman called Hervé—we'd insisted on an accent on the 'e' for authenticity. He would pick her up on his Vespa wearing a blue and white striped shirt and smoking a Gitane. As they sped off to their picnic in the park, she would hang onto him with one arm, while balancing a basket of cheese and wine in the other. And a baguette.

I smiled at the memory and guessed that was probably not the current plan. I foraged in the cupboard and found a Scottish baguette equivalent: a packet of shortbread. Three fingers down, I wondered if Glory had been hiding a Hervé. It seemed so improbable. Glory's life bore all the hallmarks of perfection. A beautiful house, stable and loving husband, adorable kids. Everyone healthy.

When they'd bought the house in Pollokshields, right after Noah's second birthday, I thought she would explode with joy. A proper, big grown-up house, with a giant garden for the boys and—yes, the thing I envied above all else—even a wisteria. She'd gone on a decorating spree, full of ideas, and only complained once, when Stephen confiscated her credit card to curb her excess. The only reason they'd been able to afford such a nice house on a civil servant's salary was because his foster parents had left him a surprise nest egg. Matched with Stephen's insider knowledge of developments in Glasgow's property market, this had allowed him to climb the ladder faster than most.

Years passed, and I believed Glory enjoyed her role. But as the documents on the floor proved, my sister's life was not what she portrayed. Along the way, she'd mastered the art of duplicity. And look where that got her.

But I owed it to her to find a way out. She was my

Glory. My Gi. I owed it to her to protect her boys, and even Stephen, from ever knowing what she'd been forced to do.

You must have had a good reason to drag me into this. A way for me to help.

Resuming my investigation, I leafed through the financial statements and left a trail of aborted calculations. My challenge was to estimate her debt to Mike.

If I checked the profits she'd retained...and maybe made an assumption about how much of a cut she could keep...I could guess at the sums laundered...and then...No. It was too complex for me. I'd never run a real business with actual goods and proper customers. No matter how hard I tried, the hidden clues would remain just that: hidden.

Deflated, I leaned back and rested my head on the sofa cushion, watching numbers dance across the ceiling in no discernible pattern. I felt an overwhelming desire to call Alastair and disclose everything. He would understand it all. He could help me with the numbers. But would he have a professional duty to report the crime? Or could you tell accountants everything without fear, like solicitors? Unsure, I thought the better of it.

As the minutes passed, what started out as a little pebble jiggling in the pit of my stomach grew into a large rock pressing on my organs. I had refused to contemplate the obvious answer because of the horrendous implications. But short of alternatives, and running out of time, I relented. The only option was to bring Dad on board.

CHAPTER TWENTY-NINE

Sunday morning traffic up to Perth flowed smoothly, as usual. I enjoyed a higher-than-normal vantage point from which to admire the fields, travelling in Dave's borrowed van. But for the second time in three weeks, I was driving up with bad news.

The decision had weighed on my mind all night. In the end, I convinced myself that the opportunity to make Glory's mistakes go away justified the fall-out from the bomb I was about to drop. The trip did nothing to change my mind, and by the time I reached the cul-de-sac, I took confidence from my rehearsed speech.

Our trusted bell announced my arrival and summoned Dad to the kitchen.

'Grace. I wasn't expecting you yet. Now is not a good... I need you to stay here. Why are you early?' He disappeared as quickly as he'd arrived.

Checking the clock on the wall, I confirmed I was only eight minutes early and felt a mild irritation at the unjustified rebuke.

On taking a seat at the table, a Which magazine invited me to check out this year's Best Buy dishwashers and accused me with giant red letters spelling 'FRAUD', which I quickly discovered was to do with contact-less cards. I moved onto the Perthshire Advertiser, to check if I recognised any names among the local events, weddings, births and obituaries. Given I hadn't received condolences from any old friends, I assumed that Glory's death hadn't been reported, which seemed strange given my Mum's fascination with the paper.

The fruit bowl stank of decay and a casual scan of the room revealed two used pans on the cooker and a jumble of dirty mugs near the sink, suggesting the local rag wasn't the only thing being neglected. My ears picked up a clinking noise and a toilet flushing before Dad walked in, drying his hands on a towel.

'Everything okay, Dad?'

Age had not so much crept up on him as sprinted in assault since I'd last seen him, his energy drained so that even his hug landed weakly. With an increasing sense of alarm, I enquired about Mum.

'Come see for yourself.' He shuffled to the door.

In the living room, I saw my mother dozing in her preferred armchair, letting out soft, irregular grunts. It looked as though her small frame was merging into the upholstery: the large image of a snowdrop cupping a drop of dew mirrored in Mum's curved white bob enveloping her face, a drib of drool escaping from her lips.

'Oh my God,' I muttered in shock. 'It's gotten worse, hasn't it?'

He nodded and placed his arm around me. 'Sorry to keep you waiting, sweetheart. She wasn't fully dressed. We don't tend to bother anymore.'

'What do you mean?'

'Darling,' he said, in a gentle voice, 'your mother isn't all there. We don't get many periods of lucidity now. Mostly she sits in the chair and looks at the garden, or sleeps.'

I crashed onto the sofa and made a herculean effort not to weep, for his sake. However difficult my relationship with my mother might have been, it broke my heart to witness her fade away. 'It's happening so fast. What do the doctors say?'

'They've been caught off-guard by how quickly the dementia has progressed. There's Glory's death, of course, which kicked it into gear, and there's the possibility she's had another silent stroke that could've made it worse. I don't know. They say the disease is unpredictable and varies from patient to patient.'

He shrugged, seeming resigned to see his wife of forty years deteriorate, as though in her vanishing she'd taken his spirit along for company.

'Is there nothing they can do?'

'No. They've arranged for some home help. She can only come twice a day and isn't much use for her...personal care.' He winced.

It was clearly awkward for him to discuss intimate matters with me. She had been such a proud woman, always immaculately presented. The thought she now needed help with bathing and the toilet filled me with sadness. For her, and for him.

'I could come up more often, to take the pressure off you.'

'Thanks, darling, but she needs more than that. I'm looking at homes.'

That bombshell dwarfed the one I had come armed with, and it floored me. As I recovered from the knock-down, I wondered if I had it in me to let off another blast.

We sat in silence, holding hands, and watched Mum doze. I suggested a cup of tea and re-joined my father on the sofa, where we sat, hands wound around our cups, huddled like campers by a fire. My rehearsed speech ready for action, I found myself mute, stalling for a better moment; one I knew wouldn't come.

'I love you, Dad,' I said, as the silence became unbearable.

'I love you too, Grace.' He patted my knee.

Growing up, our parents had always insisted on honesty. No matter what we'd done, they would rather hear about it from us. Glory and I managed to keep some secrets despite being terrible liars. But as the rules demanded that the punishment for lying be greater than the punishment for the act, we quickly learnt it was better to be open. Strict yet forgiving, our parents would send us to confession and, after some extra chores and the occasional slap, the matter would not be brought up again.

Hoping the rules still stood, I chose to speak. 'I have a story to tell you that you won't like.'

'Oh?'

'It's about Glory.'

He slid further down the sofa and turned to me with a bewildered expression. 'Is this really necessary?' he asked, in a tone reminding me that one should not speak ill of the dead.

'I'm afraid it is. Please hear me out.'

Over the course of twenty minutes he listened to my tale. He listened with gasps; he listened clutching his grey hair; he listened punching his leg; he listened while pacing and covering his face with his hands. But he listened. When I was done explaining about the money laundering and the beastly nature of the men we were dealing with, I dealt the final blow. 'And he threatened me and the boys.'

His face ashen, he informed me he needed a walk and promptly left the house, abandoning me. I knew better than to ask him how long he would be.

Mum stirred a few times in her sleep while he was out. I stroked her cheek, not so much to elicit a response—though I ached to search her eyes for signs of herself—but in the hope that she would feel my presence. I whispered, 'I'm the only one you've got now.' But there was no response.

When Dad burst through the kitchen door two hours later, he looked rebuilt, invigorated by fresh air that seemed to have inflated him back up to his usual heft. His eyes projected a steady resolve as he plonked next to me at the table I'd freshly cleaned.

'Okay. Let me have a look at these accounts.' He put on his reading glasses, reminding me of the hours he would spend inspecting the books of their own shop, when I was little.

If he had been shocked or angry or disappointed—most likely all three—his walk had given him an opportunity to digest his emotions to focus on the task of helping the daughter he had left.

Alastair's envelope emptied, he perused the paperwork, circling a few numbers across different pages, while I kept quiet to not interrupt his train of thought. I was dying to understand how he felt, what he thought we should do next. What held me back was the worry that by questioning him, I might break the spell that currently had him on my side.

'And you've not spoken to the police at all? Because you think they'll treat you as an accessory?'

'Yes. And I have no real proof other than a box of cash and a dodgy invoice. And there would be a whole investigation involving everyone. What if the guy's got the cops in his pocket, like he says?'

'And Stephen isn't aware of any of this?'

'No. As far as he's concerned, Glory's café was going well enough to pay her a small salary and not much more. I didn't have the heart to tell him. He's coping with enough.' I wished I could take back that comment straight away. Why protect Stephen over my father who was also struggling? 'I mean, this isn't just about Glory's crime, it's about hiding money from him…You said she was thinking of leaving him…What good would it do for him to find out?' I tried to rationalise it as best I could, but deep down I had a sense that the scorned husband, notwithstanding his own dirty part in getting the café up and running, would not hesitate to let me sink with the ship. At least my father would want to protect me.

'I think the solution is to pay off the wholesaler— Mike,' I said. 'I reckon it would take about thirty thousand pounds. Do you agree?'

He reviewed his notes and nodded. 'It will all depend on the interest he's been charging. Thirty will be in the right ballpark.' He shook his head. 'If we do that, we will never nail him for what he made Glory do. It's like he would be rewarded.'

His frustration was palpable, and I was relieved I had decided not to share my hypothesis that Glory was murdered. Through all my ruminations, there had been no scenario in which this information would be helpful. I'd settled on it being best to let others mourn her senseless death than to be perpetually angry, like me, because the killer couldn't be caught.

'I know he gets out of this unpunished. It makes me want to scream. But what else can we do?'

'You could continue.' His tone was bone dry.

'What?'

'The way I see it, there is no guarantee that he will leave you alone even if you give him money. And the threat of retaliation will always be there. Like you said, it's only for six months. Maybe we can take the time to build a better case, to rejig the shares so that you're not implicated. Maybe in due course we can find a fraud squad from outside Glasgow. Or it just ends.'

I heard what he was saying, but my brain couldn't process it. The words were garbled, muddled, as though in a different language. I tried to decipher it, but I was too stunned. Was my church-going, law-abiding father telling me to keep colluding with gangsters? To become a criminal? I couldn't understand it at all.

'In the meantime, we can use the extra cash to pay for better care for your mother. We owe her that,' he said. And my jaw fell.

CHAPTER THIRTY

Not long thereafter, I found myself on the hard shoulder of the M80, scrambling out of the van just in time to cross the low metal barrier and spew into the grass. The valiant battle against nausea that began in the 'royal burgh' was lost at Bannockburn. It was almost poetic, until I looked at my splattered shoes. It was also a renewed habit I could really do without. That and the raging flashes of anger, triggered over nothing. The volatility was nothing new, but why was I not able to control it like before? Before the fear and the confusion. Before nothing made sense anymore and I felt so…so…what was it? Betrayed.

My instinct had been to run to Alice after my father's shocking demand. I'd stopped on her street corner, idling like a workman on a break, watching her unpack umpteen pieces of sports equipment from her SUV and usher her high-spirited, red-cheeked kids into the house. There would be enough hot chocolate to go around and, even unexpected, I would always be welcome.

But my conscience had told me to leave. Do not ruin her happy Sunday. Do not drag her into this mess.

Though I was desperate to tap into her professional expertise, how would I begin to explain why I was asking about possible stress-induced personality changes, without revealing the whole miserable story?

No.

Move on.

Go home.

Relieved to discover a roll of paper towels in the glove box, I wiped my feet, climbed onto the elevated chair and merged into traffic.

Snippets of Dad's many excuses swirled through my mind on the journey back to Glasgow.

'I can't do this alone.'

'We didn't plan for care when we sold the shop.'

'The council expects us to pay anyway, even in a council home.'

In the final moments of our conversation, he'd tried to play down the risks as a last-ditch attempt to persuade me to give in.

'It's only six months.'

'No-one will know.'

'God will forgive us.'

Will he? I hadn't thought of God in years, having long chucked my faith in the face of inexplicable famines, AIDS, sectarianism, clerical abuse, you name it. So I didn't give a shit about God. But it mattered to Dad.

He'd invoked their vows made before the Almighty—'in sickness and in health.' Did he really think it would be an acceptable justification, come judgement day, for urging one's daughter into a life of crime?

However outraged I was at my role as sacrificial lamb, I was somewhat comforted by the rationale. It wasn't about wanting to safeguard their savings or not wanting to bathe her himself; it was about providing the best care for Mum.

'She deserves her dignity,' he'd said.

It was hard to argue with that.

CHAPTER THIRTY-ONE

On Monday morning I was on the school run and Blue-walking duties again. It was nearing the end of term and it seemed the teachers were already winding down for summer. They kept the children occupied with music recitals, art exhibitions and bake sales, all of which requiring parental involvement, which Stephen made heroic efforts to supply. Except the cakes; they were Tesco's.

While packing his bag, Noah enthused about the three-mile hike his dad had taken them on at the weekend, which had been followed by a treasure hunt at the Riverside Museum. I chortled as he described the pricey building designed by a famous architect to house the city's transport collection as 'fun and pointy' and resembling 'a squiggly line, like when they test your brain in films.' He jabbered on about the steam engines and the circular overhead bicycle installation, and I spurred him on with appreciative noises. Until he mentioned the ambulance.

'Did you know there are more than three hundred pieces of medical equipment inside an ambulance?' Caught up in his quest for trivia, as if it was the most normal thing in the world, he added, 'how many do you think they used on Mummy?'

The question landed like a left hook. Images of my sister's burnt-out car sparked across my mind: a blackened carcass of mangled orange metal smouldering in the grassy field. Panic grew inside me as I flashed back to the horrible moment the boys had been told the truth about their mother.

Breathe.

I didn't have the heart to tell him she was dead when they found her. 'I'm sure they used all the ones they had to,' I said.

This didn't seem to satisfy the little fact-seeker, who theatrically turned his smile upside down and sighed. I would need to do better. He had me torn between answering a potentially unsatisfactory 'all of them' and offering a random but precise 'five,' with the risk that he would want to know *which* five. Instead, I promised to call the ambulance service while he was at school and made a mental note to research a plausible number later.

'Where is your brother?' I wanted to bring the attention elsewhere. I'd been getting good at changing the subject when things became awkward, remembering Glory's tips for dealing with tantrums. And it was true: little boys really do have the attention span of a gnat.

'He's still upstairs.'

A glance at my watch revealed we were at risk of being late, and I bounded up the stairs to find him. The door to the eldest's room was closed and as I opened it, without knocking, he leapt up and hid his hands behind him. He reversed two steps to his bed in a discreet attempt to shove whatever he was holding under his pillow.

'What have you got there, Adam?'

His shoulders sagged. 'The phone.'

'What phone?'

He shrunk into a little ball, wincing, as if waiting to be castigated. 'Mum's phone.'

My heart quickened.

Could it be?

As if approaching a wounded bird, I drew close, my hand only partially outstretched, my voice reassuring. 'It's okay, sweetheart, you've done nothing wrong. Can you give the phone to me?'

He passed it over, the fear of a strong reprimand visibly receding as he stepped forward.

'Oh my God,' I muttered, when I saw what was on the screen. It was a game. And a game meant that the phone was unlocked. I nearly jumped for joy. 'How did you unlock this?'

'I know the swipe code. Mum showed it to me once when we were at the dentist and had to wait a long time.'

'Why didn't you tell me?'

He lifted his shoulders. 'You never asked.'

Afraid the gleaming display would extinguish again, I asked him to show me, and he drew a rectangle across the nine-dotted security feature. Stephen and I had given up hope of getting into Glory's electronic stuff, having tried multiple avenues. And yet, it now seemed so obvious. I shook my head in disbelief. Why had it never occurred to us to ask the kids?

Adam and Noah were due at school. After dropping them off, I warned Blue: 'This will only be a quick one, buddy.' The phone was burning a hole in my pocket and I hoped that Glory's emails, texts or call records might provide me with more insight. Most of the bank accounts had been found, but not those in the boys' names. I also longed to see who she had been in touch with, and how she'd communicated with her criminal contacts.

The dog and I sprinted along Terregles Avenue for a short loop home, with enough park to give a nod to Blue's insatiable appetite for tree-sniffing. Watching his wagging tail, I wondered if he missed Glory too. He had been easy in adapting to new routines and barked eagerly when he spotted me, as he did with all acquaintances, often circling my legs in anticipation of a brisk walk. Yet, he too must sense the void.

I recalled an emotional client forcing me to watch a video compilation on YouTube of dogs being reunited with servicemen returning from active duty. It was the sort of stuff designed to make grown men cry: the joy of floppy-eared pups jumping in their masters' outstretched arms, accentuated by a crescendo of violin strings. As Blue demanded a head-scratch, I apologised that he would never experience such a reunion.

When we arrived at the house, I began scrolling through the texts while preparing a cup of tea. I'd decided to stay here, keen to start my sleuthing and because it was closer to Govan, where I would collect my car from Andy later. I grabbed an envelope to scribble on from the pile of post on the side table that appeared unchanged from recent days.

I already knew my sister didn't use her mobile much, so had been managing my expectations since gaining access to it. The way she'd put it was, 'If people need to find me, they will. There are only ever two places I'll be. Home or the café.' Or, 'I see enough of my friends not to have to catch up on Facebook.' Plus, she was notoriously incapable of taking a good selfie so that was reason enough not to use it.

Casting any privacy scruples aside, I swiped the rectangular shape. The SMS messages revealed little. They consisted for the most part of exchanges between her and Stephen to do with domestic logistics. They didn't paint a picture of a healthy romance, but then you wouldn't be expected to write sonnets about running out of toothpaste. Sascha occasionally enquired about Glory's whereabouts or asked her to pick up an order from Locavore en route to work. Her WhatsApp was inundated with the ramblings of harassed mothers bemoaning lost PE kits and the lack of information about school events.

While I marched through her calendar, email and other apps systematically, my earlier excitement faded with every swipe. The electronic version of her life was all so mundane. The diary of a housewife and minor entrepreneur. Nothing indicated any illicit goings-on.

No unexpected banking App.

No secret coded messages.

Nothing.

I moped around the kitchen feeling robbed. The folder for the business contained only things I'd already seen at the venue or received from Alastair.

Where's the money, Gi? Where did you keep track of it all?

The thought occurred to me that perhaps she hadn't stored any notes on purpose. Why preserve incriminating evidence? Maybe it wasn't that hard to monitor the laundering. After all, the payments required for the wholesaler were stated in the false invoices, and any funds left over fell under her control, anyway. She pilfered a bit of her share in cash first to avoid any tax, judging by the stash in her closet, but the rest would be officially recorded in the bookkeeping.

Deflated, I cast the phone aside. The display flipped onto the lock screen, featuring a close-up of her boys. Those smiling faces drew me back in: I hadn't checked the pictures! Like any proud mother, the memory card would be full of her kids. But there could also be snaps of her and, at that moment, I wanted nothing more than to be with my sister.

I opened the Gallery and was greeted by a kaleidoscope of thumbnails. However much I had grown to love the kids, I filtered them out as I scanned the various albums, my eyes fixated on finding a blob of red hair. The stream of youthful faces was interspersed with buildings, landscapes and unfamiliar people. It was only when a grouping of random male adult figures kept popping up that I slowed down to study them in detail. What was this?

I gasped when I recognised the location of the background. Curious to make out their relevance, I catalogued all the similar-themed photos as a new set. When I was done, there were twenty-two clues for me to process.

It appeared that in the three weeks preceding her death, Glory had photographed Excelsior's frontage and the work yards at its side and rear twenty-two times. She'd captured labourers carrying all manner of boxes by hand; their work supervised by the ned I'd met, slurping on an Irn Bru with a menacing brown dog at his feet.

Taken from further away were snapshots of a shirtless, emaciated adolescent boy with dark bruises on his chest, exiting one of four caravans crowded at the rear of the wholesaler's site. Older workers, looking equally unwell, stood around smoking, the ramshackle condition of their living quarters visible through the open doors.

The series confirmed Mike would not be winning the award for 'Boss of the Year' anytime soon, but I struggled to understand what had compelled Glory to document all this. I pursed my lips as images from within his distinctive office jumped on the screen, reminding me of our unsettling encounter. What made them all the more distasteful, was that they were wonky selfies of Glory and Mike having fun: my sister and a gangster in a cosy embrace.

CHAPTER THIRTY-TWO

When I picked up the car that afternoon, it gleamed in the afternoon light, showing off its new rear window. Andy had given it a good clean and, once again, hung his foul-smelling logoed air freshener from the mirror. It was a ruse, he'd once confessed. The noxious lemon scent was chosen on purpose; so that when customers threw the thing out—which he fully accepted they would—the guilt of discarding a gift from a sweet old man would tie them to the garage forever.

'You save this for someone else.' I handed the bauble over with a wink, before sliding into the driver's seat. It was good to have my own set of wheels again. Dave's van had given me a fun vantage point from which to observe other drivers' behaviour, but it had been murder on my lower back.

Later, when Dave came to pick up his keys, I asked him to stay. We pussy-footed around my predicament, talking about his day and deciding on what to have for dinner, but it was a topic that could not be avoided for long.

'I have a plan,' I announced, as we chopped vegetables side by side. 'But I sort of feel I should get your permission.'

'How so?'

'These guys are dangerous. You said so yourself. So I want to get rid of them. Make the whole thing go away. I want to pay the wholesaler off and keep my fingers clean.'

'I see. How much are we talking?'

'A lot. And this is where you come in…I need to use what I've saved up for the flat.'

He dropped the heavy knife onto the chopping board and took a step away. 'Shit Grace, that money's important. We'll be back to square one.'

'Well where else will I get it? I won't touch the laundered money,' I said, stopping midway through a courgette. 'Don't look at me like that. Even if I wanted to, I can't access the accounts. I've only got the shoe box that hasn't been through the books. That's him basically getting her cut back. It's peanuts. The rest will have to come from me. It might not be as much as he would get if I did what he wanted, but it would be clean money, free, through the bank. That's got to be attractive for him.'

I'd mulled the transaction over a whole day: the amount, the motivations, what to say. But I was clearly failing to convince Dave, who stood watching me prepare our meal with his arms crossed.

'Why is this your problem? Why do you need to be the hero?'

'If you can't understand why I need to save my dead sister's family from misery, you don't know me.' That accusation felt unfair even as I said it. I'd never told him about the day Glory almost died. The day that triggered a childhood anxiety it had taken years of practice in emotional repression to overcome. 'I saved

Glory's life once...and there's this Chinese expression, "if you save a life, you're responsible for it." Well that's me.' I grinned apologetically.

He cocked his head. 'What happened?'

'It was the summer I was twelve. It was really warm, and our friend Alice's parents had taken us to Moncrieffe Island for the day to swim. Mum never liked going there because it was too visible from town to be in our swimmies. It's right across the bridge from one of the main streets; a little island right in the middle of the river. Anyway, this is the Tay, so it's cold and you have to be careful. But it's shallow if you stick by the main bit where other families were, too. At one point, this boy starts splashing Glory and, as far as I can tell, she thinks it's fun. She's giggling; saying, "Stop it," but in that way I could tell she didn't mean it.' I took a sip of water before continuing, cooling the heat in my temples brought on by troubled memories. 'Then next thing I know, I see the boy returning to land to retrieve his ball, but not Glory. And the panic rises. I don't see her. I call out her name and everyone starts to pay attention. The current was strong further up, but I didn't hesitate and swam on. I caught her around the first bend of the river as she was being dragged away. I managed to grab hold of a thick branch with one arm while clutching the shoulder strap of her costume with the other. I thought I was going to be torn in two. And Gi was screaming my name...'

'Oh my God, you must have been so frightened.'

'The grown-ups got us out. Dragged us to shore. Glory was shaken but okay. Probably loving the drama. Me, I threw up then walked over to that boy. And it was like I was a big ball of energy that needed to explode, you know? So I punched him.'

'You punched him?' Dave asked, laughing and looking horrified in equal measure.

'Yes, and hard too. I wasn't sure what he'd done, but the little fucker must have deserved it.'

'Woah. Remind me never to mess with you.'

'Oh, ha ha. Well, now you know…' I tossed him an onion, hoping he now understood, hoping I'd attracted him on side. 'Here, there's work to be done.'

A moment later, he asked, 'So what is it you want to do?'

'I want to pay the wholesaler off, so we can be done with this. No-one will find out. It will be over, and you and I will manage. I don't need your blessing to spend my money. I just hoped you would give it.'

'Okay, fair enough. I understand that. And it might work. But if you think he killed Glory, isn't that like letting him get away with it?'

'I don't *think* he killed Glory, I know he did. But I can't prove it. I'll never have proof. There is no CCTV, no nothing. It kills me, but I'm resigned to the fact we will never get justice.' Suppressing a sob, I placed my mountain of cuttings into a sieve and held it under the tap, my face cooling above the spray. 'Babe, I've spent a lot of time on this. There is no way to make him go down without dragging us with him. Let me at least try this. Worst case he says "no" and we consider our alternatives again.'

'But you've done nothing wrong. Stephen's done nothing wrong. So why is going to the police so bad? You can explain you weren't involved. It was all her. Your accountant chap can vouch for you. You're a lovely white lady from Perth with no previous convictions. The police would believe whatever you say. Trust me, it's only Gorbals scum like me they don't give a fair hearing.'

He wiped his teary eyes and sniffed. It was the onions. But seeing him cry made me wonder how he'd coped when they'd locked him up for two weeks. What had he called it when he first told me about it? 'A harshly punished error in judgement.' Him only a teenager. His one and only time thieving, he'd assured me. Straight as an arrow ever since.

'Even assuming that's true,' I said. 'I haven't told you this yet, but Stephen granted her landlord planning permission against the rules. If they figure that out, he could lose his job and what does that do to the boys? Would that be fair?'

His eyes widened. He shook his head and frowned. 'No, of course not.' He seemed to mull over this new piece of evidence. He pointed his knife at me. 'Fine, we'll do it your way. But I'm coming with you.'

'Good.' I lowered his utensil-cum-weapon. 'I'm scared. I've been threatened enough and, lest we forget, he murdered Glory because she wanted to expose him.'

'You don't know that for sure.'

'Ah, but I do.' I wiped my hands on the tea towel and fetched the phone from beside the sofa, opening the saved album as I pressed the mobile into his hands. 'Why else would she be taking these pictures? Look. Glory took all these photos of his guys moving boxes. She was documenting his dealings. These could all hold money. Don't you see? She must have planned to hand this in. Maybe she'd gone to the cops after all, and they'd asked for more evidence. Maybe she hadn't gone yet. We can't very well go in and ask.'

He studied the photos, zooming in on a few to explore the detail, but when the last, couply ones appeared, his demeanour changed. 'Or she was helping him.' His voice dripped with contempt. 'This doesn't strike me as someone afraid for her life.'

'He's a monster. How can you even suggest she'd have anything to do with him?'

'Because your sister liked attention. Correction. She liked attention from men. And from what I can see, she's getting plenty of it.' He held the device to my face, Glory and Mike's smiles amplified by a reflected kitchen spot light. I swatted it away, irritated that I still didn't understand what the hell Glory had been up to; irritated that she'd let herself be photographed in such a compromising way; irritated this was sabotaging my perfectly logical case.

'That's disgusting.' I tried hard to unsee Mike's hand resting on her knee.

'Sweetheart, I know you don't want to hear it. But think about it. It's conceivable, isn't it?'

For a split second, I considered the possibility that my sister had been a gangster-banging slut, leading a criminal double life in which she deviously implicated me—her loving sister—to keep her own fingers clean, while plotting to fund her escape from domestic boredom with ill-gotten gains. This fantasy brought a strange sense of relief: for that small moment, I was off the hook. I could drop her. I could move on with my life. But I shook my head. No. She was a victim, after all.

Dave sighed and placed his arm around my shoulders, still holding the phone, and gave me a gentle squeeze. I thought it was to commiserate on my ordeal, but he was preparing me for the next blow. 'I wasn't going to tell you, but she even tried to seduce me once.'

'What? No. That's not true.'

'Okay,' he acceded. 'She wasn't really interested in me. She was only persuading to get me to tell her what happened between me and Stephen when we were kids. She saw me here once and was all flirty, like, batting her big blue eyes and playing with her hair. Desperate to find out.'

'She's not the only one.' I humphed and wriggled out from under his arm. 'What did happen with Stephen?'

His eyes hardened. 'He got used and betrayed by a woman. Like now.'

He tossed the phone onto the worktop in disgust, freeing his hand to pull at his neck in a stretch. I stood motionless while he seemed to consider his options.

'Have you got any beer?' he said.

Was he finally going to tell me?

'Sure, let me get one.'

CHAPTER THIRTY-THREE

Dave settled at the breakfast bar while I grabbed two drinks and rummaged in the drawer for the opener. I didn't drink often, but I joined him. He looked nervous and I wanted to create a safe space. After his first sip, he seemed to relax and his gaze met mine.

He nodded.

He was ready.

'We were in fifth year. Stephen was in the other class. We weren't friends, but we'd never had a problem with each other either. Other guys would pick on him and the other more studious boys. To be honest, he was an easy target among the rougher crowd, but for the most part he was okay. So that year I'm seeing him more often because he starts going out with this girl called Lynda, my sister's best friend.'

As I listened I tried to picture his sister Danielle. I'd met her once at a birthday party. A year younger, she lived with a balding plasterer in Cumbernauld and their two teenage kids. She was pretty but had succumbed to the West Coast fashion of slapping on lashings of make-up and wearing short, tight dresses that turned you into a sausage no matter how fit you were. I tried to imagine her aged fifteen.

Dave continued. 'Lynda always hung out at our place. She hated going home. Apparently, her parents fought all the time and her father had a temper. Then the girl gets pregnant. She's fifteen and with her dad and all, she doesn't want to keep it.'

'How do you know this?'

'Because I caught Danielle crying one morning and she told me everything. She'd been very upset for her friend but also felt really conflicted and was struggling to keep the secret. She thought the adults should be told but confided in me instead. I promised to keep quiet. Anyway, young girls were getting banged up left, right and centre, so it was no big deal to me.'

The condensation on the beer had loosened the label, and Dave picked at the edges, rolling thin paper tatters into soggy balls that he lined up onto the counter. The thought of the counter top sputum distracted me but not enough to veer off mission. Was this where the feud with my brother-in-law would come in?

'Did she tell Stephen?'

'Yes. At first I didn't know how or when she'd gotten rid of the baby. Danielle hadn't discussed it with me again. Then one day, I'm working with my dad after school, helping him with the plumbing at the local. This was before I set up on my own to get out from under him. Anyway, I'm in the pub and I see Stephen all alone. He's clearly been there a while, and he's definitely had a few too many. It was close to exam time so him being drunk during the day seemed very odd. He was the one kid expected to get all As.'

Dave flicked the line of mushy balled-up label bits into the void with his fingers, one by one, as he spoke.

Every take-off made me flinch inside, and I memorised the exact location of each projectile, for later retrieval. I removed the vandalised bottle and offered a fresh one, even though the first wasn't finished.

'Thanks,' Dave said. 'Now because I know what's happened, I decide to go sit with him.' Oblivious to my compulsion, his hand was quick to destroy the next label. 'I remember the expression on his face. A man in need of a friend. I go sit next to him. He doesn't say much. But after a while I ask whether it's about the baby. He looks up all surprised and breaks down. He tells me how he wanted to keep it. That it was the right thing to do. But Lynda was scared to tell her dad. And besides, they didn't have any money to take care of it. Stephen's all angry, like, and starts smacking his own head real hard, cursing how poor he is, cursing his dead parents, vowing he's going to make something of himself so that money won't ever determine his fate again.'

'God, that's awful. The poor guy.'

'It gets worse.' Dave took another swig. 'He tells me he skipped school the week before to go to the abortion clinic with Lynda. How he pleaded with her one last time and even offered to marry her because he wanted to be an honourable man. But she went through with it anyway. And then he cries how now, all of a sudden, she doesn't want to be with him anymore. She says he tried manipulating her and he reminds her of her Pa.'

'Wow, that's so unfair. That must have crushed him. He was being such a good guy.'

'Well, that's what I thought, too. So then I told him something. So that he would feel better. You know, forgive himself? Remember how I said my sis shared

Lynda's secrets with me? That she couldn't keep them in?'

'Uhuh.'

'Well, turns out Stephen wasn't the father.'

I jumped up and put my hands to my face. 'Oh shit. You're kidding me on?'

'No, I'm not. Lynda had been seeing this other guy behind Stephen's back. He was in sixth form. A real dick. When she got pregnant, she chose to tell Stephen it was his, because he was nicer and would go with her, and all. And then I guess she now had an excuse to break up with Stephen—which was probably her plan all along.'

'And you told him the baby wasn't his?'

'Yes. I thought he deserved to know. He deserved not to beat himself up for the rest of his life. But he took it badly. Man, he was raging. He's sitting there spitting, thinking everybody knows, calling Lynda and me every name under the sun. But I assured him it was only me and my sister who knew. Nobody else.'

'That's so him. Worried about what people think.'

'Well, he wasn't having it. It was as if he blamed me for the whole thing. Somehow, I was the bad one; the one who'd made him look like a complete muppet. At this point I realise it had been a mistake to tell him. And I apologise. But the damage is done. He tells me to piss off and that he wants nothing to do with me ever again.' Dave shrugged and brought his beer to his lips, placing the bottle on the table with an air of finality. 'So now you know.'

'Why haven't you told me this before? All this time I've wondered why he didn't want you around. I had all sorts of visions of you as a teenage thug, or bully, or something horrible. I wasn't sure I could trust you.'

'I'm sorry. I never told anymore. It wasn't my story to tell. And then when you and I got together, it was awkward. I mean, I could understand that having me there would be a constant reminder of this horrible experience. So when Glory informed me I was banished, I let it go. I didn't want this to become a thing between you and her. I made out like I didn't mind.'

He sat hunched over his drink, sticky shreds of label wedged under his nails. It was as if the gradual unmasking of the glass had facilitated his own unburdening. I pulled him to my chest and stroked his hair.

'You're a good man. You let him have his dignity. And that is what I am doing too. Can you see why I don't want him mixed up in Glory's mess? Why he can't find out?'

'Yes, but why should I have my life messed up for his precious reputation? What about me? What about our flat? I need to come first *sometime*, Grace.'

Guilt ravaged my insides. There was no fairness, not for him. I couldn't pretend his situation was anything other than completely shit and I wracked my brain for ways to make it less bad.

'I know. I'm sorry. You're right. I can't expect you to make another sacrifice. Not without me making one,' I said. 'So maybe we'll be able to claw the money back from Glory's missing account. I know that's dirty money, and I'd be incriminating myself. But we'd only be getting back what we put in. Like a loan.' Growing more comfortable with this line of reasoning, I added, 'Call it an advance.'

He perked up a little. 'What will you do with the rest of it?'

The image of my mother, infirm in her armchair, flashed across my mind. 'I haven't decided yet.'

CHAPTER THIRTY-FOUR

D-day arrived. The morning's shower and breakfast routine progressed in a fog, our two bodies manoeuvring to avoid collision. We'd argued about the plan until deep into the night. Scarred by a flurry of ricocheting accusations of patriarchy, foolishness, insensitivity and control freakery, we'd eventually gone to bed on a fragile compromise neither of us wanted to re-examine in the cold light of day.

After a silent embrace, we got into our respective vehicles. He followed me to Excelsior where he was to behave like a normal customer, only to step in on my signal. The distance between us grew as we neared the wholesaler, so I would have a few minutes to park and enter the building before he did the same.

The cashier inspected me in the usual unwelcoming manner, and I was interested to learn with Dave's entrance that this act was reserved only for other women. She remained seated as I approached the desk. Grey roots paved a stripe across her black hair and reminded me of a skunk. Judging by the amount of perfume she was wearing, she may well have been hiding one. Her Kohl-lined eyes set on me. Would she remember me?

'I'm here to see Mike.'

'What is it this time? Bog roll chafe your sensitive tush?'

'Just call him.' I was in no mood to play her game.

She lifted the receiver and summoned the ned. I glanced around the shop for the dog I'd seen on Glory's pictures, a drooling beast I would rather not meet in person. A glimpse of Dave examining the canned foods aisle reassured me that so far, so good.

Pasty-face took his sweet time to cross the floor, popping gum and flicking his keys. He nodded to the skunk. 'Alright?'

'Aye, love.'

He looked me up and down. 'Let's go.'

When we reached the back, I jerked my elbow from his bony hand. 'I know where I'm headed.'

'Suit yourself.' He shrugged and took the stairs two at a time.

The offices along the corridor were closed but snippets of daylight escaped through slits of toughened glass, saving the hallway from complete darkness. My pulse throbbed in my throat. I concentrated on where I placed my feet to stay calm. Towards the rear, a window in the area that gave access the boss's office provided a relief of illumination. His door was shut too, and I wondered what had happened to make the place bunker down.

'On you go.' He deposited me in the antechamber, his chaperoning duties apparently over. I looked for someone to announce my arrival or a bell or something, but he jutted his chin towards the wooden door, egging me on. I knocked.

'In,' sounded a voice from the other side. Mike

stood in the left rear corner of the room, his sleeves rolled up, a cabinet overflowing with paper commanding his attention.

'Wait a minute,' he said as he rifled through the stack.

My good-girl instinct was to help him in his search or offer to return later, but I reminded myself that today I was to be a hard-nosed businesswoman. She would wait and say nothing.

'Aha!' He placed a yellow envelope on top of a perilously piled archive and shut the metal doors to prevent an avalanche. He tucked his shirt in, straightened his sleeves and his hair, and put on his tweed jacket, gradually rebuilding his beloved gentleman's persona. 'An unexpected Quality Control audit. Had us a little worried. But we passed.' His jubilant smile signalled a good mood that I hoped would work in my favour.

'Congratulations,' I said.

'Now. To what do I owe the pleasure of two visits in one week?' He gestured to the velvet-covered chairs facing his mahogany desk and grabbed his own seat. 'Sit. Sit.'

Dave and I had rehearsed my approach. I was to build rapport—by all means not antagonise like before—and explain the logic behind the proposed financial transaction. He was a businessman and a gangster; I needed to engage with the first.

'The last time I was here, you agreed to limit my "services" to six months.'

'I did, didn't I? You must have caught me on a soft day. Maybe because I was sad your dear sister died. Tell me, did you bring me one of your delicious scones?' He leaned forward, checking if I had anything with me.

Was he crazy? As if I would come skipping in here with a basket of goodies like bloody Red Riding Hood. But the question threw me. Had he been to the café? I felt as if ants were crawling across my shoulders as I imagined him in Glory's domain. But I shook them off and stuck with my script of sweetness and light.

'I'm afraid not, but I'll have some delivered to you. I think I've come with something more interesting, though.'

'What's that?'

'I propose to pay you what is left of my sister's debt. With clean money, through the banks. It would almost be the same as if I had taken over, like you wanted, but you would have the funds earlier. This week even.'

'I see. And what about the scones? Would I still get any if I leave you to run your yoga-tofu bakery in peace?'

His joking irked me, but I played along. 'I'll gladly throw in as many scones as you can eat, Mike, plain and fruit. I have to remind you, however, they're vegan and I suspect that would do your reputation no favours.'

He could no longer contain his mirth and let out a loud belly laugh. This raised my spirits, too, as I ticked off Phase 1: we have rapport. With the groundwork laid and the atmosphere in the room warming, I initiated Phase 2. I retrieved a folded piece of paper from my pocket, slid it onto his desk and leaned back. 'So can we strike a deal?'

'What's this? A number?' He chuckled. 'Did you get that from the movies?'

My stomach tip-toed into its usual churny dance as I watched him unfold the note, frown and rub his chin. Shit. Had I miscalculated? Was it not enough?

'It's tempting,' he said after a while. Then he slid the

note towards me again. 'But I can't take it.'

My internal fluttering stopped, stamped out by a giant, cold foot. 'Why not?'

'Because as you rightly pointed out, I have a reputation to uphold. Honour among thieves, and all that. And I like you. Granted, you're not quite as pretty as your lovely sister, but you have a sense of humour.'

'I don't understand,' I said, puzzled and ever so slightly insulted.

'I'm going to come clean with you: I'm not owed any money. Your sister sorted everything out ages ago.'

'But the box of cash…the invoice…'

'Oh, I didn't say she wasn't laundering money for me anymore. She was. But she did that for herself. I didn't make her.'

The story I had built in my mind of Glory's naïve mistake, of her capture and forced servitude collapsed into rubble. I scrambled across this motivational void, with nothing to cling onto. 'Why…why would she do that?'

'I don't know.' He walked to my side. 'Why not? She was getting away with it. Personally, I think she liked the adventure of it. Gave her a kick.' The man stood beside me. Dazed, I turned to face him. 'She was a wicked wee thing, our Glory,' he said with an exaggerated wink and a devious grin. 'I'll miss her.'

Before I could respond, he moved towards the door.

'I can go? We're done?' Still stunned, I remained glued to my seat.

'Yes, my lady. You can go. Our business is concluded. Well, provided you hand last week's box of cash back with your next delivery.'

It felt surreal. He was behaving as if we were

discussing the return of a library book. In the sort of casual tone that informed you to mind the gap or help yourself to a souvenir on your way out.

'But you said six months?'

'Ah. I was having a go.' His hand swatted me away. 'For convenience. I thought maybe you'd take it on. Maybe develop a taste for easy money too. Saved me the trouble of changing tack. But I've got plenty of willing takers if it's not for you. And frankly, something tells me you'd be more trouble than you're worth.' I nodded, unsure why. 'Of course, I'm only releasing you with the understanding that you will never divulge my little business dealings to anyone. I have enough inspectors crawling over this place as it is.' His tone carried the echoes of earlier threats.

I nodded again, like my body had been re-programmed to have only one setting.

'Now, get out of my office.' And he pointed at the exit.

A moment later, Dave saw me descend the stairs and rushed to the check-out with a case of sunflower oil. His concerned gaze followed me out the automatic doors as he seemed forced to engage with the woman's banter. After, he jogged to my car and I pressed to open the passenger window.

'So?' He leaned in and searched my poker face for clues.

'We're free.'

CHAPTER THIRTY-FIVE

I urged Dave to jump into his van and meet me at the flat, away from Excelsior's prying eyes; but he was running late for a job.

'It's okay,' I reassured him, 'It's over. Don't worry.'

'And the money?'

'You won't believe it, babe. I'll explain later, but it's all good. I'm good.' With no spies in sight, I grabbed him with both hands and planted a colossal kiss on his lips.

The car key quivered around the ignition slot and I had to steady my hand to motor my escape.

Could this be real?

Could I really be free?

As I drove, it was as if a heavy blanket had been lifted off me, and my vision was adjusting to the light of a bright new sun casting its rays over a fairer land. The recycling centre on the corner was no longer a convenient place for the mob to hide bodies, but instead bore testament to man's commitment to heal the Earth. The dodgy auto shop's haphazardly parked cars didn't block the street out of complete disregard for others but were evidence of the unexpected success of a valiant small business owner, to whom I wished good fortune. The teenager pushing a pram was a dedicated, sensible young mother, who had only just found that sweet-smelling cigarette on the ground and was looking for a bin.

The Panda swayed with grace through bustling scenes of urban activity on my way home. Victoria Street beckoned with an air of plenty, gold gleaming in the pawnbroker's window and market stalls abundant with blushing ripe mangoes being stroked—not squeezed—by exotic veiled princesses.

Giddy, I thought I would break into song.

I did it, Gi!

She would have been so proud, like when she used to watch me play football on Saturday mornings. I could still picture it: Glory wearing school colours in her hair, cheering me on, glowing. The sibling of the only girl on the team, she would join the other kids who had been dragged out of bed to support Perth's finest. Many of them were older brothers because, although the parents deemed a thriving high school spirit to be important, they would not trade an industrious morning for a mediocre ballgame. Historical roars reverberated in my ears. I remembered how, one day, I'd scored a splendid goal and she hollered my name and jumped up and down with such enthusiasm that she tripped and got caught by a dreamy senior.

I was left smiling at this clumsy-moment memory of my biggest fan, but my cheeks slackened as the grim awareness she had died reared its ugly head. I had bargained my way out of her mess, but this wouldn't bring her back.

My short-lived euphoria fled as fast as it had come

and the rage I'd felt towards her bastard killers these last few days bubbled up again. Rising with it, a heavy dose of shame. Only seconds ago, I had been rejoicing when, in fact, I'd let the fucker get away with killing Glory.

Verbally spitting at jaywalking pedestrians, I swerved into my road and parked my car too close to its neighbour.

Screw'em.

I strode up the stairs to fetch the necessary kit for my next client and imagined tying Mike up with the elastic physio bands and punching his annoying chuckling face with my mini-barbells, reserving the five-kilo kettle bell for an elongated swing straight into his nuts.

But something didn't sit right. I stopped my mental battery to focus on his face, his actual face; the face I suddenly recalled had said he was sad about Glory's death. That he would miss her. My brain clicked and whirred to build sense from the odd-shaped fragments of conflicted thoughts. If she worked with him out of her own free will, then she wouldn't have been a threat.

Why murder her?

Maybe it wasn't him.

CHAPTER THIRTY-SIX

As I collected my gear, I pulled the Samsung from my pocket to search the best route to my later appointment on the North side of the city and spotted two missed calls. I dialled to retrieve my messages. Only one.

'Good morning. It's Stephen. I'm calling to see where you are. I need to go, and the boys aren't ready. But as you're not there…never mind. I will bring them. Could you please walk the dog? I don't have time for that. Thanks. I hope you get this. Bye.'

While speaking in a neutral tone, his clipped sentences revealed his irritation, and I felt irritated in return. It was true that I'd forgotten about them, but it wasn't as if I'd been having a lie in. I'd spent half the night working out how to save Glory. His wife. *And* him. And on a mission to prevent us all from sinking into a criminal morass, I'd neglected my weekday tasks.

So sue me.

I shoved my trainers into the bottom of a mesh bag and suffocated them with a balled-up track suit. That'll teach them not to take me for granted.

'I never even wanted a dog,' I hissed. But the

prospect of Blue soiling the floor and the poor animal pining away, whining, transformed my recent annoyance into a Catholic's more natural state of guilt. I could make a quick detour to exercise him on my way to the café. Then help Sascha with the yummy mummy rush, and still arrive at work for one o'clock.

Packed and ready, I remembered the missing second call and queried my phone for its caller. It showed an unknown number, which I would normally have ignored were it not for the Perth prefix of *01738*.

I copied and pasted the digits into Google. It came up as the switchboard for the Perth Royal Infirmary.

Please God, no.

The line busy or mysteriously disconnected while on hold, it took ten frantic attempts to speak to a human.

The woman at the hospital was not much enamoured with the idea of giving out patient information to a supposed family member who could only assume her mother may have been brought in, but persistent begging appeared to do the trick.

She confirmed Mary McBride had been brought in the evening before and now stayed on the ward. No, she did not know why I had been called. No, she could not tell me if my mother was all right but, given I'd reached a hospital, she probably wasn't. No, she had no clue where the husband might be—had I tried his mobile?

She lost her patience when I explained that, contrary to popular belief, not everyone had been seduced by the wonders of modern telecommunications.

Cursing my father's technophobia, I rang home but there was no answer.

Moments later, driving on automatic pilot direction motorway, I glimpsed the Clyde from the Kingston Bridge and realised my mistake.

Blue.

I swerved to the next exit and crossed the river again, over the Squinty Bridge, heading South.

Back in Pollokshields, I abandoned the Panda at the gates and ran up the drive, holding my jacket over my head to shield from the spontaneous burst of rain.

The barking was louder than it should have been, and I stopped to listen for its source. I heard nails scratch decking on my right and, before I could investigate, Blue emerged from the gangway between the garage and the house, yapping away.

'What are you doing here?'

He sniffed at my shoes, wagged his tail and slowed my investigative lap of the building by circling my legs. I found the kitchen door open, explaining his escape. Testing the handle a few times, I worked out that the latch was sticky and did not always protrude far enough to secure itself into the opposing plate. With the kids notorious for not locking any doors after playing outside, this was asking for trouble. I made a mental note to inform Stephen he needed a locksmith.

'Well, at least that saves me one job. I bet you've had great fun peeing in the flower beds.'

My teasing voice prompted an excited, possibly affirmative hop, raising a small giggle from me.

'Yes. And you've pooped everywhere, too, haven't you? But guess what?'

His raised ears and wide-eyed expression seemed to reply, 'What?'

'I'm going to pretend this didn't happen. Someone else can have the pleasure of finding that particular gift.

Because Auntie Grace has got to go.'

With both hands, I pushed a very confused-looking Blue into the kitchen, double-locked the door and trotted down the slope to my car to pick up where I'd left off.

CHAPTER THIRTY-SEVEN

The Perth Royal Infirmary was a jumbled agglomeration of blue-capped rectangular extensions built around a century-old core. Parking was severely limited and, after discovering that the empty-looking lot 3B was reserved for patients with special vouchers, I gave up and crawled along the double-yellow lines, finding a lone space four hundred yards away, by the Oakbank dental clinic. The eagle-eyed receptionist visible through the window raised her head as soon as I got out, and I waved, with a guilt-ridden smile, as I thieved the space I knew they must covet for their visitors.

Large silver letters on one of the brick blocks ahead heralded the main entrance to the hospital. After consulting the floor plan in a deserted reception area, I followed the signs to the Medicine for the Elderly part of the Tay ward. I weaved through innumerable identical safety-floored corridors. The hospital administration must have been proud of the results of its recent inspection as the framed scores were exhibited at regular intervals, alongside the ubiquitous NHS posters reminding everyone that coughs and sneezes spread disease.

A sign for the Stroke Unit caused me to hesitate, having not had the opportunity to query where Mum had been admitted to. But I surmised—with no medical training whatsoever—that two strokes in quick succession were unlikely and proceeded to where they kept the oldies that were plain sick.

A middle-aged nurse in a white-trimmed royal blue uniform examined stock on a trolley at the start of yet another double-doored section. Hovering, not wanting to interrupt, I was relieved when she dropped her glasses to bungee on their cord and offered help.

'Could you please tell me where to find Mary McBride? She came in last night.'

'Your mother?' she guessed.

I nodded.

'Come with me.' She beelined to another trolley from which she consulted a clipboard, catching her specs on an upward bounce to review the list. 'Your mum's in the fourth room in the West corridor.' Her original task beckoning, she pointed vaguely, and I was left to gauge the angle of the sun's light hitting the ground from the open wards and remember whether it rose in the East or West.

Members of staff shuffled past me, engrossed in paperwork and the place operated in a state of efficient quietude, as far removed from the hive of panicked activity in A&E as two adjoining departments could be.

When I found the right place, my vision was struck by an overdose of white: the walls, the privacy curtains, the bedding, the nighties, the eight heads of withered hair. Even the sky consisted of fluffy clouds, I noticed through the full-length wall of glass. A black contour by the second bed on the left moved like my father. As

I neared the standing figure, its lines came into focus and I saw the facial ravages of a bad night.

'What happened?'

'We had to bring her in after she lost consciousness taking her pills. I propped her up until the ambulance arrived. They're running more tests, still. We have to be patient.' He moved in for our habitual hug. 'They let me call from the courtesy phone earlier. I was looking for you.'

'How is she?'

Joined at her bedside, we watched her sleep, her ashen face restful but old. Inexplicably old. She was only sixty-three.

'She was out for forty minutes. They gave her IV fluids. They said she appeared dehydrated. She doesn't like straws, but it's the only way I can get her to drink.' He seemed to defend himself against the implied neglect. 'She was very confused when she woke up, but we calmed her down. And she had a few lucid hours, which is reassuring. It's important we let her rest now.'

I stroked the skinny arm stretched out onto the woven blanket and measured her bony hand against mine. There was a time when her giant palm would swallow mine, when her arms could enshroud me completely. And now, all grown-up, I longed to feel that warmth again. I wrapped her fingers around my fist one by one and held them in place, focusing on recollections of the happy early years, before I was mature enough to see that Mum wasn't made entirely of warmth after all.

CHAPTER THIRTY-EIGHT

'Coffee?'

Dad's voice pulled me from my reverie. I couldn't remember when I'd last had a shot of caffeine; life having become an incessant stream of demands throwing my habits into disarray. 'That would be lovely. Will she be all right?'

'Yes.'

We tip-toed out of the room and he gestured for me to follow him towards the main block.

I pointed the opposite way. 'There are vending machines here, Dad.'

'No, that coffee's not worth the cup it comes in. We'll go to the Dining Hall. It will be quiet as lunch isn't served yet.'

He manoeuvred the corridors without hesitation, as if the floor plan had been etched into his mind during his daily visits last year. When we got to the canteen, it was being used as a makeshift meeting room by scattered groups of haggard medical staff. After ordering two lattes and an apple slice to share, we chose a four-person marmoleum table by the door whose sticky surface made me challenge the hospital's celebrated hygiene scores.

Dad strained to bend his body into his seat, stiff from the night in a chair.

'Is Mum eating?' If she wasn't drinking, I wanted to at least be reassured she wasn't starving herself.

'Yes, it's the liquids she's been struggling with because one side of her mouth doesn't close well.'

F-A-S-T. The leaflet we'd been given after Mum's first episode sprung to mind. The mnemonic for the signs of stroke: Face, Arms, Speech, T-something.

Hers hadn't been too severe but appeared to have kick-started an incredibly rapid decline. The mouth thing was news, but then she'd stayed asleep during my previous visit. What else didn't I know? 'Have they said how long she'll need to stay?'

'The tests so far have ruled out infection and stroke. They suspect the fainting resulted from the dementia. That happens. Or she was dehydrated.'

'And if either of those are the case?'

'Then they won't keep her here.' His eyes were downcast; his choice of words not that of a man looking forward to his spouse coming home. Her infirmity must have been taking a bigger toll than I could understand. I struggled with what to say for fear of triggering a discussion on the topic of care. Since our last meeting, Dad's startling appeal had never left my mind. Righteous arguments were batted away by calls of familial duty, only to bounce back, like a ping pong match of morality. And I was exhausted.

'There's been some good news,' I said, a small croak reflecting my anxiety that he was likely to have conflicting emotions about it. He looked up from his cup, expectant. 'I spoke to the wholesaler. The money laundering can stop now.' I omitted that no payment had changed hands. He wouldn't survive knowing his daughter hadn't been an entrapped victim but a willing perpetrator. I was still processing that myself.

'Oh.'

'So it's good news.' I continued the charade. 'Now we can sort things out and make it all look okay for Stephen. The shares and stuff.'

Glum-faced, he sipped his drink. As he moved to speak, a familiar figure strode past us towards the counter where they had started serving hot food.

'Alice!' I called, and she spun round.

'Grace. I thought I vaguely recognised your voice. Hello, Ian.'

Ian? When did Mr McBride become Ian?

'Hello Alice.'

'What are you doing here?'

'Mum's been admitted but they haven't determined what's wrong yet. She fainted.'

She grimaced. 'I'm sorry to hear that.' She looked at Dad and her face softened. 'How are you holding up, Ian?' He blushed and mumbled an indecipherable reply. She checked the clock on the wall. 'Sorry but I can't stay. I'm supervising students in the clinic and I get five minutes for lunch—no joke. But shall I come round again after my shift?' She'd lowered herself to meet his eye.

'That would be nice.' He coughed.

'Okay then, I'll phone you later for a time that suits.' She bounced up and as she walked on, she stuck a pinkie and thumb out at me and held the imaginary phone to her ear, mouthing a silent promise of a later call. A call that would be very welcome.

'You've been seeing Alice?'

'Not…um…not as a patient. But she visited soon

after Glory died. In fact, it was because you'd gone to see her that she knew. And we've had some nice chats.'

'I'm glad, Dad. It's a lot to process. For all of us.'

His generation of males incapable of showing their vulnerable side, he wasted no time in redirecting the conversation. 'She's been helping me think about your mother's care. She knows all the homes around here. Has given recommendations. She's obviously got a lot of experience of mental…issues.' My heart sank. I'd been naïve to hope it wouldn't come up. 'And she said she would be happy to put in a good word. Apparently, some of these places have their pick of patients.'

The word 'patient' stung. I wasn't ready to associate it with my mother. 'They have?'

'Yes. The better ones. The…pricier ones.' He swirled the coffee. It would be cool now. As cool as my feelings towards Alice for filling my dad's head with fancy ideas.

I felt as though everyone kept plotting against me, leaving me in the dark. Glory…Dad…now Alice. And in a weird way even Mum. At least Dave was on my side. Who would have expected the one to know me the shortest to stand by me the most?

Dad slurped the liquid off the teaspoon a few times before braving his next sentence. 'So that wholesaler chap. Would he let you keep going if you chose to?' His strained light tone was no doubt intended to soften his interest in the cash.

'I don't know, Dad.' I was torn apart. Years of training had taught me not to say 'no' to this man; but those same years had taught me that this man never made unreasonable, untenable requests like this. My pleading eyes must have had some effect: he shook his head ever so slightly.

'Grace. I know what I've asked seems irrational, at odds with everything we stand for. But you'd be doing it for the Church, in a way.'

'What?' Perplexed by this new twist, I open my hands to the heavens for a sign that I hadn't landed in a parallel universe.

'Our church is fundraising to replace the lead that has been looted off the roof, and for repairs to the internal woodwork. Before I understood Mum was ill, she'd made a large donation. Very large. I only found out one Sunday when they announced it to the parish. Everyone was clapping and thanking us. They'd even had a plaque made, Grace. What was I supposed to do? I couldn't ask for it back. So now, we haven't got the funds I thought we had, and I feel like it's fate. That somehow Glory's transgressions—you—have been sent our way to make it good.'

'That's the most ridiculous thing I've ever heard, Dad. You're saying I have to launder money because it's what God wants?'

'Well, not when you put it like that. My point is that I am at peace with it, and you should be too. Otherwise the only care we can afford is a council home. And I can't do that to her. Is that what you want?'

'No. What I want is for you to keep her home.' Feeling cornered, I'd instinctively lashed out, in an attempt to out-guilt him. I hated this side of me but I couldn't help myself sometimes.

'Well that's easy enough for you.' He rose and walked away without so much as a glance.

I collapsed into a heap on the table, guilt and anger wrestling against a back-drop of right and wrong. I wondered if he would act differently if I'd told him Glory had been murdered, that I could be in real danger too. That it wasn't just a matter of some financial hocus pocus.

Abandoned and alone, I sobbed freely, figuring there was nothing unusual about doing that in a hospital.

CHAPTER THIRTY-NINE

That afternoon, work called me to the wealthy enclave of Bearsden. My new client was married to an accomplished academic who had recently moved up from Exeter. They lived in a three-bedroom semi on Colquhoun Avenue with refreshingly easy on-street parking. The location had been chosen due to its proximity to the train station, with its frequent services into Queen Street, and the nearby private school that had the city's best provision of Mandarin for her two daughters—the professor having grand international ambitions.

All this I learnt during our introductory session, and I strained to commit these facts to memory while my mind was preoccupied with greater problems than jelly-thighs and the hindsight of having preferred the West End. Between squats and push-ups, she revealed she was bored and had expected Glasgow, given its reputation, to be more exciting. I was desperate to point out that A: she didn't actually live in Glasgow, and B: she existed in a privileged bubble. But I bit my tongue and coached her through three more reps.

When red-faced and out of breath, she star-jumped

and told me she was considering opening a café—wouldn't that be fun?—the déjà vu nearly threw me to the ground. I suggested that, what with the possibility of her husband moving them abroad, perhaps she should engage in a more mobile venture.

What was it with this pervasive suburban ennui? Could these women not see their fortune? How we who were just about managing would give an arm for their lifestyle? Unlike its male counterpart, the female mid-life crisis wasn't about buying boy toys: women sought re-invention and fulfilment. They tortured themselves with existential questions like 'Have I done enough to save the planet?' and 'Have I wasted my talents?' Well, look where that got Glory.

It had been easier when I worked at the gym, where you had a cross-section of society who left their backgrounds at the door. To me, they were all equal; equally self-conscious and equally willing to please the PT on the floor. All uniformly committed to multiple sessions each week to extract every inch of value from their monthly fee. But the gym's owners had messed the staff around, changing schedules at the last minute and demanding overtime well in excess of what I was willing to give. I'd gone private nine months before and ended up having my face rubbed daily in how the other half lived.

The next appointment scheduled and bank details given, I swung by Sutherglen Drive, feeling bad about abandoning Blue earlier. Here was a creature who enjoyed life to the fullest and never complained about a bit of exercise.

The day's intense sun made the damp grass in the park sizzle. Let off his leash and joyful, he darted from tree to tree while I walked along the paths, luxuriating in the rays. Wilted spring tulips had been replaced by roses in the central ornamental bed, and I admired the council's majestic handiwork. This dedication to park maintenance—particularly in the nicer parts of town—always struck me as an odd priority for a city with such depressing levels of poverty. But as a current beneficiary of its sweet smell, I approved.

With the weather so nice, I decided a longer walk was warranted, and coaxed Blue out of this park with the promise of a bigger one. 'We're making a small detour to the shops, buddy. I fancy an apple.' We exited on the southern end and turned left at Maxwell Park station, heading towards the small agglomeration of shops and restaurants that formed the lively part of Pollokshields.

There, five streets all come together in a jumble, making it difficult for pedestrians to cross safely. We skipped through the first section unscathed. The next would be tricky, as I needed to move forward of the parked cars that obscured the view of the oncoming vehicles, a few steps into the road. I looked in all directions and froze when I spotted the man who had accosted me in the park that first day. He stood outside the flower shop, on the corner about twenty yards behind me, his bouncer hands clasped in front of him. My stomach leapt, and I hid on the road, behind a delivery vehicle.

He didn't appear to be looking for me, standing there with an impassive expression. It made no sense. Why was he here? I thought our business had been concluded. He then moved his head left and right, slowly scanning the horizon. Unnerved, I considered all the ways I might have misinterpreted what Mike said, growing in panic that there may not be honour among thieves after all.

Blue pulled at the lead, eager to keep moving, and nearly threw himself into traffic. I stooped to grab him by the collar, losing sight of Mike's henchman for a moment. 'Stop it, Blue. Stay here.'

When I looked up again, the man had gone. I decided to stay put for now.

Ten seconds later, a small red van passed our hiding place, coming from where he had stood. My gasp made the dog jump.

CHAPTER FORTY

The next morning, I noticed the cash register's '2' was still sticky. This made it difficult to tally up the coffee orders, so I sometimes suggested an extra shot to tip the price into the three-pound zone. A freckle-faced woman in Lulu Lemon gear grinned as I fiddled with a toothpick to prop up the key.

'Sorry to keep you waiting,' I said.

'That's okay. I see you're doing your best.'

Taking a cue from the spiritual prints on the wall, I breathed in and searched for my happy place as I endured her patronising Zen smile. 'You know what? It's on the house.'

'Thanks.' She beamed, no doubt unsurprised the universe had provided again.

As I wiped the crumbs from the vacated table, tired from a night dreaming of men in black and red vans at every corner, I asked myself what I was doing there. This wasn't my world. Glory would have chatted away, complimenting her leggings or recommending she take home a packet of gluten-free cookies, to ring another sale. These stupid, expensive, chi-chi foods. But Glory wasn't here. I bit my lip. And no matter what I did, she would still be dead.

'Is it all right if I quickly go to Polmadie?' Sascha held a stack of flattened cardboard boxes to load into her car. Since making manager, she'd read up on Health and Safety, and had become obsessed with keeping paths clear and the proper treatment of waste. She'd also worked out that regular, inconspicuous trips to the dump would save on the cost of commercial recycling.

'Yes, sure. I've got this.'

'Oh, and there's a small interim delivery coming tomorrow. I did remind Excelsior we were still expecting a new invoice—didn't you ask for one? But I had to let it go as we're running low on a few things as business has picked up quite a bit.' She paused before leaving, her hopeful expression suggesting she was fishing for a compliment. Alarmed by the earlier-than-expected next interaction with Excelsior, rather than giving her what was due, I told her she should look for a new wholesaler instead.

'Why?'

'They've ripped us off.' And I left it there.

Sascha probably regretted asking me to help out in the mornings as I repeatedly blurred the lines of responsibility. She'd been doing a great job, blowing new life in the café through social media in a short space of time; whereas I would dip in and out, grumpy and only marginally helpful. If she kept this up, we might even turn a profit. A real one.

A shroud of sadness fell over me as I considered this potential posthumous success. My sister never knowing her baby was alive and well. I had planned to meet with Alastair again to discuss the café's future. He was bullish about a sale and had even offered to place it on a specialist website. But, of course, he didn't know the books were a lie. My stomach fluttered every time I considered it. With the numbers inflated, we'd get a better price than we should, and I worried I could go to prison for fraud. I wished I knew if that was possible, but it's not the type of thing you can explain to a search engine.

As if by telepathy, my phone rang and his firm's number popped up.

'Stephen has asked to meet with me to wrap up Glory's estate.'

'Oh.' I sighed. It was bound to happen. I wondered who had given him Alastair's details.

'He assumed Glory owned the café. Given your astonishment at finding out that wasn't the case, I prefer not to be the one to tell him. I've tasked him with more pressing matters for now, but he's within his rights to ask. What do you want to do?'

The pressure to make this decision twisted my guts into knots. It would be irreversible, so I had to be dead sure. I'd been running through different scenarios for days and each direction surfaced kinks in the road that prevented a clean escape. There would always be a clue somewhere, a single leftover sock from the laundry giving the game away. In weighing the different outcomes against each other, I was now factoring only two things: how easily could the clue be found, and who got landed with it.

'What would it take to put all the shares in Glory's name?'

The line went quiet for a while. 'Only yours or the kids' trusts also?'

'Preferably all.'

'For yours, it's easy. You gift them to her and we

can record that through a letter and in the company's books. I don't think I've ever had anyone make a gift to a dead person. But it should be fine since probate has not completed yet.'

All I understood was 'it's easy' and I would have to rely on Alastair to handle the paperwork. It sounded like he was approaching this with his standard professional rigour. But the poor guy had to be feeling conflicted: not a hundred percent sure who his client was, and therefore who was entitled to what information. Even though he had refused to speculate about the state of Glory's marriage, by calling me he seemed to have concluded the husband was being kept in the dark for a reason. And he probably didn't want to know. Poor Uncle Alastair. He'd made a mistake once in trusting Glory. As it was in our joint interest for that mistake to not come to light, I hoped he would trust me in reversing it.

'As for the shares for the trusts, I recommend you keep them. They are a very handy tax avoidance mechanism I'm sure Stephen would approve of, as it helps with school fees.'

Unsavoury as it was, having established there was no way to claw that money back, I had to let the tainted cash flow to the school. I took comfort in the rumours that Lochiel Academy counted more than a few dodgy characters among the parents and trusted the source of funds would never be called into question. 'These won't impact a sale in any way,' he confirmed.

Here was my chance to ask the daft lassie questions and test out scenarios.

'Can you walk me through what selling would entail, you know, in terms of process?'

When he explained the seller would need to warrant

that all the financial information provided to the buyer was correct and that an audit may be required, he hit me with the mother of all snatches. If I gave Veg&Might to Stephen pretending nothing had happened, he would dispose of it without hesitation. And that would be like him waving a big stinky neon-yellow laundered sock attracting attention.

'Can I have a day to think about it?'

Protecting Stephen wasn't the only reason I was reluctant to relinquish control. I hadn't given Dad an answer yet.

CHAPTER FORTY-ONE

Dave was struggling to follow, and I couldn't blame him. He'd come to the flat that evening to take me out as a treat and found me surrounded by scribbled sheets of A4 strewn across the breakfast bar. I'd roped him in, laying it all out, hoping that a fresh pair of eyes could spot a missed opportunity, some nifty trick. He had such a calming influence on me, too.

Well, as long as he was on side.

'So you're saying that if you give the shares to Stephen, he will incriminate himself when he sells the café. And once it's bloody obvious to the new owners the accounts are dodgy when they see the real takings, they could go after him?'

'Uhuh.'

'And if you keep hold of your shares you can carry on with the café and sell it when you think there's been a long enough period of clean trading. But in this case, you have to explain to Stephen why Glory gave the shares to you.'

'Yup.'

'Damned if you do and damned if you don't.'

'That's not funny.'

'No, I know. Sorry. What about shutting it down?'

It was an option I'd considered. But aside from the guilt I'd feel at dismembering Glory's creation, this too had its share of unsurmountable problems. 'How do I convince Stephen to flush money down the drain? Why close it when you can sell it? He's not an idiot.'

'I can see why you're stuck.' He grimaced and mirrored my slumped posture. 'By the way, what happens with the money that's meant to be yours but is in Glory's account? You know, the one in her maiden name?'

'Would you believe Alastair told me I bloody owe income tax on those dividend payments? Even though I didn't get them!'

'You're shitting me.'

'No. But bless him. Because he knows he screwed up, he said that if I put the shares into Glory's name right now, then it was unlikely anyone would spot the historical discrepancy and we could all pretend the money was hers all along. Mind you, he is only playing along with this if he gets to take care of Glory's tax filings, so that HMRC gets what it's due. I think he smells a rat.'

'I can't blame him. But we're basically left with the only option being plan A: hand Stephen the business and get him into trouble.'

I nodded. 'Unless I can print money from my arse.'

He snickered and wrapped his right arm around me, pulling me close. 'And such a nice arse it is.'

Sinking into him for comfort, my mind wandered to Dad. There was a way to print money, of course, and it's what he wanted me to do. With plan A, I was freeing myself from the burden of Dad's expectations—there could physically be no more money laundering—but it also meant being the world's worst daughter.

'You okay?' Dave kissed me on the forehead.

'As okay as I can be, under the circumstances.'

He couldn't be told about the conflict raging inside. He had enough contempt for my family as it was. And I could definitely not tell him about being followed. He'd have a fit and march me into the police station himself.

I still didn't know what those following me wanted, but I'd decided to let it play out a bit to see. I'd thought maybe they knew about the photos and wanted to keep an eye on me to see what I would do. But how could they know?

'Shall we go? What would you like?'

'I could murder a curry.'

'That can be arranged. But can we agree one thing?'

'What's that?'

'Just for this meal, can we be a normal couple having normal conversations?'

I punched him softly in the chest.

We walked arm in arm—me checking behind us occasionally—headed for New Delhi, a small family-run Indian. With a tacky neon sign and an uninspiring cream and brown decor inside, the venue's lack of glamour contrasted with the trendier restaurants popping up around it. But as its generous dinner buffet for £9.99 was an age-old neighbourhood institution, I suspected it would outlast its rivals.

'I take you to the nicest places,' Dave joked as we approached the rounded red facade. I gave him a gentle squeeze.

When we arrived, the young woman at the bar was busy handing out take-away orders and ringing up departing guests. She welcomed us with half an ear and two fingers for minutes and instructed us to sit by pointing at the cramped waiting area by the entrance. I peered into the dining room and gauged that it wouldn't be long; they were cleaning a few tables already.

We sat knee to knee. I straightened the tabloid newspapers and trashy magazines lying about, and we both picked up bits of the Scottish Record. A front-page article covered a controversial new leisure esplanade to be built on the left bank of the Clyde.

The company behind the development complained that city officials didn't show enough support for their multi-million pound investment proposal and rattled off the untold benefits the local economy could expect.

Forgetting what rag I was reading, I leafed over for the architects' rendering of the development and was confronted with a pair of giant breasts in a red lacy body stocking. Dave was thankfully engrossed in the football, and I folded page three lengthwise to help the lovely Chantayle regain her modesty—though it may have been a little late for that.

'I think it would be nice to liven up that part of town.' I guided Dave's attention to the drawings. 'Look. You could have a meal outside, right by the water.'

'For all the two days of sunshine we get!'

'No, I'm serious. Other big cities with rivers really make it a feature. We've only got Springfield Quay, and everything is facing away from the water. It's depressing.' He returned to his scores and I read on. 'Says here there will be a decision on planning permission next month and they've had loads of responses on the consultation. Mostly objections.

That's a shame.'

'Oh, it will get through,' Dave said, now perusing the racing fixtures.

'Why are you so sure?'

He laid his paper to one side and pointed at the casino on the image. 'See that? That's got a lot of people jazzed up. It's where the money is. I overhead two guys at the Prince William talking, and let's just say they were surprisingly confident the authorities would grant approval for the site.' He tapped his finger against his nose.

Intrigued by the gangster gossip, I asked, 'What did they say?'

'They pretty much said it was a shoe-in. It seems they have leverage on a guy on the approvals committee. And it's big.'

The blood drained from my face and the room started to spin. I steadied myself by placing a hand on his leg.

'Babe, what's wrong?'

'Stephen. He must know.' I jumped up and kissed him on the head. 'I'm sorry. I have to go.'

'What do you care about the council?' he called, watching me go. He'd clearly not understood.

CHAPTER FORTY-TWO

It was less than half a mile to the house, but I arrived breathless. My usual thrice weekly 10k had been severely curtailed, and I marvelled at how quickly that became noticeable. With the days at their longest, there was no excuse. I vowed to do better.

The crunching of the gravel signalled my presence to Blue, who barked from inside. Within seconds, Stephen's shape appeared in the porch to check who had bypassed the gate. I waved, and he opened the glass-panelled door while holding the dog to prevent an escape.

'Hello Grace.' My winded state must have revealed the urgency behind the visit. 'What's going on?'

'Hi. Sorry for barging in like this. I need to talk to you.'

As he stepped aside to let me in, Blue seemed to be the only one happy to see me.

'We're having our dinner. Will you join us?'

'Um, no. Best to not speak with the kids around. It's a bit of a long story.'

His face darkened. 'Come. I'll park them in front of the TV.'

As we entered the kitchen, the boys failed to look up from their plate. There was a time when my appearance would yield an excited screech; but now they saw me nearly every day, the novelty had worn off.

'Adam, Noah, take your food to the living room. You can turn on Netflix. Auntie Grace and I want a chat.'

They looked at each other with puzzled faces but whizzed off before their father could change his mind, spaghetti slipping across their plates. I got hit by the distinctive aroma of Dolmio. Their advertising slogan popped into my head—'Like Mama makes'—and my heart suffered a small pang of sadness.

'Remember Adam gets to choose first,' Stephen shouted after them. He took a large, last bite and placed his unfinished meal in the sink, red oily pasta worms spilling onto the white enamel.

While chewing, he fished two glasses from an overhead cupboard. 'Wine?'

'I wouldn't say no.'

He poured the drinks in silence and he pulled out a chair from the dining table for me to sit while he grabbed another. The cartoon noises and childish cackles floating in from the interconnected room were our cue it was safe to talk.

'What's so important?'

'I'm sorry. There's no easy way to say this. There's something I've been hiding from you.'

'Okay.' He frowned and folded his hands around the stem of the glass, resting his gaze on the yellow liquid. 'What is it?'

When I described Glory's sticky situation, it was like speaking to an ice wall. Expressionless, he took it all in without even the slightest gasp or sigh. It unnerved me, and my speech sped up as I told the story of how she'd ended up laundering money for the wholesaler. By the end of the exposé, I was pacing across the room, while he had remained immobile.

'I've been working on making it right, so you wouldn't have to know.'

At last he faced me, his eyes challenging. 'Why are you telling me now?'

'I thought you should hear it from me.'

'Instead of?' I felt a sense of foreboding, as though I was being tested. Why was he not more upset? Why was this his first question? I sat down again, assuming my answer would be met with incomprehension and more questions.

'Instead of the people behind the Left Bank development.'

'Ah.' He pushed his glass away and reclined in his seat, rubbing his neck. 'Then you're too late.'

The world might as well have flipped upside down, I was so disorientated. Here I'd been, so confident I had put two and two together, and yet I hadn't seen this coming. He knew.

I searched my brain for clues I might have missed and found nothing. No, straight-laced Stephen—who I would expect to be devastated and disgusted by such a thing—had never given an inkling.

'You knew? About Glory's money laundering? How long?'

'Long enough.'

His chilly composure was getting on my nerves. The confused swirling in my head grew into an angry storm as I replayed all my sacrifices for him, for my sister over the last few weeks. 'And at no point did you think it necessary to tell me?'

Apparently unwilling to get caught up in my emotions, he maintained a neutral tone. 'Glory assured me those activities had stopped. And then she died. There didn't seem to be anything to tell.'

'Well you were wrong. Fucking hell, Stephen—' With this, his eyes flashed in warning and swept to where his boys were. I lowered my voice. 'I've been killing myself trying to whitewash this mess, dealing with total creeps, having my car bashed up, being followed. And all this time you knew?'

'Nobody asked you to do any of this, Grace.'

His glacial voice caused all my cells to constrict. The iceberg collision crushed any certainty I'd had about my actions and my intentions. And I hated feeling like a castigated child. As though I'd been playing Grace the Hero, and it was a bad thing.

I reminded myself I hadn't asked for this: it came looking for me. And I burnt with rage at the injustice of being told off when I should have been thanked.

Our stand-off was short-lived. I had been pummelled with problems and had managed to stack them all away neatly, so I was damned if I was going to let a giant loose end get the better of me.

'So are they blackmailing you with this to get planning permission?'

'Yes. Unfortunately, I got myself into a bind when I gave Glory's landlord approval when I shouldn't have.' He looked sheepish, his earlier frostiness thawing into an acceptance of shared blame. 'They've been pressuring me for ages, threatening to have me sacked unless I did what they said. But I resisted, figuring that if push came to shove, I could blag my way out of it with my boss. It had only been a small violation. And then they came looking for a big favour—the new development—and they told me about Glory. They knew I couldn't let that come out.'

'Did Glory know about this?'

'Not at first. But I confronted her straight after they'd truly cornered me, and she admitted it. We had it out and she was very sorry. She kept telling me she never meant to damage my career. She hadn't thought it through.' He poured himself another glass. 'That bloody café. I always thought it was a mistake. Anyway, she swore it was over. That it had only been temporary, to fill a gap...As if that made it okay.'

Contempt had dripped from his lips when he recounted his wife's corruption. If he was ever to remember her fondly, he could not find out Glory had continued squirrelling money away illegally.

'When did all this happen?'

'Roughly a month before the accident, I would say.'

Working the dates in my mind, I discovered this coincided with the period in which Glory started taking pictures at Excelsior. A hypothesis was brewing in my mind, a faint shape forming through unexpected connections.

'What is it?' he asked, as he saw me deep in thought.

'Did you guys decide to go after them?'

'What? No. What do you mean?'

'There are pictures on Glory's phone from around that time. It looks like she was documenting the goings-on at the wholesaler. Like it was evidence for something. I figured maybe you were building your own arsenal to fight back with. I don't know, to stop the blackmail and save your job.'

He looked bewildered, which I put down to his being unaware of the photos and faced with my fanciful fabrications. But then he said, in a hurt voice,

'You've looked in Glory's phone?' If I could have crawled under the floor, I would have. I'd been so consumed with proving a plot, that I never stopped to think how unreasonable, how distasteful, it was to keep the phone. There were family photos on there he deserved to have.

Ashamed, I admitted, 'Yes, Adam managed to unlock it. And I found these photos of the men at the wholesaler. She was onto something, Stephen, and I'm trying to find out what. I think she was protecting you.'

'But this has nothing to do with the wholesaler. It's that son of a bitch Brian Scott who has me by the balls. His property company is part of the consortium behind the riverside development. I don't understand what you're getting at with this story of photos. Of the wholesaler.'

The landlord's name invoked a bitter taste. That bastard. My lips curled at the repugnance of his actions: first he sells off Glory, then he uses her for a loathsome double-dip. It seemed that this duplicitous lech would stop at nothing. 'We can't let him get away with this.'

'We have to, Grace. I need to let them win. And I've already told them I'll do it. The approval is due to go through next month.'

But I was still caught up in my revulsion for the blackmailer. Fragments of cause and effect, of relationships and betrayal collided in my brain and pointed, in lines I could not explain, to Glory's death. Maybe it was Brian. Maybe Glory had confronted him, when she found out. Maybe she got in the way. I stooped forward and pulled at my hair in frustration. I was certain she'd been murdered, but there were now two possible culprits, and a jumble of motives.

The words rushed out of my mouth before I could

stop them. 'I think they killed Glory.'

'What? How can you say that?'

'I do. I can't explain it, but I do.'

He reached over and placed his hand on my arm.

'Listen, I know Glory's death has been really hard on you. It's hard on all of us. And despite what I said earlier, I'm really grateful for everything you're doing to help us. It sounds like you've been under a lot of pressure. But it's nearly over now. Trust me. And once this is done, we can move on. But no more snooping into her business, Grace. And no more wild theories of murder. We need closure. I need closure. It's not good for the boys.'

I sighed and nodded. We'd get there. One step at a time. He didn't believe me now, and I could see why. I hadn't proven it to myself yet.

I wish you could tell me what happened, Gi.

CHAPTER FORTY-THREE

I'd blown it with Dave so there was no need to rush back home. 'Is it okay if I hang out with the boys?' I asked Stephen.

'Sure.'

I investigated the content of the freezer, and it took only a single shout of 'ice cream' for their little legs to sprint to my side.

Noah's white school shirt was adorned with an orange-red motif twinned by the splotch on his chin. 'Oh my goodness, Noah, did you actually get any of that spaghetti in your mouth? Look at the state of you.'

He pointed at his brother. 'He pushed me when I was trying to eat.' In return, Adam made a Pinocchio-nose gesture with the associated trumpet sound.

'Okay, okay. Well, let's take our bowls through, and I can assess the damage. Stephen, would you like some ice cream?'

'No thanks. I've got work to do, so it would be great if you could put them to bed later.'

'Of course.'

He fetched his laptop and disappeared. The three of us went into the living room, closing the doors to contain any noise.

'What are we watching?'

'*Five Children and It*. We've seen it before, but it was Noah's turn to choose.'

'I don't know that one. What's it about?'

'It's about children who get sent to live with their uncle during the war and they can make wishes because there's a hairy creature called It.'

'And a dinosaur!' Noah was never one to miss an opportunity to see his favourite reptile.

'Oh really?'

'Yes, it hatches from an egg that Horace kept warm, but It makes it come to life.'

Not that I really cared, but Adam seemed keen to outline the whole plot. 'Who is Horace?' I asked.

'He's their cousin. He lives there.'

'Okay.'

We snuggled on the sofa, me in the middle to prevent any more pushing—real or imaginary. We ate our ice cream while on the screen somehow multiple versions of the children were cleaning the house.

'Now why can't you two do that?' I teased, gesturing towards the war zone of pasta plates on the coffee table.

'It all gets messy again. The spells that It makes don't last very long,' said Adam.

Noah stopped eating. 'Auntie Grace?'

'Hm?'

'Are we ever going to have a cousin?'

His little brown eyes shone with expectation, piercing my heart as I realised that I was their only hope. Glory and I had loved visiting our cousins on the farm, stuffing home-grown raspberries down our throats and running free through the fields. Childish, conspiratorial fun could even be found in the drudgery of helping them harvest the potatoes in October. If I didn't have children I'd be robbing them; sawing the branches off an already amputated family tree. I'd never felt ready or wanting. Was my clock ticking? I didn't feel it yet. But maybe Dave had his own ideas. And now...well now the pressure was on.

'I don't know if you'll have a cousin, sweetheart. That depends on a number of things. Would you like one?'

'Uhuh.'

'Why is that?'

'Because you get more presents for your birthday.'

'And we can stay at your house on the holidays and play,' Adam added.

'Well, we'll see.'

My thoughts turned to Dave. Would he be very angry? My phone was in my pocket, wedged between other bodies. I would call him later to apologise. But I couldn't expect him to hang around forever with a shit girlfriend like me.

'Look how rich they are,' Noah said. The sound of children squealing came from the TV. In the film, the creature had magicked a bucket of gold. With a mouthful of brown creamy sludge, Adam informed me their joy would again be short-lived. 'Nobody wants to take that gold because they don't know where the children got it.'

That pickle, I could relate to.

CHAPTER FORTY-FOUR

At the café the next morning, I learnt that Sascha had placed Veg&Might in the hipster consciousness, and our loyal school run posse was joined by small groups of deftly coiffed friends and lone blog writers, test-driving the venue's vibe.

The incessant grinding of the artisan-roast beans overpowered any attempt at conversation behind the counter, so Sascha and I beavered away serving gluten-free delicacies to a colourful array of beanie hats; our movements evolving into a fluid choreography. I made a note to compliment her as soon as I got a chance.

When the rush had passed, I stacked the dishwasher and wiped the tables ready for the second coming. This job sucked as much as the Sascha-prescribed ecological cleaning products. I reminded myself it was not forever; but it had gone on longer than expected. Even with takings improving, the place could not afford more staff any time soon. I was mentally working out the maths of when our tainted books would be superseded by a more accurate reflection of the business, when someone knocked on the rear door.

'That'll be the goods.' Seeing me sigh, she justified

the visit: 'You hadn't told me to stop working with Excelsior when I placed the order.'

'I know. It's okay. Let me come with you.'

We walked together to the rear, and she opened the door. It was Marius, as expected, but the terror on his hollow face made us both gasp. Silent, he held out a bleeding hand, a long gash splitting his palm in two.

'Oh my God!' Sascha sprung backwards.

The training I'd received at the gym kicking in, I pulled the man inside and pressed with a clean tea towel to stem the flow of blood. 'Where is the first aid kit?'

She ran off to fetch it. I guided Marius to a seat.

'What happened?'

'I trip over in van. Is sharp corner on door.'

We hadn't spoken before and his foreign 'r's made his stunted phrases difficult to understand. I proceeded with simple words and enunciated with the exaggerated mouth of a Brit on holiday.

'Okay Marius, don't worry. We'll take care of you.'

He nodded and kept his eyes on me, the eyes of a pleading child. How old was he? His skin was haggard and dry, and paler than others of Mediterranean origin. Conflicting signals thwarted an exact guess. His forehead was furrowed, and crow's feet radiated from the corners of his eyes. Yet the hairstyle was youthful, and the hair full and black. I judged him to be in his early twenties, with features ravaged by a hard life. I'd seen the conditions at his workplace—in fact, I recognised him from one of the photos—and I sympathised with his plight.

The box of bandages was well-stocked and once I wiped the bulk of the blood from the wound, it didn't look as deep as I'd feared. But I preferred to play it safe. 'We should take you to A&E.'

He'd concentrated on my lips when I spoke but hadn't caught the words. 'Aynee?'

I made driving gestures and pointed at myself. 'Hospital. I take you to hospital.'

Alarm spread across his face. 'No, no hospital. Please.' He pulled his hand away and with the other reached into the bandages, waving me away. 'I fix. Is not bad. Is small.'

My curiosity screamed at me to find out why he seemed so spooked, but first he needed care. I gently recaptured his lacerated limb and gave him a comforting nod. Examining the cut again, I gauged I'd be able to do a reasonable job and relented.

'Okay, Marius. No hospital. I help you.'

Colour came back to his cheeks, and he let me take over. As I worked on him, I wondered if perhaps he worried about the cost. Then I remembered Sascha saying he'd been here for years, so he would be aware of the free NHS by now. Was it immigration? Romanian, he was part of the EU so there shouldn't be a problem; but then again, after the Brexit vote, it seemed they were being made to feel more and more unwelcome every day.

I could hear Sascha unloading the boxes on his behalf. I hoped there would be no surprises this time. Worried about potential new star-covered boxes, I sped up. Marius remained stoic throughout my bandaging, but the wound was bound to be sore.

'Do you want a pill for pain?'

'Yes. Thank you.'

When I passed him a glass of water and a paracetamol, he smiled. I pushed the rest of the pack towards him, to keep.

'You have a good family,' he said.

How odd. Maybe it was an expression from home?

'What does that mean?'

'Your mother and father are good teachers. Glory was very nice with me. And you very nice.'

'Well, thank you.' I loved hearing him speak fondly of her, and with mutual warm, wistful smiles, we bonded briefly. As we stood, I noticed he kept raising his eyes to me with a hopeful glance and then cast them down again, as though waging an internal battle. With my gentlest gaze, I offered an opening. 'Everything all right, Marius?'

For a moment, his lips parted, only to be pressed shut again. 'Yes. All okay. I must go to work.' He made inroads to leave, but I held onto his arm.

'You cannot lift boxes. You are hurt. You must tell Mike it needs a week to heal.' At the sound of his boss's name, the poor guy turned to stone. Although I didn't relish the prospect of going ahead with it, I felt I should offer help. 'I can tell him, if you like.'

He shook his head. 'No, I must work.' He tried to pull himself free.

'Marius, talk to me. Are you okay? I can help.'

'No. Glory help me and now she is dead.'

The shock from his comment made me let go. But he stayed. He swayed, and his eyes darted between me and the door.

'What are you saying? What did she do?' I stepped towards him and held his shoulder for reassurance. I needed the truth.

'Glory saw I am not free. Like the others. We must work.' He hesitated. 'We are like slaves.'

It took a second for me to make sense of his statement. The photos shot to mind. He had his shirt off and was smoking a cigarette. 'Are you being held against your will? In the caravans?' He nodded, flinching as though his masters could punish him even here.

Human trafficking? Wasn't that young girls? For sex? These were men. Big men. Grown men. How do people hold power over grown men? Not that I didn't want to believe him. It just seemed so improbable. Why not run?

But Glory had seen his suffering and taken his side. Whilst one thousand questions ransacked my brain, I couldn't get away from how he'd said, 'and now she is dead.'

'What did Glory do?'

'She said to be patient. She work a plan.'

'Did she explain the plan? She took pictures of the men at work, yes? Who for?'

He shrugged and shook his head in ignorance. Nine hundred and ninety-seven questions remained, but there was really only one that mattered.

'Marius, did your boss kill Glory?'

My thunderous heartbeat nearly drowned out his answer.

'I do not know. Is possible.'

CHAPTER FORTY-FIVE

Dave was raging. He popped round to my flat after work to have it out with me for abandoning him at the restaurant. Or so was his stated purpose when he barged through the door, leaving a trail of squished blossoms on my floor. Irked by my silence since last night's only text, he told me we needed to discuss our relationship. That I couldn't expect him to stick around if he always came second. But we didn't get to that. Instead, I landed him with the fresh pile of revelations and complications; and he'd had enough.

'Bloody hell, Grace, let it go.'

'I can't.'

'Why not? This isn't your problem. None of this is. Didn't you say even Stephen didn't want you meddling now?'

'That's not what I said. He only confirmed he didn't need my help. That he would take care of the planning permission and that would be the end of it.'

'Great. And then you give him the café to deal with—his wife, his mess—and get on with your life.'

I scowled at him for making it sound simple, when it really wasn't. Everything was linked. Every stone turned loosened another. Every decision determined a fate. For Glory's sake, I had to see things through. Finish her work. And not only that.

I'll punish the bastard, Gi. I will avenge your death.

'And what about Marius? Don't you see? Glory was onto their slavery racket and they killed her for it.'

'You don't know that.' He sighed and grabbed my shoulders. 'Babe, you have to stop. First it was the evil Mike, then you thought it was Brian who killed your sister for interfering in his blackmail, now it's Mike again but with another motive. Who's next?'

I smacked his hands away. 'Don't be such a dick, Dave. You're painting me like some sort of conspiracy theorist.'

Whether he agreed he was a dick or merely retreated to prevent a further escalation wasn't clear, but he softened both his stance and tone.

'Sorry, I didn't mean to. I know you're hurting, but you must accept Glory's gone. Whether it was an accident or not, we'll probably never know. But one thing we do know: nothing you do will bring her back. It's time to think about you. About us.'

Reluctantly, I slipped into his arms. I longed to have that luxury. Of thinking about myself. Of having a normal relationship with a normal man—one that wasn't dysfunctional like with my previous boyfriends. But had I not always picked men who needed fixing? Unlike Dave. My handsome, independent man with a clear sense of self and purpose. Would things work out better with him?

He kissed my hair. 'Promise me you won't do anything stupid.' By not moving, I hoped he'd see that as agreement. I didn't want to lie out loud. 'Grace?'

I had one more job.

'I can't leave Marius and his friends there. I owe it to him to do something. He trusts me.'

'You don't owe him shit. How many times do I have to say it? Not. Your. Problem.' He toned down when he felt me recoil. 'Listen, I get it. You're a helper. It's your natural instinct—it's one of the things I love about you. But it's not your job to save every stray. This is dangerous. You keep telling me you think they killed Glory. What's to stop them hurting you?'

His protectiveness was warming as much as it was annoying. I squirmed and admitted to myself he had a point.

'Sweetheart, if you feel so strongly about the Romanians, call 101 and leave an anonymous tip.'

'It's a thought,' I conceded.

'I'm serious. Let the professionals deal with it. They're bound to have a special department that deals with trafficking. It's rife.'

'I'll think about it.'

That seemed sufficient, for now, and we stood, holding onto each other. I felt a closeness I'd only ever felt with Glory before.

'It's nothing like they say, you know,' I said after a while.

'What isn't?'

'When someone you love dies. They always say you can feel their presence. That they never leave you. Angels looking over you. But it's bollocks. I wanted to believe it—I opened myself up to any sort of sign. I even talk to Glory in my head, hoping she'll hear me. She had a plan, Dave, and I couldn't see it. I longed for her to tell me how to make things right. Why she'd involved me. How I could help. But she's not there.'

'You've done all you could.'

He kissed me on the forehead and twiddled with my hair, while I sank further into him, into a sense of home that was new to me. I reached for his cheek and with a gentle stroke finally dared to lay myself bare.

'Please don't die.'

A large grin spread across his implausibly perfect teeth. 'Why Miss Grace McBride, is that you admitting you love me?'

'I guess it is.' I smiled and pulled his face towards my mouth, our lips finding each other.

CHAPTER FORTY-SIX

A muffled buzzing filled the room and recalled me from a shallow slumber. The sheet lay tangled around my leg and I unwrapped myself, careful not to pull it off Dave too. I slid out from under his bare thigh and wormed off the bed, the thud on hitting the floor rousing a snore from the sprawled-out nude.

On all fours, I searched for my jeans among the trail of clothes we'd teased off each other earlier. What time was it? It was still light out, but that didn't mean much in June. My stomach's rumbling told me dinner was overdue.

By the time I retrieved my phone out of the back pocket of my trousers, the caller had given up. The missed call notification showed Alastair's number, and I waited two minutes for the tape reel symbol to pop up, while gathering my undies. But there was no message, and I went to freshen up before checking what he wanted.

Once clean, I closed the door to the bedroom and dialled. Was he always as dedicated to his clients? Calling so late didn't fit the stereotype of the nine-to-five accountant.

'Hi, it's Grace. Sorry I missed your call.'

'No problem.'

'What's keeping you working so late? It's eight o'clock.'

'I'm going on holiday at the end of the week and I prefer to be on top of things. The reason for the call is that I found something in the café's post you'll want to know about. An invoice.'

Nerves tingled in my neck, on high alert, having discovered that surprises from the café were never good. Had Sascha passed on the disputed invoice from Excelsior? I hadn't had a chance—or a desire—to return to Mike for a new one, not wanting to rock the boat of freedom. But if I wasn't careful Alastair might discover the fraud.

I hopped onto a stool, crossed my legs and braced myself for the news.

'What is it?'

'It's an invoice for a monthly insurance premium. Key man insurance. I contacted the company—we do a lot of business with them—and they confirmed that Glory took out insurance for one hundred thousand pounds recently.'

'What is key man insurance?'

'It's like life insurance for a business, to protect itself in case one of their key people dies. Hence the name. The sum is meant to cover loss of income for the company. I'm not sure why Glory took out such a high cover, it feels disproportionate given the café's turnover. But here we are.'

'You're telling me the café is getting one hundred grand?' Incredulous, I'd struggled to get the last three words to pass my lips, blowing each syllable out like a dart I didn't truly believe would hit the bulls-eye.

'Well yes and no. You see, the insurance was only taken out six weeks ago. This is only the second premium. After we make a claim, it is very likely that the insurer will want to run an investigation because Glory's death came so soon. Depending on the small print, they may deem the pay-out to be invalid.'

The word 'investigation' landed in my stomach like a brick and my earlier high alert flicked to a full-blown siren in my head. What would it entail? I couldn't afford to have some claim handler crawling over the café. Would they need to dig into the books?

I wondered if there was a way to stall it. Or would that make it even more suspicious? I was pleased I'd gradually learnt to control my anxiety again, as this would've had me over a bucket.

'Grace? Are you there?'

'Yes, yes, sorry. I'm just a little shocked.'

'They're sending over the policy documentation, and I'm happy to review it. Chances are, it will be fine because her death was an accident and we can get a police statement to confirm that. But I don't want to get your hopes up.'

'No, of course. Thanks very much for letting me know. I guess I will sit tight.'

'You also asked me about transferring the ownership back to Glory, and therefore to Stephen…you need to think about the timing of that if they do pay out.'

'I don't understand.'

He cleared his throat and I sensed his discomfort.

'Well, the cash can be kept in the business, or whoever owns the shares can take it out. In some circumstances, it will be tax free, you see. So even though I said you needed to act quickly for the café to count as part of Glory's assets, you may choose to…um…not hurry too much with the transfer.'

Bless him, always looking out for me.

But what did he mean? Then it dawned on me. Always looking out for me…but not Stephen. Could that get him into trouble? Or was he just uneasy because he was suggesting I redirect cash away from a widower?

Not wanting to embarrass him further, I said, 'Thanks Alistair. I understand. It sounds sensible. I'll think about it.'

As I hung up, Dave walked in semi-naked, his gelled hair ruffled into random spikes. He roamed to the fridge, kissing me on the head as he passed, emanating the odour of a contented man.

'Who was that?'

'The accountant. It's nothing.'

A pang of guilt sprang up, demanding that I share. But I didn't think our relationship could stand more complications, more conflict. We'd only just made up. More than made up…I wondered if he'd sensed it, earlier. My shift. My jump into the unknown. With him.

He pulled out a beer. 'Drink?'

'No thanks.'

He grazed on whatever snack he found, hunched in front of the open fridge door, as I tried to shake off my fixation with the cold escaping, to concentrate on Glory's latest clue.

I jumped as Dave held his chilled bottle against my bare arm.

'What are you doing?'

'Trying to get your attention. I said, what do you want to do for dinner?'

'Nothing. I mean, I don't care. Whatever.'

Dave turned away. 'Fine. I guess that means beans.'

I vaguely heard him open the cupboard and rummage in the drawer for the tin opener.

Did you know you were going to die, Gi?

Well, did you?

CHAPTER FORTY-SEVEN

Sascha teased me when handing over her charity friend Oliver's number the next morning.

'He's single.'

I smirked in reply.

'At first I suspected he was gay; but turns out he's merely well groomed. My partner and I have been out with him a few times and he's actually really shy with girls. It's so cute. We keep trying to set him up.'

'Well that's not why I want to reach him. Besides, I'm way too old.' I dismissed her crazy idea with a wink.

'So why then?'

'Oh, I was reading about Invisible's work and I thought it was interesting. You know, those stories of human trafficking are heartbreaking.'

'You're right. They are. Often, it's migrants and we see with SAFR how hard it is to keep track of them. How quickly they can fall off the radar.'

For the rest of my shift, at every opportunity, she bored me with her activities to help refugees. Not that I didn't care, but I had enough misery to deal with. As soon as I could escape, I did, leaving her to clean up.

On the way home, I took advantage of the lack of

passers-by to scan the many newspaper billboards dotted along the road. They decried the evil Tories in unison, but parted ways when it came to the beautiful game. Glasgow would always be a city divided: Celtic and Rangers, Catholic and Protestant, Yes and No.

I skipped aside as two sisters on micro-scooters whizzed past me, pink ribbons streaming from the handles as a visual clue to their speed. The littlest one—no more than a helmet on legs—strained to catch up with the elder, while the mum walked behind, engrossed in her smart-phone. I admired her certainty they would stop at the corner and wait. They did.

One billboard heralded a new smacking ban, and I glanced at the mother wondering if that's how she got her kids to be good. Whether corporal punishment was counter-productive—as the poster claimed—I wasn't sure; but one thing I knew: this kind of discipline brought the children close together. My thoughts wandered to Glory and me, huddled in our room, her blue eyes pleading as she confessed to whatever misdemeanour it was that had Mum stomping up the stairs. I'd grown adept at defusing the situation when tensions rose, which thankfully happened with reducing frequency as we learnt to toe the line.

Why didn't you confide in me?

How many times had I posed this question to the heavens since her death? It was still the thing that made the least sense to me. Still the thing that hurt the most.

The slip of paper in my pocket gave me new hope. If Glory had been looking into modern-day slavery, she would surely have turned to the one guy she knew who worked in this field. Once I reached my car for my next client appointment, I settled in the driver's seat to make the call. But my phone rang just as I wanted to use it.

Sascha was calling from the café.

'Marius was here, unexpectedly. He was asking for a box of napkins you were meant to give back?'

My heart skipped. I said nothing.

She continued, 'Bloody cheek. Asking for stuff when they haven't even sorted out a new invoice. Anyway, that's nothing to do with him—he's only the messenger—so I gave him one from the store room. And guess what? That didn't seem to be what he was looking for. If it had been anyone else, I'd have told him to get lost—I'm really busy with customers right now—but he looked so nervous, so I showed him it was the only one here. He asked where you were. He gave me a message. To remind you about a box of napkins. So here you go. But this is all pretty weird. Grace, what's going on?'

Shit.

I'd been so distracted by all the commotion with his bleeding hand, his revelation about forced labour, that I'd forgotten to return the cash like Mike had instructed. I wondered if Marius had gotten into trouble because of it. And what Mike would do to me. Is that why I'd been followed? Or was that before? The timings were all a jumble.

'Hello Grace?'

Quick. A story. Any story.

'It's nothing. When I stacked the last delivery away, I found one of the napkin boxes was wet. Soaking. So when I phoned about the invoice, I asked for a refund for that, too. But they didn't believe me, so I said I'd send it back for proof. They're a real pain. I'll be glad when we're rid of them.'

CHAPTER FORTY-EIGHT

Four hours later, I waited for Oliver at Costa by the Gallery of Modern Art. On the phone, he'd apologised for not having an office, explaining that Invisible's HQ was in Bristol, and as a regional project coordinator, he worked from home. Owning only a rudimentary machine, he enjoyed treating himself to a nice coffee when meeting people.

My latte was served in a tall glass, which revealed how little actual coffee it contained. I remembered reading somewhere that they put an extra shot in the take-away drinks due to the bigger volume, and that you should therefore order a paper cup even if you sat in. It was the equivalent of a free extra shot. But I preferred the glass, with its dinky handle and the way you could generate a dynamic brown and white storm with a gentle stir.

All the outside tables had been taken as the square hosted swarms of students, tourists and retail workers, encouraged by a rare cloudless sky. It appeared to be 'skirt day', that widely recognised first day of the year when all the women have—in a sudden, miraculous synchronisation—stored their trousers and tights away to expose their bare legs in tribute to the sun. From my spot inside, I watched the baristas keep a cool head serving a seemingly endless self-replenishing queue.

At last, Oliver strode in and waved as he saw me. He rushed over and placed his rucksack on the chair.

'Sorry I'm late. Do you mind if I fetch a drink? It's a little busy.'

'It's fine. I'm in no hurry.'

'Shall I get you a fresh one?'

'No, but some water would be lovely, thanks.'

While he stood by to place an order, I pulled Glory's phone from my bag. Good. It had charged properly. I hadn't made up my mind on whether to share the photos yet.

Her boys' grins glowed from the lock screen's back-lit portrait, dark pixels accentuating the missing teeth. They were so alike physically, but with such different personalities. Like us. Gorgeous Noah was Glory, always excited and into something new. Whereas Adam, the older one, like me, had a more reasoned temperament. What was it someone had said about sisters? One is the dancer, the other the watcher? But as Stephen's almond-shaped brown eyes looked at me under Adam's youthful eyebrows, I snapped out of the fleeting folly that this had anything to do with me. These cautious traits were from his dad.

I put the device down, my conscience giving me an internal kicking. Why hadn't I handed it to Stephen like I said I would?

'Here we go.' Oliver took our drinks off the tray and sat down. 'I saw you the second I walked in. The same memorable hair as your sister.'

He spotted my awkward smile and changed the subject to the weather, the necessary preamble to any

British meeting. When we'd completed comparing our delight with the current heatwave, and agreeing it would not last, I brought the conversation to his job.

'We operate the Modern Slave Phoneline where people can get advice and report suspected instances of human trafficking or forced labour.'

'Does it happen a lot?'

'Oh yes. There is a common misconception about trafficking being about sexual exploitation of young women. But even though that happens and it's horrible, the reality is that most of the victims of modern-day slavery are men, being made to work without payment or means of escape. To give you an idea: in less than a year we had over one hundred reported cases of forced labour in car washes alone. We helped nearly seven hundred folk. Two of those cases were in Scotland, and I got involved.'

'Is it usually the victims that call for help?'

'No, that's rare. Only about fifteen percent of our cases are self-reported. Usually it is a member of the public who has noticed suspicious behaviour. That's why awareness raising is such an important part of what we do. To stay with the car wash example, there had been radio and media campaigns to look out specifically in that sector before we got a spike in reports.'

'So how do you then check it out?'

Oliver smiled and shook his head as if to clear it. 'It's strange. Almost a déjà vu, you sitting here asking the same questions as Glory.'

At the mention of her name, a chill ran up my spine. She'd grilled him, too. But how much had she shared? I swithered whether I should confess why I was here, about the pictures. But I'd had enough men dismissing my instincts of late that I decided to check what he knew first.

'What can I say? Same genes,' I joked. 'What else did Glory ask?'

'Lots! I wasn't really sure why, but I enjoyed her company, and her friends had made donations to the charity, so I was happy to meet with her whenever she wanted. I suspect I disappointed her a bit when it became clear I didn't participate in the actual catching of the baddies.'

'You don't?'

'No, we don't do the investigative work. We pass on any reports from the helpline to the appropriate authorities, mostly law enforcement, or the local authority safeguarding teams for minors.' He held his hands up in mock surrender. 'I'm only the conduit. No dashing knight in shining armour.'

The phone had laid on the table upside down the whole encounter, and I was about to store it away, resolving he wasn't the right guy, when something he said next made me buzz.

'She seemed keen to find out what was needed for the police to take a report seriously, and what they would do. At one point I thought she'd identified a case, the way she was talking. All these detailed hypothetical scenarios. Then the last time we spoke she hinted she might have a gift for me soon. She was being quite mysterious about it.'

'When was this?'

'Now there's a question…two months ago, maybe? It's hard to tell. I didn't hear from her again and of course, found out about what happened to her the night you and I met.'

The timing fit.

'You said she asked what it would take to get the police to look into a report. What did you tell her?'

A puzzled expression crossed his face, my enquiries probably more probing than he was used to. 'I told her a tip-off tended to be enough for the ward officer to go sniffing, but that pictures of the working and living conditions—and of the culprits—would speed things up.'

Now.

Now I was sure that's what Glory had been up to. Now it was time to share.

'Oliver, I have a theory and I would appreciate it if you hear me out.'

He shuffled forward in his seat with an air matching the seriousness of my tone. 'Okay.'

'I believe she was gathering extensive evidence of real slave labour to bring to you.'

He jerked back in shock. 'That's crazy. Why would she do that?'

'There's a chap who delivers the goods to the café. He's Romanian, Marius. He told me Grace had recognised he and some others working at the wholesaler were being exploited, and that she'd promised to help.'

'She could have given me the address...or even phoned it in.'

'I know, but I think Glory was determined to help as best she could. She took photos.' The mobile was swiped to life and Oliver sat blinking in disbelief, as I flicked through the collection of haggard men and the furnishings of their dreadful life. 'As for these with the boss, it looks like she was putting on a show to get close, to ensure they could nail him.' My cheeks warmed with a hopefully invisible blush as I explained a pose that could so easily have been misconstrued.

'I can see that. This is all valuable evidence.' A silent whistle passed his lips as he examined the images again. 'I can't believe she did this. She took a big risk.'

Didn't she just.

CHAPTER FORTY-NINE

I reported for babysitting duty later that evening, eager to share my findings; to show Stephen I'd been right. He was putting the shopping away and through the glazed doors I spotted the boys sprawled on the sofa, the beginnings of a construction project using lolly sticks and way too much glue on the coffee table.

'What are they building?'

'Noah needs to make a Viking longboat for school. I've been nagging him about it for days but, at some point, he's got to take responsibility.'

'It's okay. I'll get it done. Maybe Adam will want to help. He'll have made one for school before. Where are you going again tonight?'

Since Glory died, he'd only been out once in the evening, for a community consultation event he'd been unable to wriggle out of. Not an extrovert at the best of times, Stephen's single parent status had bolstered his resistance to social events. There had only been a trickle of his friends at the funeral and they didn't seem to have made much of an effort for him since.

'I have a dinner with the senior team. One of my colleagues is retiring.'

'Does he get a golden watch?' I quipped.

'More like a golden parachute. Let's just say he won't be missed.'

'So a bit of a hypocrite's dinner, then?'

His back to me, he shrugged while stacking snacks on a shelf. 'We need to keep him onside. Too many skeletons.'

'Who knew the council planning department would have such double-dealing intrigue.' As soon as it escaped my mouth, I gasped and covered my mouth.

I watched in what felt like slow motion as he turned around, his eyes dark and lips pursed in distaste.

'I would think you of all people would know we sometimes have to do things we don't like. And right now, you'll understand that I need to tread carefully.'

'I'm sorry, Stephen. That was really insensitive of me. I'm conscious you need to go, but I really wanted to tell you something. I know Glory got you into a tight spot at work, but she was also doing something brave, something good.'

'What are you talking about?'

'Well it's a little bit of a long story, but I found out she was working on freeing modern-day slaves from the wholesaler.

'What?'

'Hear me out. There's at least six guys there in forced labour, living in filthy caravans, and she was gathering evidence to report it to the police. You remember, no? The pictures she took at the wholesalers. This is what they were for.'

He stared at me, incredulous. 'I'm really not sure why you're telling me this.'

'Don't you see? I always thought it wasn't an accident, and now I'm sure. You didn't want to believe me, but they must've run her off the road when they found out she was onto them. I've got it all planned now and I'm going to make sure we get justice. That bastard Mike will rot in prison for what he's done.'

My presentation didn't get the reception I had hoped for.

'You're like a dog with a bone, Grace. This is all too fanciful. I wish you would stop. I have accepted that Glory died in a freak accident. It happens. Why can't you?' He saw me tongue-tied. 'Is it really better to believe that she caused her death herself? That she deserted me and her sons all because of some Mother Theresa crusade? I couldn't care less about those slaves or what you want to do to the dirty gangsters she dealt with. Go ahead and get yourself into more trouble, for all I care. But leave me out of this. Even if it's true, none of this is helping *me*. So I don't want to hear about it.'

Anger flared inside as I received his dressing down. I was right. I had to be. Why did he not want justice for his wife? I itched to have it out with him, but I knew it would do no good. It was clear that he needed closure more than justice and in that, so far, I had failed him. He was still vulnerable. He could still lose his job even if he did go ahead with the planning permission. That is, if he got found out. And I wouldn't let that happen to Glory's kids. They needed stability.

As fragments of our conversation swirled in my mind, an idea took shape. But having set Oliver off, there wasn't much time to act. I chose to play nice.

'Sorry Stephen. You're right.'

He rewarded this with no more than a curt nod.

'You'll find Quorn escalopes in the fridge. The boys will only eat them with a wedge of lemon. You can find chips in the freezer. I need to go.'

He grabbed his keys off the counter and shoved me aside to reach the door. 'And walk the dog, Grace.'

CHAPTER FIFTY

The next morning, the woman at the wholesaler's greeted me like the regular visitor I was becoming, her disdain now reduced to a medium-level you-haven't-wiped-your-feet-type scowl. As it was Saturday, it was a bit of a punt whether the boss would be in, but I had decided to give it a shot. Surely a criminal empire was a 24/7 job?

'Is Mike around?'

'Maybe. What's it to you?'

I tapped on the napkin box held under my arm. 'I come bearing gifts.'

She eyed the package with its familiar stars and accepted my presence. 'You're in luck. He's about to go home. Takes the missus shopping in Merchant City on a Saturday. Then always lunch at Rogano.'

This wasn't idle gossip; everything in her demeanour and tone suggested this excess of information was intended to remind me—perhaps on behalf of said missus—that her boss was a devoted husband who liked to spoil his wife. Maybe she thought I was coming too often for a regular a customer.

'I won't be long.'

'Right. You'll have to make your own way up. We're low on staff today.' She jerked her head towards the rear by way of permission.

'Cheers.'

The lights came on in the stairwell automatically as I bounded up two steps at a time. Along the hallway, the offices were tidy and had been cleaned with a product whose sickly pine smell reminded me of cleaning my car after my first visit here.

Feeble.

But not now.

An overwhelming desire to burn the place down was tempered only by the knowledge there was another plan in train to take care of this scum. This murderer. And I needed him. I needed his men to scare off a man who held all the cards—though not for long. When I reached Mike's door, I shifted the box to the other arm, relieving the pain in my dented rib. I knocked.

'Come in.' He was folded over his desk, reviewing papers. 'What is it?' He hadn't yet looked up, presumably expecting an employee.

'Mike, it's Grace McBride.'

His head shot up in surprise. 'Indeed it is. I have to say, I wasn't expecting to see you again. What brings you here?'

'Well, I'm a woman who keeps her promises. This morning I realised I forgot to return this box to your chappie the other day, so I wanted to make sure you got it.'

'Then we're square.' He rose and walked round the desk towards me to receive the parcel. After a brief inspection, he seemed ready to dismiss me. 'Anything else?'

'I'm afraid there is.' He took two steps back and gestured to the chair as he perched on his desk. 'So as I was saying, I am a woman of my word. We have a deal and I am determined to stick to it.' His raised brow indicated I was foolish to expect him to remember our conversation, what with him likely handing out a threat a day. 'I'm talking about the money laundering. We agreed I would keep it quiet. And I have.'

'But? There is a but, isn't there?'

'Yes. But someone else is about to blow the whistle on you. Brian Scott.'

In that instant, I had his full attention. 'Talk.'

'It's to do with the Left Bank development, which Brian's property company is involved with. I don't know if you're aware, but Glory's husband, Stephen Paterson, is one of the decision-makers for the planning permission. At the moment, with all the objections, it's not looking good. So Brian is blackmailing him. He's threatening to release information about Glory's money laundering if Stephen doesn't get the approval through.'

'And why are you telling me this?'

The morning's empowering affirmations still fresh in my mind, I inhaled a fresh batch of courage and cast my hook.

'Because we're screwed—you *and* me if this comes out. And it will. Stephen is a man who lives by the rules. I can't convince him to play ball. He knows his job and reputation are at risk, but he won't do it. He wants to call Brian's bluff. Reckons there is no way he would go ahead with it. That it would draw too much attention to him, to his property dealings.' The storm brewing on Mike's face egged me on. 'Of course, you and I know the bastard could easily make an anonymous tip-off. And it's not his business dealings we need to worry about. It's yours. You need to get Brian Scott to back off.'

'You were right to bring this to me.' He retreated to his desk without sparing me a glance. 'You can go now.'

'What happens now? What will you say?'

'That's not your concern.'

His stern dismissal made me keenly aware that I'd unleashed something I couldn't contain, a shape I couldn't quite see, and I slid out the door on a plain of dread mixed with anticipation.

CHAPTER FIFTY-ONE

My Bearsden client was now up to ten push-ups, having started on two. She was keen to learn how to best make use of the vibration plate she'd bought on eBay, believing it was the easy answer to her muffin top. During her minute-long holds in varying positions, she'd thankfully given up trying to make sentences from shaken syllables, and my mind was free to roam.

Like a director looking down on the action from a crane, I swept through an assemblage of scenes that I had set in motion, unfolding in unscripted directions. A cinematic escapade in which every righteous reel ended with the same climax: both criminal adversaries foiled and out of our lives. Forever.

A smug satisfaction washed over me as I reflected on my orchestration, the set-up. As if on order, the lyrics *'face to face'* and *'double cross'* rose from the client's play list, and I couldn't help but feel that the smooth operator being crooned about was me.

While packing my stuff away at the end of the session, my heart skipped as a text came in from Oliver asking me to call. One more manoeuvre and we were on. I rushed to the car to phone him back.

'Hi. It's Grace.'

'Thanks for calling. I spoke to my man at the specialist crime division and told him what you've got. They are very interested to talk to you. Some of the pictures I described, with the working and living conditions, could be very valuable. And they show regulatory breaches in and of themselves.'

'That's great.' Now for the tricky bit: I had to stall a little. 'When?'

'As soon as you can. Turns out they've had Excelsior on their radar for some time and your evidence might be exactly what they need to speed things up.'

'So were they aware of the forced labour already?'

'They didn't say. But DI Roberts said they've been compiling a dossier on this guy's shady business dealings and this could well be a way to get into Excelsior's books, to get the proof they need.'

My throat constricted, and a nervous flush enveloped my head, rendering me temporarily deaf. Had I heard that right? Did I just facilitate an investigation into Mike's money laundering? My heart palpitated as I witnessed my carefully constructed plan leak out of my hands, my mind scrambling for means to contain the escaped mercurial droplets heading for a target of their own. A target I couldn't let them find.

'Grace? Hello?'

'Yes, I'm here.'

'He suggested you could come see him Monday at ten o'clock.'

The day after tomorrow.

Two days.

So fast.

But I couldn't now delay without it looking suspicious. 'Whereabouts?'

'The police station on Aitkenhead Road. I could come too, if you want.'

That was right by Excelsior, so it made sense they were the ones investigating. But as if I wasn't feeling exposed enough, Mike's words popped into my head to remind me how foolish I'd been to think I was in control: 'Half of them are on the take.'

'Okay. I'll see you there. Bye.' I slumped sideways and let myself fall onto the passenger seat.

Oh shit, Gi. I think I messed up.

CHAPTER FIFTY-TWO

The alarm went off and my arm swung over to slap the snooze button for the third time. The only thing I was late for was my 10k. And after the restless night I'd had I wasn't sure if I had the energy to pull my trainers on, let alone put one foot in front of the other for a semi-serious distance.

I spat the hair out of my mouth and rubbed my face to bring some life back into it, crusty tears breaking into minuscule flakes falling like snow on my sheets. It was just as well I'd asked Dave to stay away or he wouldn't have slept a wink either.

In what felt like a giant effort, I turned the alarm off, rolled out of bed and stumbled to the kitchen for a welcome caffeine kick. To my relief, there were no messages on my phone and I skimmed the news headlines while the coffee machine sputtered. There was an odd reassurance in finding the outside world was operating as normal, when mine had been turned upside down.

The barren refrigerator shelves signalled a trip to the shops was long overdue, but I managed to squeeze enough yogurt from between the dried-out sides of the pot to create a thin smoothie. How anyone survived before Sunday trading was beyond me, but I remembered my parents being horrified when it came into effect. They'd been steadfast in their resistance to this sacrilege. But once they sold the shop, the new owners quickly capitalised on the neglected retail opportunity.

With my throbbing head, I dreaded a supermarket's bright lights and figured I could live off the bare minimum that could be provided by the local newsagent. And if I was going outside, I may as well go for my run.

Hair scrunched, leggings on and armed with a plastic bag and debit card, I left the flat and turned towards the park. I was determined to restart my running habit and not be such a loser. I didn't need the mirror to tell me I'd gained weight. It wasn't only that. My runs were my refuge, a time for my mind to wander free and let the fresh air sweep any unhappy thoughts away; but the complications since Glory's death had replaced this pleasure with a relentless stream of conflict and anxiety. Serious about reclaiming my hobby, I focused on my breathing to prevent my mind wandering.

Halfway along Queen Mary Avenue, not paying much attention to my surroundings and about to cross the street diagonally, I was shaken by a loud, continuous honk from behind. As I spun round, I saw a small red van bolt towards me, blasting its horn. I stood glued to the ground, paralysed. The charging vehicle screeched to a halt at my side and it was then that I saw Dave was the driver. My relief unclenched all the muscles in my body, to the extent I nearly let go of the pee I'd so valiantly held it in through my moment of terror. Relax. It was only Dave.

My stomach flipped however, when he jumped out and I saw the urgency in his eyes. In that instant, all the people I loved flashed before my eyes and I braced myself for what else could have gone wrong.

Mum?

'There you are, I've been looking everywhere for you.'

'What the hell's going on Dave? Why did you have to scare me like that?'

'I'm sorry. I didn't mean to. But I have some news and you need to find Stephen.'

'Stephen? Why?'

'Because Brian Scott is dead.'

'What? Glory's landlord? How do you know this?'

'I was on the job at the Prince William this morning and the bartender got a call. He sounded really upset so I got a bit closer to hear what was going on. And the guy starts making call after call telling people what happened. Grace, Brian Scott was shot in the head in his car this morning.'

'This morning?'

'Yes, not long ago. Apparently two guys jumped on him as he was setting off to work. Right in the driveway of his own house. He got shot in the head—twice— and he's dead. Crazy. Then I thought about Stephen. The council vote is tomorrow. You have to tell him he's off the hook. Do you think he'll be home? Here, jump in. I'll take you.' Lagging behind on fully digesting what he was telling me, I obeyed. 'When the guy caught me eavesdropping, he kicked me out. Man, he was in a mood.'

'Do they know who did it?'

'He never said. But babe, you're talking Glasgow

underworld here. He's bound to have enemies wanting him dead. God knows what he's done this time, but he's certainly pissed *someone* off.'

Pressing my nails into the palms of my hand to counter my rising panic, I told myself I could never tell Dave about my visit to Mike. While I comforted myself that I had only ignited the fire under an existing feud, I knew my conscience would forever remind me I might as well have pulled the trigger myself.

I had a man killed.

Then again, he was a bad man.

CHAPTER FIFTY-THREE

As Stephen closed the door behind us, he thanked us once again. Descending the steps, Dave reached for my hand and gave it a squeeze. 'That went well,' he said.

Having agonised about it on the ride over, I now felt justified in having brought Dave along to share the news. The men had greeted each other awkwardly but over the course of the conversation, Stephen saw how Dave had sought to protect him today; and maybe, by extension, also in their past. As the sun beamed down on us, I hoped this would mark a turning point for us all.

'Yes. My God, the relief on his face. He's right though,' I said.

'About what?'

'We'll have to wait until the planning meeting to see if it's truly over. Maybe one of Brian's guys will still come to pressure him.'

'Babe, with the execution the way it was this morning I don't think any of those guys will be giving any business deal a second thought any time soon. They'll be out to get whoever killed their boss.'

'I hope you're right.' In every sense, I thought, quite

happy if Mike was to suffer as a result.

The gate had been opened remotely and as we hit pavement, I saw the red van we'd come in. I'd been so distracted by the assassination that I'd forgotten my earlier fright. The hand holding mine suddenly felt constricting and, feeling the sweat build around my fingers, I dropped it.

'Dave? Whose car is this?'

'It's Tam's. He wants me to use his van when I do jobs for him, rather than my own.'

'Have you had it long?'

The question must have told him something was wrong. He stopped looking for his keys and swivelled my way with an enquiring gaze. 'What's up?'

He'd accused me of conspiracy theories before and I didn't want to sound like a loon again; but I needed the truth. With every bone in my body I believed I'd been followed. But scanning my memories for confirmation, I couldn't be sure. Could my mind have played tricks on me?

'I've noticed a red van following me lately. Is it you?'

A cloud passed in front of the sun and the temperature dropped, as we were covered in shade. When Dave bit his lip and looked at his shoes, I had my answer.

'I was worried about you. You weren't listening to me and throwing yourself into all these dangerous situations…I wanted to keep you safe.'

'What kind of creepy person does that?'

'The kind that loves you very much.' His word and earnest expression caught me off-guard and I softened my attitude as he continued his apology. 'Look, I'm sorry, okay? But you were being so bloody stubborn.'

Our little road-side argument raised a neck crane

from a dog walker across the street. I pulled my stalker boyfriend into the car to spare the posh neighbourhood's prying eyes from further vulgarity.

'I thought it was the bouncer—Mike's bouncer—that had been following me. I saw him on Pollokshaws Road again and when I lost sight of him for a minute, I saw that van.' Now conscious of my misconception, I shook my head. 'I can't believe it was you all along.'

'Babe, it was stupid. I know. But I was watching out for you. Christ, I've been making super slow progress on the drains at the Prince William just so I could listen in and make sure you were safe. But they never talked about you again. Or Glory. I even asked around my old friends—guys I don't hang out with anymore, before you say anything—but none of them had any information about Glory being targeted.'

'You should have been honest with me.' The irony of this accusation wasn't lost on me. Lord knows how much I'd been hiding.

'I was. I kept telling you you didn't know who you were dealing with. To let go. That you should leave it to the police. But no. You kept scheming away thinking you were streetwise when—I hate to break to you—you're from Perth. Possibly the most genteel place on Earth.'

'Well you finally got what you wanted.'

'What's that?'

'I'm going to the police tomorrow. I'm going to help them catch the wholesaler red-handed for keeping forced labourers.'

'Oh for heaven's sake! Why did you get involved in that?'

'If I can't get the bastard for murdering Glory, I will still get the satisfaction of putting him behind bars.'

Whether he now finally gave into my instincts about my sister's murder or not, he didn't show, and I thought the better of testing him, for fear of falling out of grace again. 'Fine. But you don't do anything by yourself. You promise? And then it's over, yes?'

'Yes.' I didn't have the heart to tell him I might have released a can of money laundering-seeking worms inadvertently.

We rode in silence for a while, his eyes on the road and mine exploring the interior of this unfamiliar, no-longer-threatening vehicle.

'Why are you working for Tam?'

'I wanted to do more hours, to have money for the flat. We're so far off. That's why I've been working weekends.' He turned to face me for the few split seconds that traffic permitted. 'I want us to be together.'

'Me too,' I said, and shut the glove box to place my hand on his knee. 'Our time will come.'

I thought about the money in Glory's hidden account and wondered, for the briefest of moments, if my role in bringing down a major criminal—strike that: *two* major criminals—entitled me to keep it.

CHAPTER FIFTY-FOUR

At 9:55 precisely, I found Oliver pacing the semi-circular steps of Police Scotland's smaller Southside station. I'd come on foot, having enjoyed my long morning walk with Blue earlier. Nothing like the shrieking sound of a small nephew practising violin in the morning to make you appreciate the soft murmurs of a summer's outdoors. I was wearing a T-shirt and leggings but had wrapped an anorak around my waist in preparation for the much-heralded end to our unusually prolonged heatwave. Any minute now.

When his eyes set on me, he raised both arms in greeting, revealing a V-shaped torso I was still convinced came from swimming.

I'd have to ask.

'Good. You're here. I've checked DI Roberts is in. But I wanted a word with your first.'

'Oh?'

'I've been going over in my mind the conversations I had with Glory. Whether there were clues…that I should have noticed her questions weren't all hypothetical. But she seemed so genuinely interested.'

'There will have been a reason she kept it quiet.'

'But if what I told her placed her in danger—'

'Oliver, it's fine, it wasn't anything to do with you. Don't worry. Let's go in.'

As I let him walk in front, I found it interesting he'd thought Glory might have been in danger. Was there something he knew?

Inside the atrium a single pendant light shone unnecessarily. Two policemen talked on the balcony overlooking the entrance, each holding the type of thin plastic cup that comes out of crappy office vending machines. I winced, anticipating undrinkable coffee.

The officer at the desk was a woman in her fifties whose blouse was revealing its length of service by the tightness across the chest; her buttons looking ready to pop off and hit the bullet-proof glass between us. Oliver mumbled something which elicited an amused snort, and she pushed a button to let us through to the inner sanctum.

'This way,' he said.

We walked along a short hallway, bland but for the notice boards lining the walls, announcing charity events and the results of the inter-district football tournament held last month. The station's team hadn't fared well and someone had scribbled a treasonous '*Losers*' on the form. At the next stop-point, Oliver pressed a buzzer, soon to be greeted by a uniformed young man.

'Visiting DI Roberts?'

'Yes,' Oliver replied.

'Come with me.'

It amazed me that the access to meeting rooms took you through the open-plan offices. People beavered away in the sweltering heat created by full-width windows, no doubt designed by an enthusiastic architect to give the passing public a sense of the force's transparency. But the only transparency I witnessed was in their sweat-soaked work shirts.

There was paper everywhere, and it seemed that, despite a fortune being spent on government digitisation, law enforcement still heavily relied on piles of multi-paged printed reports. After passing a few closed doors, the man ushered us into a small, windowless room and offered refreshments.

I wasn't going to risk it. 'Water, please.'

Oliver sat at the table, on the side with two chairs. 'I'm sure he'll be here shortly.'

'Have you been here before?' I joined his side even though it gave the setting an us-against-them feel.

'Yes, twice.'

The door swung open and a middle-aged policeman walked in, as broad as he was tall. Oliver jumped up, and given the gravitas exuded by the inspector's face, I was compelled to stand to attention as well. We shook hands and introduced ourselves. A few steps behind him entered a younger, slimmer chap who merely stated 'Armstrong, CID.' We were instructed to sit.

DI Roberts arranged his notebook and pen on the table, released the tie caught in the fold in his stomach, and clasped his fingers together. 'I'm deployed to the national human trafficking unit, based at Stewart Street. But I wanted to meet here with my local colleague. He is our resident expert on Mike Catach.' The expert gave a nod in acknowledgement. It was the first time I'd heard Mike's last name. 'Now, Miss McBride, Oliver here tells me you have information pertaining to a plausible case of forced labour.'

'Yes. Well, it was my sister…She died.' I fumbled to retrieve the phone from the pocket of the anorak swinging in the void under the chair.

'I'm aware of that. My condolences.'

'The delivery man for Excelsior, Marius, confided in her about his slavery situation and that of the other Romanian men with him. There are six of them. So Glory set out to get evidence. You see, Oliver told her you would need photos of their working and living conditions.'

At the mention of his involvement, Oliver squirmed. 'She'd asked me about a hypothetical situation. I never advised her to go in like this.'

DI Roberts patted his shirt pocket and trousers, which I guessed was him searching for reading glasses in vain, because he then flicked through the photos holding the device at arm's length and using his thick fingers to zoom in on each one. I had been very tempted to remove the cosy-looking images of Glory and Mike. People kept getting the wrong idea. But as Oliver had seen them, that might have raised suspicion. As expected, Roberts paused on one of those.

Armstrong sat with his arms crossed in front of him and craned his neck for a better view. 'What was your sister's relationship with Mike Catach?'

'A customer. Excelsior is the wholesaler for her café. Veg&Might on Pollokshaws Road. As you can see from the dates, these inside ones were taken at the same time as the others. It's obviously part of evidence gathering. You know, because Oliver said you'd want pictures of the men in charge.' He seemed unconvinced and I jumped to defend her further. 'I suspect she used her charm to get close. Glory could be very charming.'

'I can believe that,' he said. 'Good thing Mrs Catach didn't see these. She'd have her for breakfast.' He snickered, oblivious to his insensitive comment.

'So you're running an investigation into him?' I asked.

'The force has been after Catch for ages. Everyone knows he's a major player, but we could never get anything to stick so far. He's a master at covering his tracks and letting others take the fall.'

'What's his crime?'

'You name it: drugs, bribery, intimidation, money laundering—' He stopped as if he'd divulged too much and fixed his gaze on me. 'You seem exceptionally interested in Mike Catch and his business, Miss McBride. Is there something you want to tell me?'

I felt the blood drain from my face and I hoped it didn't show.

Back-pedalling as elegantly as I could with one foot in my mouth, I lifted the phone off the table and pointed at the labour conditions. 'I guess I was curious what kind of man could do this to another human being. And, you know, it's my first time talking to the police about criminals. So forgive me for being a little over-interested.' After emitting a coy smile, I turned to catch the eye of DI Roberts. 'Were you aware of forced labour taking place there?'

'Actually, no. But human trafficking is a priority for the force so we're grateful that you've come forward.' Roberts was about to take charge of the conversation again when his colleague interrupted.

'We weren't aware either. Catch's main guys tend to be local lads and we're all over them. We've never focused on the workers—they look like any other immigrants doing menial jobs in that part of town.' The way Armstrong dismissed the victims smacked of an attempt to justify his team's failure to spot their plight.

Roberts' stormy glare told me his DI rank trumped Armstrong's.

Oliver chimed in. 'There is a misconception that victims fall into forced labour due to their employers having control of their immigration status. People don't expect it to apply to Eastern Europeans who can live here freely. But we find, in fact, that many of our cases here in Scotland involve Romanians. Sometimes Poles. Other nationalities don't seek help because they fear being deported. But as that's not the case for our EU friends, people can't understand why they don't just leave.'

'Yes, it was easy to miss,' Armstrong said. 'We've been focused on making the case with the hauliers.' With Armstrong being on the defensive, I sensed an opening.

'The hauliers?'

He bit; a wounded male ego chomping to re-assert its importance. 'Our investigation points to a multi-million-pound money laundering racket, involving several wholesalers across the Glasgow area and a haulage company under the control of Catach that we believe transports drugs.'

'And you think these pictures will help you get into his books?'

'Yes, their records are the last piece of the puzzle. We'll finally be able to follow the cash flows between his wholesale firm and the hauliers. And with what we've already got, we'll lock the scumbag up for years.' This raised an eyebrow from his superior and he found his place again. 'And, of course, free the Romanians…ahem…Poor guys.' He didn't speak again for some time, leaving the talking to DI Roberts.

'The photos clearly evidence breaches in Health and

Safety for workers, which in and of themselves warrant a visit. See here: they're not wearing gloves and have no equipment to help them shift the boxes. When you couple that with the decrepit living conditions, and the fact the men live on site, you have tell-tale signs of a forced labour situation. But ideally we need a real witness. Miss McBride would your delivery man—this Marius chap—would he speak with me?'

'You can't expect him to come in here!'

Oliver clarified. 'DI Roberts means for you to set up a secret meeting at the café.'

'You mean like get him in with an order, so you can have a chat at the rear?' I asked.

'Exactly,' Roberts said.

Perhaps over-sensitive to the security of the women in his life, Oliver said, 'You don't need to, Grace. You've done a lot already. The police could take it from here once you give them the photos.'

'Indeed, we don't want you to put yourself in any difficult situation. But it would speed things up,' nudged Roberts.

'Thursday. He delivers on Thursday. I can bring him in for a while.'

'Are you sure?'

Oliver's slimy concern was getting on my nerves and I blurted out something I probably shouldn't have. 'Yes, I'm sure. I want to nail the bastard.'

The two policemen looked at each other in alarm while Oliver's eyes darted between them, curious for a response. My stomach had not only sunk but collapsed straight through the chair and hit the ground with a big fat thud.

'What's it to you?' Armstrong's interest had been re-awakened.

Why had I not kept quiet? Now I had to tell them there was more to it. 'You'll think I'm moronic. And there's nothing to support my claim. But I suspect Catach killed my sister.'

'Why?' the DI asked, a fatherly expression on his face. Comforted by him holding his arm against Armstrong's chest in anticipatory restraint, I opened up. Worst case, I was some mad grief-stricken woman. Best case, I was right.

'Because she was snooping around. He must've caught her and wanted to get rid of her.'

By now, Oliver had moved away from me, rubbing a very raised forehead. Armstrong chewed his cheeks in contemplation. 'I would say that seems a little excessive, detective inspector. Not really his style,' he said, keen to reassert his expertise.

'I know I sound a little crazy. And I know it was a car accident. But I can feel it, you know? I can feel it in my deepest heart of hearts. She was murdered.'

Roberts conceded to my pleading. 'Why don't we do this: you set up a meeting with Marius this Thursday and I will read through the file on your sister's accident. Deal?'

'Yes. Deal. Thank you, detective inspector.'

CHAPTER FIFTY-FIVE

Sascha was miffed when I asked her to place an order at Excelsior after she'd so diligently procured another supplier at my request. But when she understood why, it changed everything. And now that the delivery day had come, she was following me around and fussing over me as if I were a visiting dignitary. A heroic freer of men.

I hadn't planned on telling her, but she'd met Oliver at an event and he'd apparently not been able to contain his admiration—or perhaps incredulity—for the selfless efforts of these two sisters. Still, it made it easier to explain why I was going to let strange people into the kitchen or why I was still hanging around the café at this time.

DI Roberts and a female colleague of similar age sat at the table closest to the counter, sipping coffees in their civvies, looking very much the part of an ordinary married couple. Less ordinary, but unlikely to be noticed by a casual observer, was the fact that they'd been sitting there for two hours already. We never knew what time Marius would come, as it depended on the day's delivery route, so we had to play a waiting game. I took their latest order. Having started with espressos, the pair had moved onto decaf and Roberts' attempt at a third pastry was thwarted by his companion, seemingly applying a hint of method acting to her role of spouse.

Our hipster visitors vacated the window-side seats and glowed with self-satisfaction when donning their trendy caps as they stepped into the rain. Outside, normal service for Glasgow's skies had resumed and made up for its dry spell glitch by pelting us with unremitting showers, with only dark clouds for cover. Sascha was mopping the area surrounding the entrance again when the knock on the rear door came.

As planned during the morning's run-through, I went to let him in. Roberts waited two minutes before getting up and walked towards the toilet—for the benefit of the lone real customer still on site—only to slip into the kitchen once out of sight. His companion, who worked in Victim Support, would stay in place and be called upon if needed. Sascha would continue to man the front of house.

The door opened, Marius slunk in like a pet expecting a beating. He carried a box of tinned chick peas—at an angle to relieve the pressure from his injured hand. The state of the bandage confirmed it hadn't been changed in some time.

'Come in. It's okay. It won't take long.' I took the box from him and steered him towards the table where I'd treated his wound before, away from any prying eyes. Roberts entered and Marius cowered behind me. It didn't help that the officer took up the whole width of the kitchen, effectively blocking us in. With an arm around the frightened informant's shoulder, I introduced the two.

I listened as Roberts reassured Marius, with a gentle manner and a speech he must have used on many others. 'You did the right thing in calling for help. It is important that you understand that you are the victim of a crime. You are not in trouble. Do you understand?' Marius nodded. 'You have every right to live here in Scotland. You have done nothing wrong. I am here to help you.' I could feel Marius's body relax in my hold and nudged him forward to encourage his participation. 'But to help you, I need you to talk. About the men at Excelsior. About you and your friends. Do you understand?'

Marius nodded again, but he still emitted an air of preoccupation. 'I have no house. Where do I go?' Those eight words brought home the vulnerability of these forced labourers. However bad their circumstances, they had nowhere else to go.

'After you give me more information today, we will plan a raid on the wholesaler to rescue you. You and your friends will be taken to a safe house in North Glasgow and have the opportunity to give formal evidence, so we can charge the men who did this. There are other Romanians there who have been rescued like you, and people from Migrant Help whose job it is to get you on your feet. They will call the Romanian Consular Office in Edinburgh who can contact your family in Romania for you. And help you get new papers, assuming they were they taken.' Roberts had spoken slowly for the benefit of our foreigner. It was a lot to take in for anyone.

'Yes. No papers. When do you come?'

'That depends on how much you can tell me today, but it could be very soon. I know it's difficult, but you will need to be patient.'

Shaking his head, he insisted, 'My friend Emil, he is sick. He has bad lung problem. He coughs a long time and...how to say? *Scuipat.*' He pretended to spit, to show us. 'They treat him bad. He must see a doctor. You must come quick.'

Roberts frowned and massaged the rear of his thick neck. 'Well then, let's talk. I want you to name the men on these photos.' Marius joined him to look at the print-outs and started his journey to freedom.

When all the requisite information had been collected, Roberts confirmed they'd have enough to move. Marius was thanked and discharged to finish his delivery, but he requested one more thing. 'When you come. I need Grace there.'

'We can't take civilians along. It's too dangerous.'

'Grace is my friend. She is there,' he pressed, 'I am afraid.'

'I'll see what we can do.'

With no promises made, DI Roberts left to re-join his colleague, Marius stepped into his van, neither asking me what I thought.

CHAPTER FIFTY-SIX

True to his word, DI Roberts sought approval to have me along for the raid, but he received a vociferous 'no.' As he explained this in a call two days after meeting at the café, he also addressed his earlier promise, which was to dig into Glory's crash.

'Officers at the scene of the crash evaluated the condition of the vehicle to determine the probable cause for her coming off the A809. The vehicle suffered extensive damage when it flipped over on the sloped bank, so they couldn't say for sure, but there were no signs of a second vehicle being involved, like a different colour of paintwork present.'

'I see.'

'That stretch of Stockiemuir Road is a known black spot. We see incidents there all the time.'

Not quite ready to give up, I asked, 'What if someone nudged her off the road, you know, not actually hitting her?'

'Well, I guess that's possible in theory, but it's difficult to accomplish in practice, particularly without leaving a mark. Unless the target isn't a very competent driver.'

'No. Glory was a good driver. She loved her Bug. She could manage the roads to the Trossachs no problem.' I remembered how she loved taking the boys on day-trips. I joined them on a drive once, and she'd chatted away while navigating the tortuous roads along Loch Lomond to go watch the seaplane take off. I savoured the memory, then packed it away. 'So it really was an accident.'

'That does appear to be the case. A tragic waste. But hopefully I've given you closure.'

'I guess. Thank you.'

'Take care, Grace.'

'Wait. About the raid. I feel so bad for Marius. He wanted me there and I have no way of communicating with him. What if I came alone and stayed out of the way?'

'No. I can't possibly agree to that.' In a less formal tone he added, 'But then the police cannot reasonably object if a member of the public is coincidentally present where an operation is taking place at o-seven-hundred hours on Wednesday.'

That brought a grin to my face. 'Good luck, detective inspector. Bye.' I held the idle phone to my chest, mulling over his clever choice of words to cover his arse.

'Who was that?' Dave strode into my living room, freshly showered, and loaded the pockets of his cargo pants with his keys, phone and wallet from the kitchen counter.

'DI Roberts. He says they're raiding the place the day after tomorrow.'

'Wow, that was quick.'

'Yes, apparently the photos and Marius's testimony got things moving. That, and one of the men being ill.'

'What did he say about you going along?'

'He told me what time to be there.' Technically not a fib. 'But don't worry, I will stay out of sight.'

'Fine. But I still think it's a terrible idea to expose yourself like that.'

'Breakfast?' Anything to avoid this conversation again.

'No, I've got to go. I'll get something at Greggs.'

'Dave. For crying out loud. How many times do I need to tell you to stay away from that junk?'

He shrugged and poked me in the tummy. 'And how many times have I told you to stay out of trouble?'

'Touché!' I smiled, though my lips wouldn't curl up as much as usual.

'What's up?'

'Oh, nothing. Roberts looked into Glory's file.'

'And?'

'And it's time I accept her death was an accident.'

'Oh babe.' He wrapped his arms around me and kissed my hair. 'I hate to say I told you so. But at least now you know for sure and you can move on. And think about it: even though Catach didn't kill her, he's still vermin and you girls will have played a part in taking him down. That's got to count for something, right?'

Right.

CHAPTER FIFTY-SEVEN

Stephen responded well when I told him I wouldn't be able to help with the kids in the morning. It had been a week since the front pages shouted about the council's decision to reject the planning permission for the Left Bank development; and he behaved like a new man, regaining an interest in life, and in his kids after this period of crippling uncertainty.

The fear of reprisals for the planning rejection had gripped us for a few days after the announcement, but nobody came. Before Dave got the door slammed in his face for not having the job done yet—when surely, the drains couldn't possibly take that long—he had confirmed that Brian Scott's men were too flustered dealing with anxious creditors and business partners storming the Prince William to juggle anything else.

I'd scoured the news for mentions of Brian Scott, holding a morbid fascination for details on the progress of the investigation. The police never tied Brian's murder to Mike. And I wasn't about to point them in the right direction.

It would soon be over. At least, that is what I thought as I put on a black outfit of jeans, T-shirt and jacket, to try to blend in at the raid. I looked for my black hiking boots—a search taking in every corner of the flat—then remembered I'd brought them to the house when I got fed up getting soggy trainers walking the dog in the perpetual damp of Maxwell Park.

My hair was fixed in a loose bun that I stuffed inside my beanie. I checked myself in the mirror and snorted that not only did I look like a prowler, but the hat's Under Armour logo had a bit of Spiderman to it.

After some wrist flicking moves and associated 'Spidey' sound effects the boys would be proud of, I grabbed my car keys and set out to witness justice being served.

By 6:45 I'd reached my observation point. The same place I'd monitored the wholesaler from on my first scoping visit. That felt so long ago now. When the closest I'd come to Glasgow's underworld was dancing at The Cowshed. When white was white and black was black. And there was no doubt on which side I stood. Still now, I prided myself on standing in the lighter shades of grey; acting on what was right, what *felt* right.

Visibility was reasonable. The sun had been up for two hours already and the drizzle was light enough that I did not need my wipers on.

There was movement in the side yard, but I was too far away to make out the individuals. Being trade, the place opened at dawn, but I guessed the police must have timed the operation to catch more people on site.

As my watch beeped for the hour, four punctual people carriers parked in quick succession in front of Excelsior. White, with high-vis blue and yellow checks and '*POLICE*' spelt in giant letters on every side, their function was unmistakable.

I watched as officers streamed out of the vehicle

like a disrupted wasp nest, swooping in silence to take position on the perimeter of the site. The twenty stab-vest-clad and helmeted men waited for a signal I did not hear or see, but when it came, they dispersed at once. Half of them swarmed around the building and the other half pounced inside.

My gums were nearly numb from nerves as I watched the professionals do their thing. It was suddenly very real.

An additional patrol car drove up, accompanied by two silent ambulances. DI Roberts hoisted himself out of the Vauxhall's passenger side and took visual stock of the situation. On spotting me, he acknowledged my presence with a curt nod but also pushed his open palm down to instruct me to stay put.

Almost as quickly as they'd moved in, men returned from the rear of the property, their number swelled by their haul. My familiar ned shuffled forward handcuffed and hunched, pushed by a baton at his bum. It would have taken a trained eye to distinguish in such a hurry the skinny, pale yobs from the sickly trafficked victims, but I was thrilled to see the baddies being dragged by their handcuffs while the Romanians were being gently ushered to freedom. Marius and his friends remained calm and yielded to directions willingly. Even though they would have known their release was imminent, it must have been torture having to be patient and not knowing when.

Like an excited family member held in the glazed pen at an airport arrival hall, I waved to catch Marius's attention from the confines of my car; but his searching eyes missed me at every turn. Until the operation was complete, I was stuck here and hoped I would be able to speak with him before the medics carried him away.

Seconds later, people poured out of the shop and the scene exploded as if someone had un-muted the volume. The mouthy cashier lady hobbled effing and blinding in unison with two equally outraged office workers being guided to the vans.

A lone raider remained to guard the door. When he clipped a padlocked chain around the handles, I was struck with panic. Where was Mike? Had he escaped?

The front ambulance, with the sicker men, left straight away with its lights flashing. When the rest of the commotion had died down and the convoy drivers jumped into their seats, Roberts motioned the coast was clear. I ran across the street, straight to the second ambulance.

'Marius! Marius, I'm here,' I cried to prevent the doors being shut. The paramedic looked at me in confusion but made way when the DI shouted his approval.

My friend's eyes lit up when I appeared in his sight. 'Grace!' He said something I couldn't decipher to the three others, who then faced me and showered me with thank-yous.

'I see you soon,' he promised, glowing with happiness, when the doors folded to a close and the engine revved for departure.

I felt a large hand on my shoulder and turned to see DI Roberts with a satisfied smirk, which turned into a fatherly expression of concern when he saw me wiping away a tear.

'Are you all right?'

'Yes. No…I mean, it's…' How could I explain the relief, with him unaware of the full scale of the burden I'd carried?

'It's a lot to process, Grace. But don't worry. The men will be well taken care of.'

My nerves stayed on edge, however. The job wasn't finished, as far as I was concerned, and a pulling in my chest nagged that something smelt off. 'Where is Mike Catach? Why was he not here? Had he been tipped off?' The barked accusatory questions took Roberts aback and his face clouded over.

'No. We got him at home, with his wife, in a parallel raid. They're gathering his files there and his laptop, and we'll send someone in here today to fish out evidence. Now, go home and let us do our job,' he said, in dismissal. 'I can assure you we'll get what we need.'

But would I get what I needed? The lightening from seeing Marius freed was weighted down by a visceral tension I could not shake. I resented that I missed the main event; missed being witness to the despicable man's ripped-from-bed humiliation; missed the opportunity to stand in his line of sight to show him who had turned him in.

But as I visualised my revenge through an imaginary run-through of his capture, I realised what I resented most was not getting justice for Glory's death—as there was none to be had.

CHAPTER FIFTY-EIGHT

The Sunday roads provided another smooth run up North, my first in nearly three weeks. My mind replayed my last conversation with Dad, in hospital. I fought every instinct to turn back and avoid such torment again, and pushed the pedal resolutely to hit the permitted seventy miles per hour and stay on course.

I'd received a short, reassuring message on Mum's release from the PRI but found it too difficult to proactively enquire about her condition; to face a possible misery it had been in my power to prevent. No. It was easier to don a shield, to hide, to stick my fingers in my ears and sing 'la la la.'

With Mike now gone, I hoped to be able to wash away the guilt. Raising money for her care illegally was no longer an option. Rationally Dad could no longer be disappointed in me for refusing. I tried to repress the anxiety I felt that our relationship may be doomed already. That my motives could never truly be considered pure: was putting the man behind bars merely a convenient sabotage?

As I exited the Broxden roundabout, I took a deep

breath and exhaled to expel the grains of insecurity that scratched inside. Once past the high school, I had gained comfort with the concept I had done nothing wrong. Quite the opposite. And not only should I not be a disappointment, dammit, I was coming armed with a tale of heroism to restore Glory in his eyes.

Dad's car stood in the drive. I had expected them to be home, but it was a relief to see it confirmed. The square patch of immaculate grass was bordered by budding pink roses and majestic feathered dahlias. A line of purple lupines stood at attention, fronting the house. Exiting the Panda, I soaked in the colourful harmony. Whatever disease or neglect lay behind the door, it hadn't yet disgorged outside to Dad's cherished garden.

Bracing for what I would find, I pressed the door handle and stepped inside. Dad was sitting at the kitchen table, watching the tennis on the portable TV. It meant Mum was awake. Through the throbbing of my heartbeat in my temples, I hardly heard myself say, 'Hi Dad.'

'Hello, Egg.'

My joy leapt so high it pressed against the back of my eyes to spill out in liquid form.

Egg.

He'd called me Egg.

It instantly transported me to this same kitchen in a 1980s decor, a dark wintry sky, and the frantic preparations for a large family meal. Mum bossed the three of us around. We were running behind for her parents' Christmas visit. Glory glazed the carrots as I peeled potatoes, one vigorous stroke after another.

There was a small spot above my right elbow where I could still, decades later, feel the nudge against the bowl of whipped egg whites for Mum's prized pavlova. When it fell to the ground, it was as if time had stood still. I remembered how one hiccuped breath kept me going as I turned to see my mother's eyes expand in anger. I made myself small and waited for the fall-out. Glory slid out of the room. Before the dreaded screech came, a thunderous male laugh stunned everyone. 'Oh thank God for that. I hate pavlova.' On seeing my mother's puzzled face, Dad added, 'I didn't have the heart to tell you—you were always so keen to compete with your mother's.' As if by contagion, this revelation made my mother sputter and before long we all howled in glee around the spilt white clouds.

Dad had cleared his throat. 'Of course, that was very clumsy of you, Grace. For punishment we'll call you "Egg" until the new year. And then forgive and forget.'

Ever since, the name Egg had become analogous with forgiveness and, as it sounded today, there existed no sweeter word. I moved in for a hug, which he gave—though hesitantly at first. In the distance someone grunted. An umpire yelled 'in.'

'Is Mum awake?'

'Yes.' He moved my hands from his shoulders and got up. 'Come.'

Mum's complexion was still pale and her skin looked paper-thin. But her eyes sparkled as they took in Coronation Street. Dad whispered in my ear. 'You've caught her at a lucid time. They come and go, but she's been good all day so far.'

I inched forward into her field of vision. 'Hi Mum.'

'Hello darling. Were we expecting you?' She looked at Dad for confirmation.

'No. But it's Sunday. And I've decided to come see

you every Sunday.'

'Oh that's nice. We had the grandkids over yesterday. I'm sure Stephen is doing the best he can, but Glory used to dress those boys better.' She seemed to fish for the remote around her lap. 'Can you turn this off?' Her frail arms succeeded in pushing her onto her feet. 'I'll make us a nice pot of tea.'

'It's okay, Mum, I can do it.'

She batted me away. 'Don't fuss, Grace.'

Banished and bemused, I joined Dad on the sofa.

After a while, cautious not to jinx it, I said, 'She's looking well.'

'As I said, it comes and goes, but it is a little better than before. The doctors said she had been dehydrated, which wasn't good for her body but also accounted for the increased confusion. The nurses put her on fluids and gave me some tips on keeping her drinking. It's not always easy.'

'I'm sorry,' I left open-ended what for.

'I know.'

'Will you be able to keep her at home?'

'Maybe for a little while, but don't let today fool you. She is not well.'

'Does she know?'

'Yes. We've had the conversation when it's been possible. And she's at peace with it. She knows what we can afford. I never mentioned why. And don't you dare.'

'No, of course not.'

The tinkle of cups and saucers neared, and we repositioned ourselves in casual expectation.

'Here we are.' Mum walked in and deposited the tray on the coffee table. 'Here is some tablet, also. It's from a neighbour down the street. She insists on making it and then hands it out to everyone. This batch is thankfully quite edible.'

Dad chuckled.

'The reason I came today is that I've come to share amazing news about something Glory did. Well, and I helped.'

'Oh?' they said in unison, and the floor was mine.

As I described the sequence of events since discovering the photos on Glory's phone, my mother sat transfixed and muttered the odd 'my goodness.' Dad's eyes widened at the first mention of Excelsior and we exchanged warning looks. I avoided any hint at why Glory might have been closer to the wholesaler than most other customers and focused on her discovery of Marius's plight and decision to do something about it—never mind why. By the time I reached the climax of the Romanians safely inside the ambulance, Mum was holding her clasped hands under her chin, gripped.

'They're in a safe house now, for a few days, where they will get the help they need to rebuild their lives,' I said.

'Isn't that marvellous?' Mum asked of Dad. 'They'll be rejoicing in heaven, won't they, dear?'

'Yes, God bless her.' It seemed as though he was humouring her, not yet convinced of his daughter's saintliness himself.

'It should make up for the criminal money things, don't you think, dear?'

I gasped and nearly dropped my cup. Dad's head darted back and forth between us two, as if he'd missed a whole conversation.

'What are you talking about, Mum?' I enquired in a light and airy tone.

'What?'

'That thing you just said. About Glory.'

She shrugged. 'I don't know. I've heard you two talking. It was complicated. Did I say something wrong?'

Had she been awake after all? And lucid? It wouldn't surprise me if she'd heard the whole thing—what Dad asked of me—but chose to pretend. My parents and their incredible skill of suppressing the unspeakable.

Dad redirected. 'I'm very proud of what you did, too. Very proud, the way you picked up what Glory had started.'

'Thanks. That means a lot.'

'Will you take the last piece of tablet?' Mum asked.

'No thanks. In fact, I've got to go see Alice. I called to say I'd drop by.'

'How are those cute little girls of hers?'

'They're big teenagers now, Mum.'

'Oh.'

'I'll be back next Sunday, okay?'

Mum nodded, then summoned me with a wave. 'Come here.'

I walked to her armchair and bent through my knees to be at eye level. 'What is it?'

She placed both palms on my cheeks, cocked her head and stared at me intently. What was she doing? She pulled gently, and I let her guide my head to hers. Then she pressed her dry lips on mine. 'Good girl.'

The shock knocked me off balance and I nearly fell on my bum. I couldn't remember the last time she's been affectionate with me—childhood, for sure.

She was already looking away again and motioned for Dad to help her out of the chair. I placed my fingers on my lips, where hers had been. Not another word was said.

Dad held Mum's elbow as she got up and shuffled to the kitchen.

I put my shoes on to leave and wrapped my light-blue scarf around my neck. Mum began circling like a dog trying to catch its tail.

'Where is it?'

'Where is what, Mary?' Dad asked.

'I had the PE bag in my hand a second ago,' she said.

My nerves jumped to attention. 'What PE bag?'

'The one Glory forgot to take to school. You can bring it to her. She's always hiding it. I swear, this girl has missed more sports than she's ever done.'

Dad sighed and shook his head.

Faced with this baffling switch, I experienced an overwhelming urge to not upset her. 'It's okay, Mum. I have a spare set. I'd better go, or I'll be late for class.'

'All right but tell her we'll have words when she comes home. Now shoo.' She swatted me out the door before I was able to say goodbye to my poor dad.

CHAPTER FIFTY-NINE

Alice's girls were lounging in the kitchen in onesies, legs draped over the rattan armrests, so engrossed in their smart-phones that my presence went unacknowledged.

'I swear they have been in that exact position since the moment school broke up on Friday. I have no idea what I'll do with this bunch all summer.' Slapping a series of feet, Alice said, 'Girls, say hello to Grace. And go shower.' The fluffy creatures mumbled greetings and dragged themselves away while their mother opened the glazed patio door for air. 'That's better. You remember listening to Nirvana? Well, this is what teen spirit actually smells like.'

'You're mean.' I chuckled.

'No, I just tell it like it is,' we chanted in chorus, paying tribute to an age-old gag about her predilection for tactless candour. A flush of warmth filled my chest, toasty snippets of intimacy and laughter, the flints of a twenty-year friendship.

Once the kettle had boiled, she enquired about Mum's condition and I described the changes I had witnessed moments earlier, from her usual self—

stinging criticisms and all—to her unexpected affection and her sudden, upsetting detachment from reality.

'Judging from Dad's face, that wasn't the first time things had changed so quickly.'

'No. Probably not, given where she is at. Still, sounds as though the new hydration regime is working a little. And he appears to be managing okay, for now.'

'Yes, for now. Dad still thinks he'll put her into a home, though.' My tone held an accusatory note. Not just for Dad. Also for her, for her role in planting the idea of expensive care homes in Dad's head.

'I know it's hard to imagine. But you haven't experienced the day-to-day demands of dementia. I'm sure he's doing his best. He's the most devoted husband I have met. He'd do anything for her.'

Didn't I know it.

'Anyway, that's not why I came today,' I said. 'It's been an incredible two weeks, and it all kicked off when I found some strange photos on Glory's phone. Listen to this…'

This was my fourth time running through the story—first with Dave, then Stephen, then my parents—but it did not lose its shine. My heroic sister freeing the shackled slaves. It also never failed to floor the listener.

'Wow.' Alice reclined into the seat, digesting the tale.

'Isn't it wonderful?'

'Yes. Yes, it is.' A crinkle in her forehead hinted at a question.

'What's up?'

She shook her head and flashed a reassuring smile. 'Oh, nothing.'

'No, I can see it. There's something.'

'I was trying to picture Glory going through this and it seemed a bit out of character, that's all.'

'How so?'

'No, really, it's nothing.'

I poked her in the rib. 'Come on. Spit it out.'

'I feel it would have been unlike her to keep everything so quiet, to be so secretive about it. But then I suppose Glory died before getting a chance to bask in glory, so to speak.'

'What's that supposed to mean?' I challenged her, sensing a veiled insult.

'Oh, shush. Trust you to jump to her defence. Have you noticed you've totally downplayed your role in this rescue? You made this happen, too, Grace. Don't forget. You should be celebrated.' She patted my hand to reinforce my contribution. 'All I'm saying is: she wasn't the type to do things purely out of the goodness of her heart—'

'That's unfair.'

'Is it? I'm curious…Is this Oliver guy good-looking?'

It seemed an odd question, at first. 'Well, yes, I guess. He's tall and athletic. But he's got a beard.' I scrunched my nose in disgust. The memory of Glory's penchant for facial hair popped up and made me uncomfortable, like a perturbing grain of truth. 'What's your point?'

'Last time you thought she was bored, maybe seeing someone. Is it possible she was hoping to impress handsome Oliver with this escapade into human trafficking?'

Rationally, I knew she could be right; but viscerally it felt wrong, disrespectful. 'Don't say that.'

'That doesn't make her a bad person, Grace. We all

have different personalities, our own quirks. Nobody is all good or all bad. If my job has taught me anything, it's that people are a product of their character as much as of their circumstance. Put someone in a stressful situation and they may act contrary to their nature, but for the most part, people are who they are. And Glory wasn't like you, always jumping in to save others.' I frowned at this simplistic characterisation. 'Glory needed attention, and that drove a lot of her actions. Particularly attention from the opposite sex. If you're being honest with yourself, you know it's true...But it's fine. I'm not judging her. I loved Glory too. I miss her too.'

'You're speaking as if she only cared about herself. But she cared about others, about me. She was always there for me, too.'

'She was. I'm not saying she wasn't. I saw how close you were, how much you loved each other. And how could you not? The saviour and the narcissist mutually reinforcing this feeling of togetherness. But I equally saw that whenever she "was there for you"—or for me, for that matter—there was usually also an audience.'

The finger quote-marks she used infuriated me. But I was prevented from lashing out by new scratchy grains joining the first at the speed of memory, sinking me into a quicksand of truth. Reshaped recollections: there had always been an audience, or some boy.

'I'm sorry,' she said. 'I've gone all psychotherapist on you. An occupational hazard. But I accept I've completely overstepped my boundaries. Please forgive me. I don't know why I even opened my mouth. I guess with you picking up so much of Glory's load, and with your parents, I'm worried about you. It may not be obvious right this minute, but I just want you to be happy. And for you to do what you want. Not what you think you owe your sister or what someone else needs from you.'

'I understand. You meant well. But you're wrong. And whatever you or anyone says, I'll remember Glory my way.' I squeezed her knee and got up to leave. She rose, but I gestured for her to stay. 'Don't worry. I'm okay. Really.'

And I meant it, figuring that by now I'd survived the worst.

CHAPTER SIXTY

The next morning, the café buzzed with kids frolicking around, their mothers seeking strength in caffeinated coping potions on what was the first official day of the summer holidays.

Sascha's diligence and skill were clear not only from the latest till receipts, but from the way she floated through tables, like a chatty fairy casting healthy-but-delicious treats in all directions. Perhaps because my attempts at bonhomie weren't as genuine, they were met by stone faces. I determined I wouldn't keep this job up much longer. Watching our committed manager, an idea brewed in my mind.

A party of four was leaving as Stephen entered with the boys, and I waved for him to grab the table before someone else did. Adam and Noah knew the place well, as they'd occasionally hung out here after school with Glory, but they wouldn't have seen it so vibrant and the buzz seemed to infect them with excitement. Stephen looked surprised, more than anything, but he would never have visited during working hours anyway.

'Hey guys. Lovely you're here.'

'Hey Auntie Grace. That boy there, that's Hamish. He's in P2C.' Noah pointed at a blue-eyed child, crowned by a cascade of golden curls, doodling on the kids' place-mats with a coloured marker. A picture of angelic perfection that would blow the springs off any woman's biological clock. Even I felt a hint of a twinge in my lower belly.

'Well, we are very near school, perhaps he forgot it was the holidays and came this way out of habit.' I flipped my finger across his nose to underscore my joke, which elicited a giggle. 'What can I get you gentlemen?'

'I'll have a cappuccino please. Can you get the boys an elderflower cordial? And can they share a brownie?' Four little eyes lit up at that last word.

'Sure thing. What's planned for today?'

'I'm off work so I can take them to the Science Centre. Then from tomorrow they go to camp. It's conveniently at the high school. Oh, and because it starts at eight, I can take care of mornings.'

'And Blue?'

'I'm good. Thanks. The walker who takes him out at lunchtime says she can jump in whenever I need, but while the weather is nice we don't mind a little walk in the morning, do we boys?'

I cleaned their table, each wipe sweepier than the last, reflecting the gradual unburdening of my daily routine. Soon, my life would be mine again.

Cups balanced in hand, I flowed past the clientele to the rear. While preparing their order, I drank in the scene of my sister's family, with a melancholic smile.

They're okay, Gi. They're going to be fine.

Against these soothing thoughts, my heart constricted. They were going to be fine—without me.

One of the customers signalled to pay, and I was pulled back to reality. A reality I had by now accepted did not consist of black and white. A reality where it was the exception, rather than the rule, to be free from perpetual conflicting emotions. Reality was grey.

I asked Sascha to take care of the woman while I rejoined my kin. As the brownie was being torn from my hands, my attention was drawn to an unexpected but welcome shape in the doorway: Marius. My new friend scanned the café and burst into a smile when he noticed me, only for his face to sink as his gaze dropped. In a blink, he spun around and exited onto the street. Alarmed by his sudden retreat, I rushed through the door.

'Marius! Marius, wait up!' He walked South, and I caught up with him after two shop fronts. 'What's wrong?'

Everything about him projected fear. 'That man at your table. He cannot see me.'

'Stephen? The man with the two boys?'

'He is a friend?'

'Yes, that's Glory's husband. His name is Stephen.' He gasped and covered his mouth. 'What is it? Tell me.' I pried his lips clear by pulling at his wrist.

'I see him with bad men.'

'What bad men? At Excelsior?'

'No, a delivery place. I see things. They think I do not understand but I hear. The men are criminals. Glory's husband I saw with big gaingster. I remember he turn around—cold eyes—he see me.'

Despite his mispronunciation, I understood straight away he meant Brian Scott. 'Oh, g-A-ngster,' I corrected. 'Yes. Don't worry, Marius. It's okay. Yes, they are bad men, but they were bad to Stephen. They were blackmailing him. Do you know what that means?' He nodded. I shook my head in an exaggerated motion. 'Stephen did nothing wrong. He was a victim, like you. He is a good man.'

He seemed unconvinced.

'And it's over now,' I said. Come. Come and have a coffee. Tell me how you've been. About the safe house.' I tried to steer him by the elbow, but he resisted.

'No. I not come now. I come tomorrow same hour for you. Okay?'

'Okay,' I said, since he wouldn't budge.

As he strode away, I wondered how long it would take for him to trust again.

CHAPTER SIXTY-ONE

Alastair requested I pop into his office between clients. Unable to find any nearby on-street parking and running late, I rerouted all the way to the NCP garage on Mitchell, hoping to God I could return within an hour, before the rate doubled to an eye-watering £8.

Large strides brought me to West George street within minutes, the streets clear of obstructive pedestrians given it was wet and windy out. The receptionist offered me a cup of tea in the small meeting room and subtly slid the box of tissues in my direction. I felt a pang of panic thinking she knew of bad news to come, but then understood she'd meant for me to dry my face.

Of course the receptionist wouldn't know.

I became conscious of the drips from my ponytail onto the velour upholstery and slipped to the edge of the armchair to avoid soaking the back cushion. The purpose of the meeting was woolly. He'd only said he had news and some paperwork for me to sign. With the parking clock ticking, I ambushed Alastair with questions as soon as he arrived.

'So? What's the news?'

Such dispensing with social niceties took him aback, but he smiled and jumped straight in.

'It's excellent news. The key man insurance is paying out. It took a few emails and the police report, but they have accepted that Glory dying so soon after taking out the cover was nothing more than a statistical fluke.'

I felt elation like I'd only ever experienced racing down a zip-line before. I couldn't believe my luck.

'Oh my God. The hundred grand? You said I would be able to take it out of the business. Is that true?'

'Yes. That's a choice you can make. Since you've not yet transferred the shares to Glory's estate.'

'No, I haven't. There's been no time.'

'This means it's essentially yours to keep in the café or to pay out in dividends. If you do, you get eighty-five, in proportion to your shares, and Glory's estate gets her fifteen percent.'

'Wow.'

'There will be tax implications, and I can talk you through how to mitigate…Oh.' A glimpse of my wet eyes stopped him from divulging his accountancy tricks further. He got up and moved towards me. But tall as he was, no bending of his limbs could result in anything close to a hug so, instead, he stood next to me, with his hand on my back, as I hunched over and wept. 'Please tell me these are happy tears.'

'Yes, yes.' I sniffed, wiped my eyes and regained my composure. 'I'm just in shock, you know? This will make all the difference to Mum and Dad.'

And to my conscience.

'Is that where it's going?'

'Yes, to give Mum the best care there is.'

'That's very generous of you. Good for you. What

a lovely thing to do. I'm sure Glory would approve.'

Once the paperwork was signed by me as new director, I bounded down the hill, tripping over my feet as if in zero-gravity, the weight of weeks of guilt gone. I whipped out my Samsung when I entered the car and called home—parking rates be damned.

My parents were not in and I cursed as the line rang out, their technical ineptitude often disabling the answer-phone. Bursting to share our good fortune, I dialled Dave's number.

'Hello?'

'Dave! It's me. You won't believe—'

He interrupted, sounding as though he was speaking from deep inside a cavern. 'Babe, I can't talk right now. I'm elbow-deep in sludge.'

'Oh, okay. Sorry.'

'But listen. Come by my flat at six. I've got a surprise for you. Gotta go. Bye.'

I let out a scream of frustration. My energy needed a release and when banging on the steering wheel wasn't enough, I got out of the Panda and ran a lap of the parking structure's third and second floors.

CHAPTER SIXTY-TWO

The Gorbals. Once known as the most dangerous place in the UK; an overcrowded area of social housing where unemployment and crime went hand in hand. Mouldy, concrete high-rises with limited outdoor space had given it the unenviable reputation of a lower life expectancy than Iraq. It was no wonder people from outside Glasgow—and many from inside—had an unflattering view of the area and its people without having set foot there. It was also no wonder Stephen had escaped as soon as he could.

What a place to grow up.

But my boyfriend had stayed put, loyal to the origins that shaped him. Having learnt the trade from his father, he'd set up his own plumbing business aged nineteen to prove that he could stand on his own two feet and be the kind of man his father was. Humble. Industrious. Traditional, but with a respect for women that would have been uncommon in those days; instilled by Mrs Baker as she juggled raising her two children, her work at the launderette and helping her Women's Aid group run a refuge for battered wives.

Nowadays, the place wasn't as bad. The Glasgow

Housing Association demolished the worst, most poisonous structures and was in the midst of a big redevelopment. Though judging from the weathered tarpaulin lining the construction sites, it was progressing at a snail's pace.

I'd been to Dave's flat a few times when our relationship began but had used an early act of vandalism on my windshield wipers as an excuse to make him come to mine instead. Unlike most other structures, his place looked out onto something green: the Gorbals Rose Garden. With only a small patch of blooms it was undeserving of its name.

As I secured my car—with gear stick lock—I noticed the park was otherwise well-maintained and the two mothers pushing prams were not teenagers, for once. There's hope, I thought.

His red brick and grey metal building had four floors and Dave lived at the top, which an estate agent with a sense of humour had called 'a penthouse.' The black door shone with fresh paint and for once the doorbell button did not stick when pressed.

He opened with a wide grin on his face. 'Welcome, honoured guest.' A kiss later, he gestured for me to enter. The first thing that struck me was the clean window. There was actual sunlight coming through. But as I took off my shoes, I saw the new flooring and a pair of immaculate magnolia walls.

'Surprise!' he said.

'You've redecorated? Wow.'

'Yes. Come look.' He pulled me by the arm into the lounge, where I had a clear view of the open-plan kitchen, a gleaming worktop framing a polished steel hob.

'It looks amazing. When did you do this?'

'I've been working on it ever since we started talking about moving in together. But it was going very slowly. With the extra work for Tam at weekends and evenings, I've had the money to speed things up.' While his trusted worn-out kettle bathed the new cabinets in steam, he showed me the smooth closure of the drawers. 'I tell you, I'm knackered. I've been at it every given opportunity, for months.'

'What a transformation. I'm really proud of you.'

'I'm glad you like it.'

An uncomfortable silence hovered as the tea bags brewed, him gazing at me in expectation, and me worried he wanted me to move here.

'So? You had news…when you called,' he said.

'Oh.' So that's what he was waiting for. We'd need to have 'the chat' at some point but for now I was delighted with the change of subject. 'You won't believe it. I hadn't mentioned it to you before because, to be honest, what with everything else, I forgot. And the accountant had managed my expectations to be so low it hadn't really registered, you know? But turns out Glory took out a hundred-grand insurance through the business and they're going to pay out…and there's nothing to stop me using it for Mum's care.'

'Jesus, Grace. That's insane. Just like that?'

'Just like that.' I could hardly contain my glee. And when Dave spoke again, I knew I had most definitely found my man.

'Wow. That's wonderful. I'm so happy you get to help your Mum. Sure, it would have been awesome to get to keep it for a better flat when I sell this one, but this is such a wonderful gift.'

After we kissed, and all the trouble he'd gone through, it would have been rude not to sleep in the freshly refurbished flat. But that did mean getting up extra early in the morning to swing home for clean clothes.

Come that time, sunlight streamed into the room through the thin blinds, and despite appearing to be asleep, Dave managed to clutch the rim of my pants as I stepped out of bed.

'Stay.'

'I've got to go.'

'Nooo. Stay.'

'I've got the café and two clients this morning.' I pried myself loose and he sat up as I covered my breasts with a T-shirt.

'Can we do something fun later, in the afternoon? You're always off taking care of others...'

'Great idea. Why don't we go up Ben Lomond? It's meant to be a nice day and there won't be many tourists yet.'

'Sure. What time?'

'I need to pass by Glory's house to pick up my boots. Why don't you pick me up there at one o'clock? We'll stop for a sandwich on the way up. It's only about an hour's drive.'

Plans made, I left to fulfil the morning's duties with a spring in my step.

CHAPTER SIXTY-THREE

Ben Lomond's 3196 feet beckoned, with its rewarding views along the loch and far into the hills to the North. All morning, I was energised by the prospect of an afternoon of fresh air and physical activity, and the bagging of my fourth Munro. Even my client in Bearsden couldn't dampen my spirits with her excuses to avoid actual-heart-rate-raising routines and her habit of ordering miraculous no-effort body-shaping gadgets she'd bought online. I was going to climb a hill with my gorgeous boyfriend. What wasn't to love?

I dropped the Panda at home and walked to Glory's. The billboards outside Sainsbury's Local bore images of picnics and summer berries, which seduced me in, and I stocked up on goodies to power today's ascent.

By the time I reached the house, my arms had been outstretched with the weight of two brimming plastic bags for so long, I struggled to bend them back. I rubbed the strained inside of my elbows once at the gate to punch in the code, and noted the nice definition on my biceps.

A narrow plank of wood lay nearby, which I placed against the sensors to keep the gate open for when

Dave came. The gravel crunched twice under my feet before triggering Blue's welcome. The walks no longer a daily burden, I confessed to myself I missed his unwavering enthusiasm. I considered taking him climbing with us, but remembered he now had a dog walker whose unknown schedule I did not want to disrupt. Maybe we should get a pet, I thought. After all, we'd soon have our own place, which I mentally filled with puppy paws and floppy ears.

My trusted greeter jumped against the door as I unlocked it, practically throwing me off my feet.

'Calm down, boy.' I quickly placed the bags onto the worktop to prevent them ripping as he stuck his face in. 'Hello, buddy.' I shook his furry cheeks. 'Miss me? I'm only here real quick. For my shoes.'

He cocked his head as though interested.

'Yes, that's right. My boots. Have you seen them? Go look!' That set him off, which in turn set me off laughing, shaking my head as he hopped about the room like a rabid animal.

His dopiness stopped being fun when his tail wagged the seemingly permanent pile of post off the side table, sheets sliding down like a waterfall. I used one hand to dam the chute and the other to assemble the paper spread across the floor. The collection had at least all been opened by now, but I grumbled it was time for Stephen to file this lot away.

The golden logo of the Highland Arms crossed my sight, and I let out a melancholic sigh.

Aw, your spa day. I'm sorry you missed it, Gi.

I lifted the letter to place it back, but the one underneath caught my attention. It was from the NHS, addressed to Glory and inviting her for her three-yearly cervical examination.

I guess they haven't updated your records.

I didn't feel it was appropriate for this to be lying around where the boys could find it, even if they wouldn't understand what it meant. In fact, this pile really had no place in the kitchen at all and I picked the whole lot up to bring it to somewhere grown-up: Stephen's study.

As I bent over to pick up a letter I missed, I saw that it was from the Clydesdale bank, sending Noah a new authorisation code for online banking. Noah, who was too young for a regular bank account. In a flash, I figured this must be the trust. And as it was dated after Glory's death, it could only have been Stephen who requested it.

So he knew.

What else did he have?

A nagging feeling of unease washed over me. Why had he not mentioned it when I'd come clean about the money laundering?

His study was at the front of the house, a somewhat hidden, tiny former pantry behind the guest toilet. Glory had instructed me early on it was off limits.

Sorry, Gi, not today.

I ventured into the windowless room and saw a compact desk and a wall with three shelves carrying books, boxes and lever arch files. A large grey jumper hugged the chair, and I imagined him in here, late at night, catching up on work; the electric heater angled to blow warmth in his direction.

On the table, multiple heaps of paperwork bordered a clear area narrowly big enough to fit a laptop, but currently populated by chewed-off nail fragments. I wondered if this was a recent habit, as I'd not had him down as a biter. The overflowing bin further showed the cleaner avoided this room. As I moved to set the letters I'd brought in on the desk, I tripped over a bag. It was a blue holdall. Glory's PE bag.

That's it!

Like Mum said, you were always hiding it. Why hadn't I looked for it before?

There were lots of papers inside. I held a manageable stack in my hands and, like a flip-book, let the pages fall from under my thumb, stopping at the red ink of the Clydesdale. As my fingers tried to extract the red from the rest, I spotted a troubling image and my heart jumped. It was a colour print-out of a photo. A photo of Glory and Mike deep in conversation. Why did Glory have this? Or was it Stephen's? Had this been part of the blackmail? To prove Glory's money laundering? It wasn't the same one as on her phone. I searched for more pictures. There were none.

That lech Brian Scott's face popped into my head and I shuddered, a bitter taste flooding my mouth. It had never been my plan to have him killed, but I'd grown comfortable with the fact that he'd deserved it. Like the wholesaler getting caught. Even though he didn't kill Glory, he had still crossed her. He was still scum.

I examined the red logoed bank statements and, as I'd suspected, discovered they belonged to the children. And they had way too much money in them to be a simple savings account. No wonder I hadn't been able to find them. They were here all along. Or were they? Maybe he'd only just found the bag. All this proved was that Stephen knew of the trusts. But the proof I needed was not *that* Glory had been hiding things from him, but *when*. And as my brain alternated between the 'before Glory' and 'after Glory' scenarios,

I realised that's what mattered the most.

I plopped into the chair with the statements to check their dates, buzzing with the prospect of a discovery that could change everything, but the spit-out nails in the middle of the desk distracted me. I wiped the disgusting, flaky body remnants with a sheet of paper, trying to catch them with another so I wouldn't need to touch them. A few fell on the ground. I stooped under the desk to collect them, their uneven ridges snagging on the carpet as I picked them free. That's when I noticed, through the mesh of the metal bin, the unusual letter formation '*Zolp*' on a folded piece of paper midway down. Reaching inside with care, I managed to extract the square without letting anything else fall out.

Once I saw what it was, waves of nausea rolled in from the swirling pool inside my stomach and I had to build up breath after breath, like sandbags, to stem the flood. Memories of that first night raced through my mind: Stephen's despair; how he'd crumbled; how he'd clung to me for help. The next morning: how he'd explained Glory's sleeplessness and his concern. It all seemed so genuine, so plausible and yet…The delivery note from Pharmacy4U.com for a pack of sleeping pills was in *his* name.

Why the pills?

What did I miss?

What did he do?

I wracked my brain for any indication that would fit a new theory brewing and it spat up 'Marius.' Marius had warned me against him and I'd dismissed him. I grabbed my phone and dialled the mobile number they'd given him in the safe house.

'Hello?'

'Marius, it's Grace.'

'Hello. Good to hear from you. Are you—'

'Sorry Marius, I don't have much time. I need to ask you something, Okay?'

'Okay.'

'When you told me you saw Stephen with the bad man. The big boss. Was that at the Prince William?'

'No. I do not know a Prince William.'

It was, by now, what I'd expected to hear.

'So where did you see him?'

'At the Royden Tavern. Why Grace? Is there problem?'

'Why do you say they're bad men?'

'Oh, they are. I have new friend here, Mihai. He is also in safe house. He worked there and tell me bad stories. They had slaves and prostitutes. They break legs of people.'

'Would they kill someone? Would they run someone off the road in a car?'

'Like in Glory accident?' The penny had dropped. 'I do not know. I ask Mihai. Please wait.'

The silence lasted an eternity. I heard muffled noises. Questioning voices. Insistent tones.

'Grace?'

'Yes, Marius, I'm here. What did he say?'

'Mihai says yes. Mihai say they kill people for money. With guns. And with accidents. But Mihai say he not want to. His boss not happy. He punish. Mihai did not do these things.'

But somebody did. Deafening cries pressed against my temples. Screams for a dead sister; the banshee that wailed too late. I knew it. I fucking knew she'd been killed. And now I finally knew how.

I stuffed the incriminating pharmacy note in my

pocket.

Slowly sounds came through my ears again: 'Grace?' on the phone and then a 'woof.'

'Woof woof woof.' Right by the front door. Blue! I snapped out of my dwam and realised this meant someone was coming. And it wouldn't be Dave. Or a delivery. Because that dumb dog only ever barked at friends.

Shit.

Stephen.

CHAPTER SIXTY-FOUR

An incendiary burst of adrenaline coursed through my veins as I heard the familiar male voice calm the dog nearby.

Now what?

Why was he home? It was only lunch time.

I quickly turned the light and the phone off, planning to hide, and hoping to God he wouldn't need his office. But then I remembered the groceries on the kitchen counter. They would signal a presence. With an encounter unavoidable, I reckoned if I darted into the next-door toilet, I could pretend that's where I'd been.

I followed muffled sounds across my mental map of the property. When the right moment came, I spurted to the door and closed it behind me at lighting speed. For stage two, I zipped into the toilet, careful not to let its handle click, flushed, and stepped out again. For added effect, I continued straightening my clothes as I ambled into the heart of the house; a picture of casual solitude, until Blue re-joined my side.

Scrambling sounds came from the utility room off the kitchen, which meant he would have passed the food. I ran my trembling palms through my hair, clearing loose strands from my moist temples. The plan was to make it through this and beeline to DI Roberts with what I'd learnt. Would it be enough?

Please God, let there be enough.

As the wide-shouldered frame of my murdering son of a bitch brother-in-law came into view, I shook with fear—not of him, but that he could go free. That he would not suffer for what he'd done.

'Hi.'

'Oh hey, Grace. I thought that stuff must be yours. What are you doing here?'

'I left my boots here a while ago and I'm going hiking today.' I headed for the shoe rack as he searched, in a huff, through a mountain of clean laundry divided into multiple peaks by the drier. 'There they are. What are you doing home?'

'Camp called to say we forgot Noah's trunks, and he's had a meltdown. He really wants to go swimming. And I can't bloody find them. I'm so annoyed. This is not what I want to be doing during my lunch hour.'

'Would they not be in his room?'

'No, they're here somewhere.'

'What about his dirty basket?' I hoped that if he went upstairs, it would be easier to leave, and he wouldn't catch Dave coming to pick me up any minute.

'No, I said, they're here somewhere.'

'Would he fit in Adam's trunks? Those may be upstairs.'

'Jesus, Grace, can you please just butt out! Mind you own business, for once.' He remained doubled over, head down, fingers picking a multitude of yellow items out one by one.

Anger flared inside. I was hit by a sudden, violent fantasy in which I smothered his face in the clothes until he suffocated. So vivid was it, that I felt his resistance in my hands, the pressure as I held his flailing body. I curled my fists and returned his unwelcoming outburst with a more measured, 'Fuck you, Stephen.'

He jerked up to face me, and a fire burnt in his eyes. 'Don't you talk to me like that in my own home, Grace. I've had my fill of you always being around. Fuck you yourself. Go away. I don't need you.'

That landed like a giant slap. Clearly, the heartless bastard had forgotten I'd saved his arse from losing his job. That I'd even gotten someone killed for him. That smothering fantasy was becoming more appealing by the second, but I clenched my jaws to contain my rage.

'Fine.' I grabbed my boots and strode past him to the exit, unable to resist knocking my shoulder against his upper arm. He teetered but stayed upright, steadied by a hand against the wall.

An insulted look overtook his face as he retaliated, like a juvenile, with a shove. 'And don't come back.'

'You can't keep me away' I squared up to him. 'I get to see the boys. Glory would want me to be with them.'

'Well Glory is dead.'

I tried.

I really tried. But the nonchalant way in which he dismissed Glory's death—a murder by his own hand— tipped me over the edge. I swivelled around and propelled my right fist into his jaw. This lifted him off his feet and made him drop to the floor. He pushed himself up with his arms behind him and scuttled spider-like in retreat.

'Jesus, Grace. What's gotten into you?'

'She's dead because you killed her, you sick bastard.'

His shocked expression did nothing to convince me of the contrary. I'd feign shock, too, if I were him. Or maybe he was shocked I'd found out.

'Are you crazy? I loved her.' On his knees now, he wiped his hands on his trousers and set his right foot down, preparing to rise.

Adrenaline primed my muscles as I towered over him, confident of my greater physical strength. 'I know you did it. I know you hired a man to run her off the road. And I've got proof. The minute I leave this house, I'm phoning the police.'

His eyes narrowed. I retreated to the glass panelled door dividing the utility from the kitchen. As he motioned to get up, I slipped to the other side, intending to lock him in. Shit. No key.

Stephen's dark, rising frame filled the width of the glass, while I clung onto the handle with both hands, preparing for a tug of war. I gauged the distance to the rear door to see if running was an option.

'Open the door, you bitch.'

I let go and sprinted away. At the same time, Blue charged into the kitchen, attracted by the commotion, and obstructed my path. I danced around him to free my legs. A forceful yank at my hair pulled my head back, spraining my neck. Stephen grasped my bra strap through my T-shirt with his other hand and tugged me backwards before throwing me aside, slamming my head on the island. I screamed out in pain. Blood gushed from my split lip and I gasped for air. My windpipe was pressed onto the worktop.

Stephen thrust his forearm into my neck and held me down. I pushed against the worktop with both hands. The harder I pushed, however, the more I struggled to breathe.

'How did you know? Hm? Who told you about the hit?'

It was true.

Dark circles obscured my vision. Channelling all my strength into my arms, I gave one monster push and, this time, broke free. He was still clutching my hair. I ducked my head, turned under his arm and punched him in the chest, instantly followed by a kick in the groin. He doubled over. I grabbed his head and slammed his face against my knee, releasing him when he collapsed onto the floor.

Blue was going wild, jumping about and barking, shoving his muzzle into my adversary's groaning face. I needed to restrain Stephen and reached for the first thing that came to mind: the dog's lead. When I took it off its peg, Blue mistook it for an invitation and raced to me, biting at the green leash in excitement.

'No, Blue. Get off.'

Having had time to recover, Stephen stretched out his leg and kicked my ankles, swiping me to the ground. On all fours, I fought off Blue, who seemed to think this was all a fantastic game. But he growled when Stephen stomped onto my lower back. The pain radiated like a shock wave across my body and collided violently with a counter-shock as Stephen plonked the knee from his other leg on my shoulders. Along with his full weight. I cried out, laying spread-eagled.

'You couldn't leave it alone, could you? What am I going to do with you now?'

I stretched my limbs out to attempt an escape but remained flat and helpless like a turtle caught in a sand bank. He hovered over my face, my right side pinned to the cold tiles.

'Why did you do it?' I asked, drool sliding down one side of my mouth. 'What did she ever do to you?'

'Ha! I thought you knew everything. She betrayed

me. She betrayed me lying about her bloody café, getting herself into so much trouble that she dragged me along. Risking my job!' His breath invaded mine as he spat his disdain in my face 'And the lies! Pretending it's all over but all the while planning her escape. Hiding money with you and the kids so I wouldn't find out, so I couldn't touch it. Going off with that lowlife wholesaler. Flaunting her affair to the entire world.'

'No! You're wrong. She didn't have an affair with Mike.'

'I saw the pictures.'

'They were a set up. She was doing it for the police.' I twisted my neck as far as it went to face him straight on and saw a flicker of doubt. He hesitated. I quickly shook my hip to throw him off balance. His foot slipped but he caught himself with both hands on the floor and quickly replaced the load on my back with a second knee. He straightened up. Fully kneeling on me, his bum on his feet. The pain was excruciating.

'So now what, bitch? I can't let you go.'

'You fucking bastard.'

Stephen leaned sideways, and I lost him from my field of vision. When his weight was centred again, I spotted something red in his hands. As he hoisted it above his head, I saw what it was. The fire extinguisher that always stood in the corner. I let out a piercing scream. Startled, Blue pounced free through the unreliable rear door.

'I wish you'd stayed out of it.'

Defenceless, I shut my eyes and waited for the blow. His knees dug into me as he elevated himself to increase the force. I winced, bracing for the end.

Dave's voice came out of nowhere. 'Grace!' My eyes sprung open. I watched him hurl himself onto

Stephen's outstretched torso without a second thought. They landed beside me, Stephen's head hitting the ground. As he dropped the extinguisher, Dave jumped on him and, on all fours, grabbed his arms and secured Stephen's legs with his calves, immobilising him in a tight grip.

I leapt up.

'Hold him, Dave. He killed Glory.'

Dave turned to me in confusion. 'What?'

Stephen seized the opportunity of Dave's distraction and raised his legs in an attempt to release himself. But my man was on him again in a flash and contained him in a full-body lock. My heart pounded in my ears. Hyped up, charged with electrical impulses, and deaf to Dave's 'You're going nowhere, pal,' I lifted the extinguisher.

Dave yelled, 'Grace, no!'

But it was too late. The red metal cannister hit Stephen's skull with a harrowing crunch and all resistance left his body.

CHAPTER SIXTY-FIVE

'Call an ambulance!'

My limbs leaden, I stood bolted to the ground, dazed and mute, as I watched the scene unfold in an echoey fog: Dave chanting Stephen's name and checking for vital signs in his lifeless body.

'Call an ambulance, Grace, he's still breathing.'

The third scream of my name jolted me back. I fumbled inside my pocket and struggled to steady my phone while it tried to recognise the lines of my trembling fingerprint. I dialled 999. 'What do I say? Oh, my God. I did this.'

'Say there's been a fight. Say a man was hit on the head, is breathing but unconscious.' He placed Stephen in the recovery position. 'They'll send the police, too.' I dropped the phone in shock—or perhaps in unconscious sabotage. Did I want him saved? Dave swiped it and instructed the operator while continuing to prod Stephen with his foot.

Afterwards, he came and put his hands on my shoulders. A gentle shake drew my distant mind to him.

'Babe. It was self-defence. He was going to hurt

you. You said he killed Glory.'

'But you had him…You'd pinned him down.'

He drew me into his arms, stroked my hair and shushed. In a resolute tone, he threw me the ultimate lifeline. 'They don't need to know that.'

Two of the precisely six minutes and forty-seven seconds it took for the ambulance to reach the property from the Queen Elizabeth University Hospital were wasted with a lingering embrace, as I broke into grateful tears. But with time ticking, and my innocence at risk, I had to pull myself together and concentrate on getting our stories straight.

Our shared tale had to be plausible. It had to start with the truth: Dave hearing a scream through the open rear door and finding Stephen sitting on me and about to slam the extinguisher into me. And it had to end with my blow to his head, cloaked in irrefutable self-preservation. We acted out a sequence of actions, only to find the continuity was physically impossible. Then we tried again, and again, until we arranged a credible flow that worked, just as the sirens approached.

'Punch me,' said Dave. 'They won't believe he knocked me out unless there's a bruise.'

I winced and fired my first into his jaw. 'I'm sorry.'

He stumbled sideways but stayed on his feet. 'Wow. You've got some hook.' As he rubbed the side of his face, I apologised again and rushed to hold him tight. After we kissed, I stared down at the immobile shape.

'What if he wakes up?'

'He's still a killer, Grace.' He joined my downward gaze. 'Plus, I somehow think he won't.'

At that moment, Blue bounded in, erratic and excitable, which reminded me the first responders wouldn't know to come to the rear door. I sprinted to the front entrance to usher them in, pulling both glazed panels open in welcome as they ran up the drive.

The rest was a blur.

In the kitchen, the paramedics packed Stephen up in an almost surreal demonstration of professional efficiency, casually throwing Dave an ice-pack on their way out.

Four police officers mulled about taking pictures and hurling questions at us in quick, but illogical succession. The fat one had separated me from Dave, and I clung onto the image of his last loving look, for comfort.

'Please. I have to speak with DI Roberts,' I said.

'Ma'm, please answer the question. Why were you in the victim's house?'

I wished they'd stopped calling the bastard a victim. He was a murderer and had it coming. Frustrated, I searched for Dave and saw a skinny brunette escort him out by the elbow.

'But my boyfriend—'

'Ma'm, your boyfriend is being taken to the station. And as soon as my colleagues have finished scanning the house for other victims, we'll be on our way too.'

'Get DI Roberts. He's in the human trafficking unit. He knows about my sister. Tell him it was murder. Tell him I have proof.'

CHAPTER SIXTY-SIX

Confirmation came five days later when DI Roberts visited the café. Preparing his espresso, I signalled to Sascha to take over the other customers, threw in a cookie and joined him by the window. I'd been waiting to hear from him since our conversation at the station, when his colleague had finally called and allowed him to join the interview. And with him now here, my heart fluttered in anticipation.

'So?' I clutched the cup between my hands.

'It took some work. To begin with, this isn't my area, but given our history, they gave me the go-ahead. And the guys at the lab weren't happy when I asked them to run toxicology again. However, what with the assault, and as you'd mentioned zolpidem by name—which is not something they routinely look for—they couldn't refuse. By a stroke of luck, they hadn't disposed of Glory's samples yet. There's a dispute with the medical waste firm that has created a backlog.'

I displayed a polite grin, which fronted a jumpy impatience.

'And?'

'And they found it. You were right. The report says

Glory had ingested a sleeping tablet within a half hour to an hour of her accident. Nobody does that before getting in the car. But it would explain why she could be run off the road so easily. And you said the husband had given her a cup of tea before departure. With your testimony of his confession, and the Romanian chap pointing fingers on his side, we have a murder case.'

I exhaled a breath it felt like I'd held for years and dropped my head into both hands. 'Thank God.'

'I'm sorry we missed it before.'

This time my smile was genuine. 'It's not your fault. I would probably have thought I was a crazy lady too. After all, I wasn't even a hundred percent certain she'd been murdered. And I thought it was Mike Catach.'

'True. What's the husband's condition?'

'He's still in a coma. They had to open his skull to address the internal bleeding,' I said.

'A craniotomy.'

'Yes, that's the one. He's stable but they can't tell yet if there's any brain damage. Besides, they wouldn't really know the full extent of it until he wakes up.'

'Yes. Well, I know the hospital has been instructed to alert us the minute that happens.' Roberts bit into his cookie and flicked the crumbs from the side of his mouth in a backwards sweep of his thumb, like my father did. 'How are you holding up?'

'It's been tough. I'm staying at the house to take care of Adam and Noah, but I am filled with dread whenever I enter the kitchen. It's like he's still there. And the poor boys can't understand what's going on. They've been to see him in hospital, but I haven't got the heart to tell them how he got there, or why. Is it wrong that I wish him dead?'

'No, Grace, it's human nature.' He stroked my

forearm. 'You'll get through this.'

'I guess.'

'I'd better get back to the station.' He rose. 'I'll keep you in the loop on any developments.'

'Thanks.'

When I was clearing up, I noticed the morning rush had subsided. Are rare opportunity for Sascha and me to talk. My near-death experience had prompted me to review what I wanted out of life, out of my second chance. One that Glory never had. I'd spoken to Alastair. I couldn't blame him for being puzzled. Why would anyone make such an unusual non-profitable decision? But it was within my rights, as majority shareholder, and the documents had arrived by post in the morning.

'Sascha, shall we go through the papers?'

'Coming!'

She returned from the rear and set the clean crockery down while I retrieved the envelope from below the counter. We settled in the nearest seats and I walked her through the accountant's instructions. Alastair had laid it all out in a check-list, in simple language, and pasted stickers highlighting where to sign. When the moment arrived for her to write her name next to the first sticky arrow, she looked at me and frowned.

'Are you sure?'

'Yes, Sascha. I'm sure.'

'You're not still in shock or anything? And won't later decide you made a big mistake?' She was one of few people I'd told about the altercation with Stephen and I trusted her to keep it quiet for the children's sake.

'Believe me. I'm sure. You're a natural. You're the one making this a success. It's only fair. I want you to have the café.'

'For a pound?'

'Yes, for a pound. I'd give it to you for free, but Alastair says that's not tax efficient. So one pound, please, if you will.' I held out my palm and she laughed, shrugged her shoulders and pulled change from her summer dress. She placed a single gleaming coin on the table. 'And free coffee for life,' I said.

'But of course. Free coffee for life.'

Sascha lifted the pen to the dotted line and with one neat blue scrawl wiped away all but the last stain from Glory's crime.

CHAPTER SIXTY-SEVEN

The bell rang, and I walked to the front window. It was difficult to see who was at the gate, since the shape was wearing a big winter coat and a hat. But given the parcel in the figure's hands, it was probably Amazon again.

'Are you expecting another delivery?' I yelled at Dave in the other room.

'No, I don't think so. I think all the Christmas gifts are in.'

'Shush. Keep it down. The boys might hear.'

I buzzed the gate open and waited by the glazed front door while the visitor's boots sank into the snow with each step up the drive. The door was held open only for as long as it took to place my signature and haul the box inside. We needed to keep the warmth in. Glory's house was murder to heat. We'd learnt that the hard way when temperatures started to drop mid-Autumn.

Dave appeared in the hallway. 'What is it?'

'I don't know. The label is handwritten, which is a bit odd. And it's got tonnes of tape on it. I'll need scissors.'

Stephen's old office was on my right and as I

entered, I nearly tripped on one of the many boxes on the floor.

'Goddamnit, Dave, when will you put your stuff away? If you don't want it in the house, then please put it in the garage. I'll break my neck one of these days.'

I shoved aside some junk. Why did he have to take so long to unpack? It was as if he never moved in. He'd sold his flat thee whole months ago. It only took me a few days—and I'd moved in when things were still chaotic: within a week of Stephen landing in hospital, the instant the police confirmed there would be no further action against me.

The tape came away easily once I'd snipped down one side of the parcel. There was an envelope on top of a package wrapped in festive green paper with stars on it. My heart skipped on seeing who'd sent it.

Dear Grace, I am well. I hope you are too. I have job in biscuit factory in Dunfermline. They are good to me. I live with friends in nice flat. This is the best biscuits we make. They call it Prestige. I hope Adam and Noah like it. I thank you for your help of me. Merry Christmas. In Romania we say Crăciun Fericit. Your friend, Marius Agarici.'

Dave was reading his magazine when I brought the box into the living room.

'It's from Marius,' I said. 'Isn't that kind? He's doing well. He's got a new job in Dunfermline.'

'That's great news.'

'Could you shout up for the boys please? We should all go for a walk. It looks nice out. Where's Blue?'

'I think he's upstairs. He's taken to jumping along when the boys are playing with the Wii.'

'Are they on their games again? It's morning! I wish you'd never brought that thing in.'

'Hey. Lay off it,' Dave said. 'It's been great for them.

It got them through the tough times.'

'Yes, I guess that's true. But still…'

I placed the present under the tree, so it could be opened with all the others in the morning. The card I brought into the kitchen, where it was pinned onto the cork notice board. Prime position. Right next to the thank you from Invisible. I ran my fingers over the formal letter.

'…*Your generous donation was the largest the charity has ever received. It will help us have a tremendous impact on the lives of the victims of human trafficking…*'

How would Oliver be doing? I remembered handing over the cheque only weeks after giving the café to Sascha. Alastair had made a herculean effort in getting me access to Glory's bank account. What else could I have done with the dirty dividends? It had felt so right.

My phone tinkled in my pocket. Another notification from the WhatsApp group for school mums. I chuckled. Now what? More pictures from last night?

A shot of Susan filled the screen, literally pulling her hair out, with the words '*Help! I need batteries. AAA. Anyone got any left? The local shop is all out!*'

I checked the pantry and found four left over. I took a photo of them and typed, '*Me. We're off for a walk. I'll drop them round. After all, if it wasn't for you I would have never known you're meant to put them inside the toys before you wrap them. Or even what to buy for Adam. Clever Santa, you. He's going to love his pressies. xxx*'

The phone pinged again. '*Thanks doll. You saved Christmas morning! Now, when are we going to hear you belt out Waterloo again? Karaoke was ace!*'

Another chime from another mum. '*My head still*

316

hurts! Bloody kids are driving me insane. Where are the babysit elves when you need them? I still have so much to do!

Susan replied, '*At least you don't have your mother-in-law staying with you for TWO WHOLE WEEKS!*'

I chuckled as I placed the phone back in my pocket. To think I used to dismiss these women and their 'mummy problems'. I now knew it wasn't nearly as easy as it looked.

The ceiling above me shook as the boys stormed down the stairs. I walked to the hallway to meet them.

'Can we go to the ice rink again, Auntie Grace?' Noah asked.

'No, twice in one week is more than enough.'

'Aw. Please?'

I play-punched him in the arm. 'You know begging doesn't work with me. Now put your coats on. Dave? Are you coming?'

'Yes, coming.'

We all crammed into the cloakroom. With our thick down jackets on, we were like Michelin men colliding, jostling for position over the box that held hats, scarves and gloves.

Blue raced out the door as soon as it opened. I watched him sniff the ground. Dustings of snow stuck to his grey velvet nose. Silly dog.

The boys followed him out and threw speedily manufactured snowballs at each other, that disintegrated before hitting the target.

'Ready?' Dave asked.

'Yes,' I said and let him lock the door behind us.

We walked towards Pollok Park, greeting passers-by on the way. Adam and Noah up ahead. They seemed to be competing for who could exhale the largest amount of steam into the cold air. I hoped one wouldn't keel over trying to win.

'Remind me to take the cake out of the pantry so it doesn't dry out too much,' I said.

'I'm not sure that will help much at this stage.' Dave winked.

'Oh ha ha. How was I supposed to know you need to soak the fruit for six weeks in advance? I think I deserve credit for remembering to ask Dad for Mum's recipe at all. It's the first year she hasn't been able to make them.'

'I know, babe. You've done great. All this effort to give the kids a great Christmas. All the little touches.'

'Wait until you see what Adam is getting in the advent calendar tomorrow. I saved the best treat for last, just like Glory used to.'

'Yes, well, Glory had a little more time on her hands than you do. You didn't need to go through all the trouble of making sweets yourself, you know. I'm sure they would have been fine with chocolate, like everybody else.'

It wouldn't be the same though, would it, Gi? Without your traditions. But we couldn't expect him to understand.

My mind elsewhere, I jumped when Dave groped my bum.

'When do I get my special treat?' he said.

I laughed and slapped his hand away. 'Stop it, you perv. The kids are right there.'

Adam and Noah were only a few steps ahead in the park. They'd stopped a few times to pick up sticks to throw for Blue, who never seemed to carry them all the way back.

'I can't help it if my girlfriend is a fox.' He flashed his gorgeous set of teeth. 'Besides, how else are we going to make one of our own?' he said, indicating the boys with a nod.

'Ha! What am I going to do with a baby? Balance it on my head? I've got my hands full with those two already—not to mention Blue.'

His smile vanished and he faced forward again.

Had he been serious? I re-adjusted my hood, which had slipped backwards as we'd talked, and reached for his hand. Would he understand that meant 'maybe?'

He accepted the invitation and we walked on, using our clasped hands for balance as we crossed the ice patches on the path.

Dave lifted his free arm and looked at his watch. 'What time did you want me to drive you to the hospital?'

'Sorry. I just hate driving in snow. I feel so stressed about losing grip.'

'That's okay.'

'I was thinking four o'clock. It would be a bit awkward to take the boys on Christmas day. I don't want visiting Stephen to ruin it.'

'Like he ruined everything else?' Dave shrugged.

He was right.

'I hate going there.' I sighed. 'I hate it with a vengeance. I can't believe the doctors got it so wrong. "Coma's don't last more than a month," they said. Well it's been six and it's anyone's guess if he'll ever wake. And in the meantime, I have to bring his sons to him and tell lies about how he got like this. Because Glory would want me to protect them from the truth. It's like I'm the one being punished when he should be. I wish he would die. He deserves to.'

'Grace!'

'What? An eye for an eye. Isn't that what they say?'

CHAPTER SIXTY-EIGHT

I was elbow-deep in stuffing, bits of onion oozing their way under my nails as I pressed the sticky mixture inside the bird. I wiped my hair away with my sleeve and looked at the clock. Seven thirty.

A sleepy Dave came up behind me and stroked my hips. 'Good morning. New skirt?'

'Yes. I got it in the sale. What do you think?'

'It's nice. Very pink.' He scanned the kitchen counter. 'How's it all going? Need some help?'

'No, I'm fine. Everything's on track. The boys will be up soon. Did you make the Santa footprints with the flour?'

'Yes. Want a coffee? Not sure I can cope with the great pyjama-clad avalanche about to hit us without one.'

'I'm okay, thanks. Bless. I can't wait to see their little eyes light up when they open their presents. But I've got tonnes of work to do before then.' I washed my hands and got to work on the parsnips.

That afternoon, the main event kicked off with red paper hats and the stinging scent of exploded crackers.

'What happens to the elves when they are naughty?'

asked Noah holding up his gag. He paused only briefly before revealing, 'Santa gives them the sack!' The rest of us groaned appreciatively, like every family across the country was doing at this exact time.

'Now mine,' said Adam. 'Why did they let the turkey join the pop group?'

'I don't know, why did they let the turkey join the pop group?' we asked in unison.

'Because he was the only one with drumsticks!'

'Badaboom.' Dave simulated a drum roll, and we all laughed.

Until I panicked.

'Drumsticks. The turkey. Where is Blue?' I'd remembered I left the turkey cooling on the kitchen table, within reach. On hearing his name, the dog appeared, innocent, from behind the sofa and walked over to the table, sniffing as if expecting a treat. 'Oh my God, what a relief.'

Dave sliced the turkey and the children wolfed down everything. Even the sprouts.

After the pavlova, the fire was lit. We watched the Queen's speech and cackled with laughter as we stuffed chestnuts in our cheeks to copy her posh accent.

'Are you sure you want to go upstairs?' I said. 'The Sound of Music is on next.'

'That's boring,' Adam said.

'Yeah, we want to play with the new Nerf guns,' Noah said, turning to run up to the attic play room. The war zone.

'Don't think you're getting out of cleaning up the kitchen!'

I tried to blank the future mess from dozens of foam bullets from my mind, as I luxuriated in the peace and warmth.

Dave reached down for an embrace and murmured into my hair. 'You did good.' I snuggled into his chest. He must have sensed my exhaustion. 'Why don't you have a little snooze?'

'I'll try.'

And for the first in a very long time, I let go.

When I woke, my neck ached, and it took a few seconds to find my bearings. The embers were still red, meaning I hadn't been out long. Strands of staticky hair crackled against my cheek, caused by the woollen blanket that someone had placed over my knees. Someone who loved me. Dave. I smiled and stroked the soft knit. My hand passed over my lower belly just as I heard the boys' laughter from upstairs, triggering an odd twitch in my womb. Maybe. Maybe someday.

I scanned the room. A disaster. There were glasses everywhere. Crumbs. All the gift wrap was bunched into a big ball. I sighed; I'd have to remove the metallic stars before recycling the paper.

How long before I could get rid of the tree? That flashing multi-coloured lop-sided affront to my senses I had endured for the sake of its tiny, proud decorators.

A nice clear out. That's what was needed.

When I stood up and got to work, Blue obstructed my legs, generally being no help. 'Buddy. I love you too, okay? But please let me do my thing.' A quick kiss on the muzzle seemed to satisfy him enough to retreat behind the sofa again.

I swept up the pine needles for the umpteenth time, a futile exercise that reminded me of the effort I'd wasted on some of my clients. A grin spread across my face as I pictured my new job in January. How much more rewarding it would be to run a fitness programme for the disabled and disenfranchised. No more pandering to the insecurities of well-to-do women. Life would be good.

It had been Dave's suggestion to apply, after he'd seen it advertised in the Gorbals community centre.

Where was Dave?

Through the glazed doors I saw that both the dining room and kitchen were deserted. I found him sitting midway up the stairs, pulling at the brown tufted carpet; pensive.

'Hey. What are you doing?' I joined him on the step and smoothed the plucked fibres down.

'Nothing.'

'Everything all right? You look sad.'

'Don't worry about it.' He clasped his hands in front of him.

'Hey. Talk to me.'

'I don't think it's the right time, babe.'

'Well now you have to tell me.' I poked him in the arm, as if to prod it out. 'Spill.'

'Okay…It's…I didn't expect it would be like this.'

'What?'

'This. Stephen's coma. Everything.'

'Oh.' A shaky unease formed in my stomach. 'I know it's not ideal, hon. But is it so bad? I'm quite getting used to this cushy lifestyle.' I stroked the lush flooring to accentuate the joke but he frowned.

Shit. Tears accumulated behind my eyes, barricaded only by the idealistic belief this would end well.

It had to.

'No, it's not bad. But it's not my life. Can't you see? I am living another man's life. Not my house. Not my kids. Not my money.'

'You have me. I'm yours.'

'I do. But sometimes…I don't know how to say

this.'

My heart sank. Why? Was it that bad?

'Go on. You can tell me.'

'Sometimes it's as if I'm not sure it's you. I sometimes feel like you're hanging onto Glory so much—wanting to be like her for the boys—that it's like you're turning into her. And it's just weird. Even this skirt…'

All I heard in my head was a stream of 'no's.

No. No. No.

I couldn't believe this was happening. What was he saying?

'But it's only temporary,' I said. 'It will settle into being our life. You and me, like we planned. Like before. I could change. I mean, change back. We could get our own dog…maybe…maybe have a baby.' I threw these phrases out like lifebuoys, trying to catch him as I felt him drift further away.

Did I even mean them? Oh God, what did he want? My anxiety grew with every one of his slow, silent breaths.

'Come on, Grace. Don't kid yourself. If Stephen dies, the kids will have no-one. If Stephen wakes, he'll go to jail, and the kids will have no-one. The situation has always been that, and it was always going to come down to you stepping in. Permanently.' He faced me dead-on. 'You somehow thought this would become normal. And it was still such a tough time when you asked me to move in. I thought maybe I could get used to it. But let's not pretend. This is where we are.'

'But—'

'Let me speak now. You made me speak. So I'm speaking.'

I felt my pulse throb in my throat. Where was this

going?'

'They're great kids, Grace, and you're being amazing. But I've really been struggling with this lately. I don't think I can do this anymore. I'm sorry.' He straightened his back. 'Listen, I'm going to go and stay with my mum for a while—she'd wanted to have me for Christmas anyway—and we can talk in a few days. Maybe after Hogmanay.'

'No!' I shouted. He stepped down the stairs. 'No. You can't.' I reached out to stop him but missed, the distance between us increasing as he ignored me and floated off. 'You can't leave me.'

Nearly by the door, he turned and winced, his handsome features wrung into an insulting expression of pity. 'I'm sorry, Grace. I just need some time away right now.'

'But what about us? What about your promises?' A torrent of injustice coursed through me and propelled me to him. I slammed my fists on his chest with ever-greater intensity as my rage grew. 'You're the one who wanted to be together. I'd resisted. I bloody resisted. You lured me into this. We had a plan. It's not right! You can't abandon me. You owe me.'

He caught my wrists to cease the battering. 'I owe you? What a weird thing to say. How on Earth do I owe you? That's not how this works. And after all I've done? Shame on you. Look, I know you're hurting right now, but I can't stay here.' He kissed my fingers.

'No. You can't leave…I won't let you.'

He released me and shrugged. 'Babe, this isn't something you can control. However much I know you need to. I have to figure things out for myself. I'm sorry I've ruined Christmas. I'd meant to wait with this.'

Why was he talking about ruining Christmas? Like it was nothing. My God, did he not see he was ruining my whole future? One that he'd promised me. How long had he been planning this? How long had he strung me along?

No. I wouldn't have it.

Clusters of anger that had built up across my body merged in vengeful unison, chanting threats of retribution like a lynch mob. Punish him!

But how?

'No you can't go…you…I…If you leave me, I'll…I'll tell the police you assaulted Stephen.' I surprised myself with what had come out of my mouth. But it could work. Right?

'What?'

'And that it was not self-defence,' I added.

'Why would you do that?'

'Because…because you can't betray me like this. We had a plan. We had it all mapped out…I love you.'

'Jesus Grace, you've got a bat-shit crazy way of showing it. I didn't betray you. Relationships end. That's all. And I wasn't sure ours had. But with the way you're behaving, you're making the decision very easy for me.'

No.

As I puzzled through the practicalities of my startling threat at lighting speed, the pieces fell into glorious place, painting an infallible roadmap to justice. And it felt *right*. How dare he leave me like this?

'I mean it. I'll call DI Roberts and say you came in out of nowhere and picked a fight. You two have a history. And then you whacked him with the extinguisher. And we concocted a whole story of how it was me—to protect you. But now I'm conflicted and

I want to come clean.' Satisfied my plan made perfect sense, I rubbed my hands as if done with putting things in order. 'Yes, that'll work.'

'Wow.' He raised his arms in surrender and walked backwards towards the exit. 'Fuck me. You've officially lost it.'

No.

'No Dave, you've lost. Because I vividly recall you saying the police would believe anything from me. Remember? It will be your word against mine. Who will they believe? The Gorbals scum with a criminal record or a lovely white lady from Perth?'

His face fell. 'You're serious, Grace?'

I hesitated. His pleading eyes nearly pulled me back. Into a world I could not control.

No.

I needed to teach him a lesson.

'You think you're free? I said. 'You're not.'

Nobody is.

LETTER TO YOU

Dear reader,

When I set out to write this novel, I never expected anyone to read it outside of my immediate family and circle of friends. Yet here you are.

I am humbled and grateful that you were willing to invest so much of your time in this story. I hope you enjoyed the ride.

Reviews are essential for the success of any book and I would be ecstatic if you were to leave one on Amazon or Goodreads.

As this is my first novel, and I'm not sure I know what I'm doing yet, I would also love to hear your thoughts directly. If you're gentle, I may even write another.

Keep in touch:

www.heleenkist.com
@hkist.

Best wishes,
Heleen

ACKNOWLEDGEMENTS

Writing 'In Servitude' felt like bouncing between extremes.

On the one hand, I was never so lonely as when huddled away in my garden office, every day for months, forcing the words to flow—something which was inexplicably helped by wearing a pink woollen hat made by my daughter.

On the other hand, I've never felt as encouraged, loved and supported in my life. For that, I am hugely grateful.

By the time I posted on Facebook that I'd completed my first draft (512 likes!) nearly a full year after announcing my intention to write a novel (only 158 likes—perhaps they didn't believe me), I'd reconnected with friends from various periods and locations in my life: the Hague, Minerva, Brussels, Stanford, London, Scotland. Their virtual cheers rose despite, in many cases, decades of silence between us. On top of that I made new writer friends online willing to share tips, laughter, and commiseration any time day or night. A shout out to the James Patterson Masterclass group, and the lovely peeps in the Writer's Murder Club.

When I started, I considered this book a bit of a folly; the midlife-crisis-achievement-seeking equivalent to racing at Iron Man or climbing Everest—but for someone who prefers a soft seat with a bar of chocolate within reach. It was only after its first readers, book reviewer Shalini G and developmental editor (and author) Ray Banks, sang its praises, that I realised I had written a real book. A proper book. I want to thank them for their contribution and this early validation, which got me to take the book seriously and seek further, much valued, editorial assistance from Anna Hogarty and Sara Cox.

Then came my posse of beta readers, each giving their unique take on the story and its characters. A big thank you to Alice, Sascha, Jill, Kaben, Kerry, Mary, Pauline, Laura, Karen, Katie, Tania, Kyle, Sheila, Ana, and Zoe.

I also want to thank my parents Floor and Lyda for giving me a snippet of their literary DNA, and for tricking me into believing that I can do anything I set my mind to. A begrudging thanks to my brother Floor and sister Martijn for each having a book out already; sibling rivalry thus requiring me to do the same.

Immense gratitude to my husband, Grant, for staying married to me while I became a needy, insecure, brainstorming-partner-seeking monster for a while.

And lastly, my love to Marcus and Delphie. Thank you for listening to my chapters when you didn't feel like it, for telling me I'll be 'the best author ever' because that logically followed from being 'the best mum ever,' for inspiring *and* acting out the fight scene, for the cups of coffee, and for the many cuddles along the way—the most precious gifts of all.

Lightning Source UK Ltd.
Milton Keynes UK
UKHW042208211118
332752UK00001B/107/P